A BRIDE BY
Christmas

FOUR STORIES OF EXPEDIENT MARRIAGE
ON THE GREAT PLAINS

VICKIE MCDONOUGH
KELLY EILEEN HAKE
THERESE STENZEL
LINDA GOODNIGHT

BARBOUR
PUBLISHING

ISBN 978-1-60260-119-2

All scripture quotations are taken from the King James Version of the Bible.

This book is a work of fiction. Names, characters, places, and incidents are either products of the author's imagination or used fictitiously. Any similarity to actual people, organizations, and/or events is purely coincidental.

Photograph: Maria Taglienti/Getty

Published by Barbour Publishing, Inc., P.O. Box 719, Uhrichsville, OH 44683, www.barbourbooks.com

Our mission is to publish and distribute inspirational products offering exceptional value and biblical encouragement to the masses.

ecpa Member of the
Evangelical Christian
Publishers Association

Printed in the United States of America.

AN IRISH BRIDE FOR CHRISTMAS

by Vickie McDonough

Defend the poor and fatherless:
do justice to the afflicted and needy.

PSALM 82:3

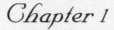

Chapter 1

Prairie Flats, Illinois, 1880

W here's Mama and Poppy?" Rosie hugged her rag doll to her chest and stared up at Jackson with worried brown eyes.

Unshed tears blurred the view of his niece as Jackson knelt in front of her. He blinked them away for fear of scaring her. He could handle his own grief, but seeing his niece crying for her parents nearly gutted him. How could he make the four-year-old understand that they'd just buried her mom and dad—that they weren't coming back?

Help me explain it to her so she'll understand, Lord.

He picked up Rosie and hugged her tight, needing solace himself. "Remember when Bandit got bit by a snake and died?"

Rosie looked up at him and nodded. Her eyes shimmered with unshed tears.

7

Maybe she understood more than he gave her credit for.

"We had to bury him, and then you and your mama put flowers on his grave and your poppy made a cross for it. Remember that?"

Rosie's lower lip trembled, and she nodded. "He's in doggy heaven. Poppy said so."

"Well, that's what happened today. Your mama and poppy died in a stagecoach accident"—he didn't want her to know they were shot by robbers—"and now they're in heaven with Jesus."

"But *I* want them." Tears dripped down her cheeks.

Jackson hugged her tight. "So do I, sweet pea; so do I. But Jesus needed them in heaven with Him. I'm going to take care of you now."

Jackson swayed back and forth as Rosie clung to his neck, crying. Why couldn't it have been him who died instead of Ben. Instead of Amanda.

God, I have to say I don't understand this. I know You see all and know all, but why this? How am I supposed to run Lancaster Stage alone and raise a little girl? Rosie needs a mother and a father, not an uncle who knows next to nothing about caring for a child.

He raked his hand through his hair. He'd agreed to keep Rosie while Ben and Amanda went to a nearby town to celebrate their fifth anniversary, but he didn't know they wouldn't return. Now Rosie was the only family he had left in the world. He needed her as much as she did him.

Jackson looked around the small room where he lived

behind the stage office. It smelled of leather and saddle soap from his evenings spent polishing harnesses and bridles. He hadn't had time to sweep the floor all week. The windows were so dingy he hadn't needed a shade to cover them, and there was only one bed. He hated all the reminders of his big brother and his sister-in-law in their house—a house left to him and Ben when their mother had died—but that was where Rosie should be.

He flipped the quilt back and laid Rosie on the bed, pushing back his emotions. He didn't understand why God hadn't protected Ben and Amanda during the stage robbery. It seemed a simple thing for the God who created the universe to deflect a few bullets.

But Jackson knew his brother wouldn't sit by and watch another of their stages being robbed. Most likely, Ben had tried to stop it—and now he and Amanda were dead.

Rosie was an orphan, and he had a two-man business to run alone.

He drew the carpetbag out from under his bed and blew the dust off. He'd pack his things while Rosie slept and then take them back to the neat two-bedroom home next door.

A few minutes later, he took a crate from off the back porch and packed up his coffee, sugar bowl, and cup and plate. He rarely ate there, preferring Amanda's fabulous cooking and open invitation to dine with them. What would he and Rosie eat now? He wasn't much of a cook.

Setting the crate by the door, he put the carpetbag on top of it. Rosie would miss her mama's homemade sugar cookies.

Maybe one of the church ladies would let him chop wood in exchange for some.

Entering the door to the stage office, he stared at the map with pins in it marking the four places where their stagecoaches had been robbed in the past three months. Why had they been targeted? They were just a small-time operation, transporting people and freight that arrived in Prairie Flats, Illinois, by train to the small area towns where the train didn't go. They rarely carried anything of great value, although someone seemed to know whenever they had a payroll shipment on board. With a shaking hand, he picked up a pin and stuck it in the spot where Ben and Amanda had died.

He dropped into a chair. Lowering his head to his arm, he let the tears he'd held back for the past few days flow.

Jackson awoke to someone knocking on the stage office door. He glanced around, wondering why he'd fallen asleep at the desk. Suddenly everything rushed back to him.

The rapping increased.

Rosie! He dashed into his room, and his heart slowed when he saw his niece curled up on his bed, hugging her dolly.

Someone pounded again, and Rosie stirred. Jackson hurried through the office, wiped his damp eyes, and opened the door. Judge Smith, the mayor, and the mayor's wife stood on the boardwalk. They seemed an odd trio to offer condolences, but he hoped they would do it quickly.

The judge cleared his throat. "May we come in, Mr. Lancaster? It's warm for late November, but that wind is stiff."

"Of course." Jackson stepped back, allowing the three to enter. Rosie appeared at the door between the two rooms, hair tousled from sleep, and leaned against the jamb.

"How can I help you, Judge?"

He glanced around the office, and Jackson noted when the man's gaze landed on Rosie. "Perhaps it would be best if Mrs. O'Keefe took the child in the other room while we talk."

Rosie's eyes widened, and she raced toward him. Jackson scooped her up, concern mounting. What could these men have to say to him that they didn't want Rosie to hear? Had someone discovered the identity of the robbers?

Mrs. O'Keefe ambled to the back of the room and peeked through the door to his private quarters. Jackson narrowed his eyes at her rudeness.

"Tsk tsk. Would you look at this, Judge? You'll see for yourself what I've been talking about. This is no place for a child to live."

To Jackson's surprise, the judge and mayor joined Mrs. O'Keefe at the door of his room. With the news of the two deaths, a funeral to plan, and a precocious young one to care for, he hadn't gotten his normal chores accomplished. Sure, his place was a bit disorderly at the moment, but what did that matter to them?

"I don't see nothing all that much out of the ordinary here. He's a single man, Maura."

"But he can't raise a child in a place like this. That's my point." She eyed Jackson over the top of her glasses, pressed her lips together, and shook her head.

Jackson shifted Rosie to his other arm. "Just what is this all about?"

The judge sighed and turned to face him. "Mrs. O'Keefe has petitioned the courts to get custody of your niece."

"What?" Jackson backed up against the door, clinging to his niece. She wrinkled her brow and looked from him to the judge and back. "Now you listen here. Rosie is *my* niece. My flesh and blood. We belong together."

"You sure you want to be talking about this in front of the child?" The judge lifted his brows.

No, he didn't, but he wasn't about to let Mrs. O'Keefe get her paws on Rosie. "Not really, but there's no point discussing it. I'm all the family she has, Judge." Rosie must have sensed his distress, because she laid her head down on his shoulder and hugged his neck, nearly choking him.

"You're a single man, living in a—a hovel, for lack of a more decent word. A little girl has no business living here and being raised by an unmarried man. Isn't that right, Harvey?"

Harvey O'Keefe gave Jackson an almost apologetic glance before nodding at his wife. The man had yet to utter a single word. Maybe Jackson had one ally in the bunch.

"I've made my decision, Mr. Lancaster. Rosie is a young and impressionable child. You're a single man and shouldn't be tending a little girl. It isn't proper. I'm giving temporary custody to Mrs. O'Keefe."

Jackson's already-crumbling heart shattered in two. "You can't do that. We're family, and family stays together."

The judge laid a hand on Jackson's shoulder. "I know this

is a difficult thing, son, especially after losing your—" He looked at Rosie. "Um. . .well, you know. You can see your niece regularly, but you've no business tending to her physical needs. If you know what I mean."

Jackson shook his head. This couldn't be happening. He wanted to run out the door with Rosie and leave town, but his business was here. He had people and clients who relied on his service. And if he left, he'd have no way to support Rosie and no home.

"This isn't right."

"Let me have the child." Mrs. O'Keefe held out her hands, a smug smile on her plump face.

Rosie whimpered. Jackson cast the judge a pleading glance. "There must be something I can do. She needs me. I'm the only familiar person left in her world."

"I'll give you the chance to get her back. If you marry in the next month—say, by Christmas—I'll grant you permanent custody of your niece. Otherwise, she'll stay with the O'Keefes." The judge put his hat on and buttoned his coat.

"Can't this wait—at least until tomorrow? We just buried Rosie's parents this morning." Jackson searched his mind. There had to be some way to fix this nightmare.

"Prolonging the matter won't make it easier. You have until Christmas." The judge reached for the door, and Jackson stepped aside. He turned the handle then stopped. "Hand over the child, Mr. Lancaster."

"No," Rosie cried.

The tightening in Jackson's throat had nothing to do with

Rosie choking his neck. He'd never broken the law before, although he was highly tempted now. But if he ran with Rosie, what kind of life could he give her? As much as it pained him, he had to follow the judge's orders.

He untangled his niece's arm. "It will be okay, sweet pea. You go home with this nice man and lady; then I'll come see you every day until you can come back home."

"I have cookies and milk waiting for you." Maura O'Keefe smiled congenially for the first time and held out her arms.

"I like cookies. Can Uncle Jack have one?"

"Maybe when he visits tomorrow." Mrs. O'Keefe patted Rosie's head.

"Can Sally come?"

Mrs. O'Keefe wrinkled her brow. "Who is Sally? Not a dog, I hope."

Rosie shook her head. "No, she's my dolly."

Jackson's legs trembled and his head ached. Rosie had never known a stranger, and that alone could make this horrible situation bearable. He couldn't stand the thought of her crying for him and him unable to console her.

"I can come to your house and eat cookies." She wriggled, and Jackson reluctantly set her down. She took Mrs. O'Keefe's hand and waved at him.

"You'll bring her clothes to the house later?" Mrs. O'Keefe lifted her brows at him.

He nodded, too stunned to move. Silently Mr. O'Keefe followed his wife outside. Shutting the door, Jackson slid to the floor, unable to digest all that had happened.

He'd lost everything he held dear in one day. A frigid numbness made his limbs feel heavy, weighted.

Why is this happening, God? How will Rosie get along without me?

"And how in the world am I supposed to find a bride by Christmas?"

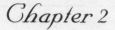

Chapter 2

Larkin Doyle stared with her mouth open as Maura O'Keefe strode into the house with a little girl in tow. What in the world had the woman done now?

"This is Rosie Lancaster, and she's going to live with us. Rosie is in need of cookies and milk." Maura eyed Larkin with her brows lifted, and Larkin understood the silent message.

The lass tugged at Larkin's skirt. "I like cookies." The brown-eyed urchin stared up at her.

Reaching out a hand, Larkin smiled. "Then, wee one, we must go find some."

Rosie took Larkin's hand without hesitation. "You talk funny."

"Aye, 'tis true. I come from Ireland, which is why I talk as I do." The charming child won Larkin's heart immediately.

Larkin put a shallow crate upside down on a chair and set the child at the table. She gave her two gingersnaps and a glass half filled with milk. As Rosie nibbled the snack, Larkin studied her. The girl's brown eyes were so dark Larkin could barely see her pupils, and her wavy hair was only a few shades lighter. What a lovely lass she was. "Is that good?"

Rosie nodded. "Mama makes sugar cookies."

How sad. Did the lass not understand that her mum was gone? Larkin brushed a strand of hair from Rosie's face and tucked it behind her ear.

Wilma, the O'Keefes' cook, entered with a bucket over her arm. She glanced at Rosie. "Well, what have we here?"

"This is Rosie. She'll be stayin' here awhile."

Wilma pursed her lips and set the bucket down. She leaned toward Larkin. "Not another attempt to replace the baby Maura lost?"

Larkin shrugged, hurt by Wilma's callous words. "Rosie, I must go talk to Mrs. O'Keefe for a moment. You stay with Wilma."

Rosie scowled but nodded. She dipped the corner of her remaining cookie in her milk then stuck it in her mouth.

Larkin gave her a third cookie then patted the lass's head. "I shall be back in a minute."

Rosie picked up another cookie and waved at her.

Larkin hurried through the dining room, past the elaborate table, and into the parlor. Mayor O'Keefe sat in his favorite chair, hiding behind his newspaper as he often did. She located Mrs. O'Keefe in the spare bedroom, tapping her index finger against her thick lips.

"I was going to give this room to the girl, but I simply can't have her destroying the décor. This furniture was far too costly to allow a child to live here. Too, if we have guests, I'll no longer have a place to put them."

Larkin didn't ask but knew that meant Rosie would be sharing her room. She didn't mind but would have liked to have been asked rather than having Mrs. O'Keefe instruct her as to how things would be. But wasn't that always the case?

You're a servant here, not a daughter—and you'd best remember that, Larkin Doyle.

As much as she'd hoped for a loving family to live with after her parents had died, that hadn't happened. The O'Keefes had taken her in and given her a nice place to live and decent clothes to wear, but she was not an adopted daughter. Perhaps Rosie would fill that coveted position.

"May I ask why the lass is here?"

"You may." Mrs. O'Keefe sidled a glance her way as she closed the curtains on the lone window. "Rosie's parents were buried today. A single man the likes of Jackson Lancaster isn't fit to raise a child—a girl, at that. Besides, he didn't want the responsibility, so I very graciously offered to take in the orphan."

" 'Tis a sad day when family refuses to care for family." Larkin's ire rose at the uncle who coldly turned his back on such a darling child. What a horrible ordeal Rosie must have been through.

"Give the girl a bath after she eats her cookies, and find something to put her in. Her uncle was supposed to deliver her clothes here, but with the lateness of the hour, he may not come until tomorrow."

"Aye, mum." Larkin hurried back to the kitchen. Wilma

nodded toward the table. Larkin's heart stopped when she saw Rosie's head leaning against the table. Poor lass. Larkin lifted her up.

"I want Uncle Jack!" Rosie suddenly went rigid and struggled to get free. Larkin set her down for fear of dropping her. The lass slumped to the ground, tears pooling in her eyes. "I wanna go home."

Larkin clutched her chest as the memories of her parents' deaths came rushing back. She knew what it felt like to lose those she loved and to become an orphan.

Cuddling the girl, she patted her back. "There, there, 'twill be all right."

Uncle Jack. The poor child must be crying for the very man who'd refused to care for her. What a horrible beast he must be. Even though she was a Christian woman, if she ever got the chance, Larkin intended to give him a piece of her mind.

❧

The sun peeked over the horizon, sending its warming rays across Jackson's back. He knocked on the O'Keefes' door then rubbed his hand across his bristly jaw. He should have taken the time to shave this morning, but after another nearly sleepless night, he'd been anxious to see how Rosie had fared and to get her clothes to her so she'd have something fresh to wear. Shoving his hands in his coat pockets, he waited. Maybe he was too early.

A noise on the other side of the door indicated someone was coming. His gut tingled with excitement while at the same time he worried about Rosie's well-being. Had she cried last night? Had she asked for her mama? For him?

A pretty young woman with thick auburn hair opened the door. Her green eyes widened at the sight of him and then narrowed. "Might I help you?"

He brushed the dust from his jacket and smiled. "I'm Rosie's uncle. I've brought her clothes and have come to see her."

The woman's cinnamon-colored brows dipped. "She's not yet awake. The wee lass had trouble getting to sleep last night, so I thought it best not to awaken her this morning. I'll take her clothes."

Disappointed, Jackson handed the small satchel to her. "Could I come back and see her later?"

She scowled and stared at him as if he were a weevil in a flour sack. He glanced down at his clothes. Did he look that bad? Or had something else twisted her pretty mouth like a pretzel?

"You'd best come back after the family has had breakfast. Mrs. O'Keefe can talk with you then."

She started to shut the door, but he stuck out his foot, holding it open. "Wait. I don't need to talk to the mayor's wife. I just want to see my niece and make sure she's all right."

"The lass is fine, other than having a difficult time sleeping in a strange bed. I tended her meself. Really now, I've other duties to attend to. Come back later."

Jackson stared at the closed door, feeling empty and alone. He looked up to a window on the second story, wondering if Rosie might be there. Would she look out and see him?

Backing away, he stared at the big structure, one of the few brick houses in Prairie Flats. White columns holding up the porch roof gave it a Southern flair. The house was much nicer and probably warmer than Ben and Amanda's clapboard cottage. But strangers couldn't love Rosie like he did.

Please, Lord, show me how to get her back. Comfort Rosie, and help her not to fret.

Shoving his hands in pockets, he crossed the street to Pearl's Café. He'd get breakfast, check on today's stage, and then go back to see his niece.

At the café, he pulled out a chair and stared out the window. He could just make out one corner of the O'Keefes' home from here. He thought of the gal who'd opened the door. She was a pretty young woman, even with that pert nose scrunched up at him and her eyes flashing daggers. What had he done to upset her so?

Maybe she hadn't had her morning coffee yet. He remembered seeing her walking down the boardwalk and shopping at the mercantile on occasion but had never met her before. Her singsong accent was unexpected on the Illinois prairie, but it was lovely and intriguing.

Two hours later, Jackson knocked at the O'Keefes' fancy front door again. The wood-carver had done an excellent job on the twisted columns. Jackson tapped the dainty gold door knocker several times then pounded on the wood with his knuckles.

Finally, the Irish gal opened the door, her eyes widening again at the sight of him. He was glad he'd taken the time to shave and change clothes.

"Wait here and I shall get Mrs. O'Keefe." She closed the door in his face, not even allowing him to step into the parlor. Was she always so rude?

Jackson slumped against the jamb, anxious to see Rosie. The longer he waited, the more his anxiety grew. Were they purposefully avoiding him? He glanced at his pocket watch.

The door creaked and suddenly opened. The mayor's wife pulled a shawl around her shoulders and stepped outside, her lips pursed.

"What is it you need, Mr. Lancaster? Surely you must know that as the mayor's wife I'm a very busy woman. I can't have you disturbing me constantly."

Jackson lifted his brow. Two visits constituted constantly bothering her? "I'm here to see Rosie."

Mrs. O'Keefe let out a tsk. "It's not good to trouble the child. She's been through enough."

"Seeing me won't upset her. She loves me, as I do her."

"Yes, well, the judge gave me custody, and if she sees you, she'll just want to be with you—and not being able to do so will frustrate her. So, you see, it's better if she doesn't see you at all."

Jackson ground his back teeth together as his irritation rose. "The judge said I could see her every day. I want to see Rosie now."

Mrs. O'Keefe backed up a half step but glared over the top of her wire-rimmed glasses at him. "I simply can't have you interrupting things here at your leisure. We will go talk to the judge and get this matter settled now."

She disappeared back into the house. Jackson wanted to ram his fist through her glass window but knew that wouldn't accomplish anything other than proving that he wasn't fit to care for Rosie. He gazed up at the cloudy sky. "God, I need help here. I can't lose Rosie."

Moments later, he followed Mrs. O'Keefe as she marched toward Judge Smith's office. Jackson prayed the man wouldn't be in court so the matter could be settled quickly. He had his own work to do.

The mayor's wife stormed into the judge's offices, past the surprised clerk, and knocked on his private door.

"Now see here, madam, you can't—" At Mrs. O'Keefe's glare, the thin clerk slumped back into his chair. Mumbling under his breath, he yanked off his round wire glasses and polished them.

Mrs. O'Keefe knocked harder. Jackson had never been in the judge's offices and glanced around the opulent room. It smelled of beeswax and leather furniture. Two chairs sat on either side of a small round table, and a fine Turkish rug decorated the shiny wooden floor. The clerk's cherrywood desk was nicer than anything Jackson had seen in a long while.

"Come in, Andrew." The judge's deep voice resounded through the closed door.

Mrs. O'Keefe opened it and plowed right in. "It's not Andrew, Roy. It's Maura."

Jackson sighed and followed her. *That's just great. She's on a first-name basis with the judge.*

"Roy, Mr. Lancaster here was at my door this morning at a

most inappropriate hour, demanding to see his niece. I simply can't have that man coming and going anytime he chooses. As the mayor's wife, I'm a very busy woman."

The judge lowered his spectacles and glanced at Jackson. "That true, Lancaster?"

Jackson shrugged and resisted the urge to fidget. "Yes, sir, but I thought Rosie would need a fresh change of clothes when she arose. That's why I went so early."

The judge turned his gaze on Maura. "Sounds reasonable. The child needs her clothes."

"Yes, but then he returned in a few hours."

"That's because I didn't get to see Rosie, and that helper of yours told me to come back. I was worried how she fared last night." Jackson crossed his arms, irritated that he had to explain why he wanted to see his own niece.

"You see, Roy, we have guests constantly, and I can't have this man coming in and upsetting the girl when I have a dinner party to prepare for."

Judge Smith sighed. "I can see your point, but you can't keep the child from her uncle."

Jackson's hopes rose for the first time.

"Lancaster, I'm guessing Sundays are slow for you. Am I right?"

He nodded, unsure what that had to do with anything.

"How about Wednesdays?" the judge asked.

"Sometimes busier than other days, sometimes not. Just depends." Jackson swallowed, not liking where his thoughts were taking him.

"All right. Maura, you let the man see his niece twice a week—on Sundays and Wednesdays."

"But—," Maura squeaked.

"That's not—" Jackson stepped forward.

Judge Smith raised his hand. "I've made my decision. Lancaster can see his niece for two hours every Sunday afternoon and Wednesday evening." He smacked his gavel down as if he'd made a court decision.

Jackson's heart plummeted as the sound echoed in his mind. He combed his fingers through his hair, holding them against his crown. He promised Rosie that he'd take care of her. She would think he'd lied to her—that he'd deserted her.

A ruckus sounded in the clerk's office. "Someone said Jackson Lancaster is in seeing the judge. That true?"

Jackson recognized the voice of Sheriff Kevin Steele and stepped into the other room. The sheriff's steady gaze turned his way. "Sorry to have to tell you, Lancaster, but your stage has been robbed again. The driver's been shot."

Larkin squirmed in her chair as Frank Barrett leered at her over his cup of cider. She broke his gaze and pushed her carrots around on her plate, uncomfortable with his attention. Even though some might find the man of average height with sleek dark hair and pale gray eyes handsome, something about him gave her the shivers. She couldn't help comparing him to Jackson Lancaster's rugged, often disheveled appearance that made him look like a boy in need of a mother's care.

"It was very benevolent of you to take in the Lancaster orphan. Must have been quite a shock for her to lose both parents at once." Frank turned his attention to Maura. "How is she adapting to life here?"

"As well as can be expected. Although I do believe Judge Smith made a grievous error allowing that scoundrel uncle of hers to visit. He had the nerve to return her a half hour late, and then the child pitched a royal fit when it was time for him to leave. I simply don't understand what she sees in him. He didn't want to keep her, after all."

"I can see how his visits would be disruptive and not in the best interest of the girl."

Maura picked up her glass and lifted it as if in a toast. "Exactly how I feel. The child has enough worries without pining for the very uncle who gave her away and refused to care for her. His visits will only prolong her healing process."

Larkin narrowed her eyes but focused on her plate. Maura allowed her to attend the O'Keefes' dinner parties but made it clear that she was to remain silent unless directly asked a question. To Maura, Larkin represented a trophy of the woman's hospitality and generosity. Taking in an orphan somehow set her above her peers—at least in Maura's mind. And now she had two.

Larkin took a bite of mashed potatoes covered in Wilma's thick beef gravy, but its flavor was wasted on her. Why did Maura always refer to Rosie as "the child" or "the girl" but never by her name?

Had she done that when Larkin first arrived? Searching her mind, Larkin couldn't remember. She'd been a distraught twelve-year-old, having lost her parents to illness only a few years after they had arrived in New York. The deplorable conditions on the boat from Ireland had caused her mother to take sick, and she never recovered. Then her da caught the same sickness and died.

She didn't dislike living with the O'Keefes and was grateful to them for taking her in, but at nineteen, she longed for a home of her own—a family of her own.

Maura wanted Rosie so badly that she was willing to offer her a home when nobody else would, but one spilled glass of milk and Rosie had been relegated to eating in the kitchen. Thankfully, dinner tonight was later than normal to accommodate Frank Barrett's busy schedule, so she'd been able to sit with Rosie while she ate and had put her to bed before dinner.

"Don't you agree, Miss Doyle?"

Larkin's gaze darted up at Mr. Barrett's question. One she hadn't heard. "Um. . .'tis sorry I am, but I did not hear the question." She swallowed hard, irritated that her accent thickened whenever she was flustered.

"I said that the Lancaster girl is far better off here than with her uneducated uncle. Don't you agree?"

Maura stared at her as if awaiting her agreeable response. Larkin knew it was better to deflect her answer than step in that miry pit. "Why do you refer to Mr. Lancaster as uneducated? He speaks clearly and runs a successful business. I wouldn't think an uneducated man could do that."

Mr. Barrett's brows lifted at her defense of Jackson Lancaster. She wasn't even sure why she defended him, since she despised the way he had abandoned Rosie.

"You'd be surprised what a man can do when he sets his mind to it." Frank narrowed his eyes at her.

His interest in her was undeniable, but she did not return the attraction. A sinister air encircled the man, and even though he was a friend of the O'Keefes, Larkin intended to keep her distance.

"I'd best look in on Rosie and make sure she's sleeping

soundly." Larkin pushed back from the table, and Mr. O'Keefe and Mr. Barrett both rose.

"There's no need for you to check on the child, Larkin. I'll have Wilma do it."

"Beggin' your pardon, mum, but you asked me to tend Rosie. I wouldn't want Wilma to be off helping in the bedrooms when you might have need of her here." She rushed out of the room before Maura forced her to stay, grateful to be away from Mr. Barrett's leering.

In her room, she found Rosie still asleep, with both hands under her cheek. Larkin brushed a lock of hair out of the girl's face. She was such a pretty child. And resilient, even after all that had happened. Larkin's heart warmed. Maybe someday she'd have a sweet daughter like Rosie.

❧

Rosie bounced on her toes and ran to the door. "Is he coming?"

Why was the lass so eager to see the uncle who didn't want her? Perhaps she was unaware that he had abandoned her. Larkin shook her head, finding it difficult to understand why the man wanted to spend time with Rosie now. Did it ease his guilt? She looked through the tall, narrow window at the front entrance. "Here he comes now."

She tied Rosie's cloak under her neck and opened the door. The lass raced outside. "Uncle Jack!"

He picked her up and tossed her into the air. Childish giggles echoed in the quiet of the late afternoon, warming Larkin's heart. She was so glad to see Rosie smiling.

"I sure missed you, sweet pea."

"I'm not a pea." Rosie locked her arms around his neck and hugged him tight.

"Ready to go?"

Larkin's heart skittered as he turned to walk away. "Mrs. O'Keefe needs a word with you, Mr. Lancaster."

His dark brows dipped down. A muscle ticked in his jaw. "Why?"

Larkin shrugged. "She didn't tell me. Only that I must inform her when you were here."

He sighed, and his broad shoulders drooped a bit. He shifted Rosie to his right arm. "All right. Let's get the inquisition over so Rosie and I can have our time together."

"We going home?" Rosie patted her uncle's clean-shaven cheek.

"We'll see, sweet pea."

Larkin ushered him into the parlor. "Please have a seat and excuse me while I find Mrs. O'Keefe."

Darting out the door, she swiped at the band of sweat on her brow. Odd that she would be perspiring in early December. She located Mrs. O'Keefe upstairs in the spare room where the woman was sorting her Christmas decorations.

"I'll have to order some new ornaments this year. Some of the old ones weren't packaged properly and got broken."

The look she cast in Larkin's direction told her that Maura blamed her for the damage. "Mr. Lancaster is here. He's anxious to be off with Rosie."

"Hmm. . .we'll just see about that."

Downstairs in the parlor, Rosie's uncle stood as they entered. "Good day, Mrs. O'Keefe."

"Humph. It's been a busy day." She glanced at the mantel clock. "Since Rosie was half an hour late returning last Wednesday, you may only keep her an hour and a half today."

Mr. Lancaster's eyes shot blue fire. Rosie cast worried glances from one person to the next and clung to his neck.

"Now see here, I was only late because one of my coaches cracked a wheel. I had to see about getting it repaired since it was due to go back out the next morning."

Maura waved her hand in the air. "No matter. I want the girl back by six o'clock so she can get her dinner."

"She can eat with me." He stood rigid, like a soldier, holding Rosie in one arm.

"That wasn't part of the judge's deal. Also, I want Miss Doyle to accompany the child on her excursions with you."

Jackson Lancaster looked as if he could have strangled Maura.

Larkin stared at her, stunned by her declaration. "But, mum—"

Maura zipped an angered glance her way. Larkin swallowed, remembering the times as a child that she'd been punished for her disobedience. "Aye, mum. As you wish."

"No! Rosie is my family, not yours." Mr. Lancaster headed for the door. "The judge made no conditions and said nothing about my visits being supervised."

"You can accept Miss Doyle's chaperoning or not see your niece at all."

"We're leaving." He slung open the door and stormed out.

"Go with the man. Make sure he returns the child on time tonight."

Hurrying to do Mrs. O'Keefe's bidding, Larkin donned her cloak and followed the pair outside, feeling like an unwanted stepchild. He didn't want her company, but she didn't dare refuse Mrs. O'Keefe's orders or she'd be out on the streets. Hurrying to keep up with his long-legged gait, Larkin took two steps to his one. Rosie peered over his shoulder and waved. Larkin smiled at her.

Mr. Lancaster stopped suddenly, and Larkin plowed into his solid back. He turned quickly, grabbing her arm and steadying her. "Sorry. Look, Miss Doyle, I don't need anyone watching over my shoulder during my time with Rosie."

Larkin studied the ground rather than his fierce blue eyes. "I don't doubt that a'tall, but you wouldna want me to get into trouble for not complying with Mrs. O'Keefe's wishes, would you, now?"

Indecision darkened his gaze. Finally, he heaved a sigh. "I guess not. Follow me, then."

She hurried to keep up, running a bit to draw even with him. He loosened Rosie's arms from his neck and tossed her in the air again, gaining a wide grin from his niece.

"Do it again, Uncle Jack."

"One more time." He tossed her high, this time catching her and cradling her in both arms as one would hold an infant. Leaning down, he pressed his lips against Rosie's cheek and blew, making a sputtering noise.

Melancholy washed over Larkin. His actions reminded her how her da had played with her as a child.

"That tickles." Rosie giggled and rubbed her cheek.

Jackson Lancaster chuckled for the first time, and it took her breath away. A dimple in his tanned cheek winked at her before it disappeared as his expression sobered. She found his ruggedness appealing, much to her dismay. She didn't want to like the man after what he'd done.

Something didn't add up. Was Maura wrong in her opinion of him? Who told her he didn't want his niece? From what Larkin had seen, the man was willing to fight to spend time with Rosie.

They approached a small clapboard house painted a cheery buttery shade. Rosie peered over her uncle's shoulder. "That's *my* house."

Larkin nearly stumbled. This was Rosie's home? There was nothing unsavory on the outside of the cute cottage, other than it being much smaller than the O'Keefes' overly large house. Mr. Lancaster opened the door, then stepped aside and allowed her to enter first.

The house had a slight musty smell, but it *had* probably been closed up since Rosie's parents' deaths. A stairway led up to the bedrooms, most likely. A simple kitchen was to her left, and on the right, the parlor was decorated with a pretty floral wallpaper and a colorful rag rug. A small settee looked abandoned under the front window. Two rockers sat turned toward the fireplace. Everything was neat and tidy. All it needed was a family.

Surprised at the emotion that swept over her, Larkin crossed to the parlor window and looked past the lacy curtains that were held back with a matching tie to the cozy front yard. This was just the kind of place she'd dreamed about whenever she thought of having a home of her own—something simple but cozy. She felt a tug on her hand and looked down.

"Come see my room." Rosie's wide gaze beseeched her to follow.

Larkin looked at Mr. Lancaster, and he shrugged. "Make yourself at home. I thought Rosie might like to get a few of her toys to, uh. . .take back with her."

Larkin didn't miss the huskiness in his voice when he thought of having to return his niece. Like the morning sun bursting over the horizon in all its glory, she realized the truth. This man dearly loved Rosie and was pained by their separation. So why didn't he keep her?

"C'mon, Larkin." Rosie leaned sideways and pulled her along. He followed them.

Upstairs, Rosie went into her room, but Larkin stood out on the stairway landing, looking in. The furniture in Rosie's small room consisted of a little bed and a chair. Three crates turned on their sides held her few toys and another pair of shoes that looked to be her Sunday best. A book of children's stories leaned sideways in one crate, and a ring-toss game sat across from it. Another crate was filled with more than two dozen blocks of various sizes. Three empty pegs were attached to the wall at a height that the girl could manage.

"Would you like to take a book, game, and blocks back to the O'Keefes'?" Mr. Lancaster asked.

Rosie shook her head, her braids swinging back and forth. "No. They need to be here for when I come home."

Larkin couldn't help glancing at Mr. Lancaster. The longing look in his blue eyes took her breath away.

❧

If *she comes home*, Jackson couldn't help thinking. Miss Doyle looked uncomfortable in the doorway. He'd made it clear that he didn't want or appreciate her presence, but he hadn't thought what it meant for her. Mrs. O'Keefe sounded like an ogre, and he didn't doubt that she'd be quick to punish Miss Doyle if she refused to accompany him. Obviously she hadn't wanted to come with him any more than he'd wanted her to join them.

Ignoring her, he dropped to the floor and picked up one of Rosie's books. "Come here, sweet pea, and I'll read to you."

Rosie complied and sat on his lap. He couldn't help glancing at Miss Doyle. She stared at him with a surprised look. What? Did she think he couldn't read?

He tried to forget she was there as he read the story *The Three Bears* from *Aunt Mavor's Nursery Tales*.

Miss Doyle's soft floral scent drifted through the room when she untied her cloak and laid it over her arm. She leaned against the doorframe, watching him. Feeling guilty for being so rude to her, he looked up. "You can sit on Rosie's bed, if you like, or in the parlor."

Relief softened her pretty features, but she didn't enter the room. "If you're sure 'tis all right, I *would* like to sit in the parlor. . .and give you and Rosie some time alone."

Appreciating her consideration, he nodded and watched her leave.

Rosie nudged him in the belly with her elbow. "Read more, Uncle Jack."

After he read three stories from the children's book, she wanted to play with her blocks. He built several towers, and she knocked them down, laughing with delight.

Being with Rosie made him realize he'd missed her more than he thought. Staying busy with work had helped keep his mind off the situation, which angered him whenever he thought about it, but working sure hadn't helped him to find a bride. He simply had no time to court, not that there were many unmarried women *to* court.

"I'm gonna build a house." Rosie collected her blocks in a pile and started stacking them.

It bothered Jackson that she didn't seem to miss him nearly as much as he missed her. In fact, she seemed to be getting along quite well without him. He stared at a knothole on the wall. Children were adaptable. Not so with adults.

He stood, and Rosie looked up at him. "Go ahead and make a house. I need to talk to Miss Doyle for a few minutes."

"Her name is Larkin."

He smiled. "That's a pretty name."

With the tip of her tongue in the corner of her mouth, Rosie carefully set another block on her growing stack.

Jackson entered the parlor and found Miss Doyle in Amanda's rocker. He wanted to be irritated, but instead, he thought she looked as if she belonged there. He walked closer and noticed her eyes were shut. For the first time, he wondered how hard Mrs. O'Keefe worked the girl—and surely having an active four-year-old had only added to her burden. How had Larkin Doyle come to live with the O'Keefes?

Jackson stepped on a board that squeaked, and Miss Doyle jerked and opened her eyes. "Ach, sure now, you frightened me. I fear I must have dozed off." She sat up and ran her hand over her hair.

Jackson dropped into Ben's rocker. A shaft of longing and sadness speared him. He missed his brother so much. Not just because of the business, but because Ben was his best friend.

"Are you all right, Mr. Lancaster?" Miss Doyle leaned forward in her chair.

Jackson nodded, irritated that she'd witnessed his grief. He turned his face away from her, trying to force back the tears stinging his eyes. He lurched to his feet and went to stand by the window.

"I want you to know, I'm sorry for your loss."

He couldn't respond with his throat clogged as if someone had shoved a rag down it.

The rocker creaked as she stood. He could sense her standing behind him. "I lost both me folks in a short while, leaving me an orphan, like Rosie."

Jackson didn't want her comfort—didn't want her in Ben's home. She was a member of the enemy's camp. He whirled around so fast that Miss Doyle took a step backward, her eyes wide. "Rosie is not an orphan. She has me."

Miss Doyle blinked her big green eyes. "Then why did you

give her to Mrs. O'Keefe?"

Jackson clutched his fists together. All the anguish and pain of the past week came rushing to the surface. He leaned into Miss Doyle's face. "I never gave Rosie up. She was stolen right out of my arms."

Confusion, and maybe even a little fear, swirled in her eyes and wrinkled her brow.

Guilt washed over him for taking his frustrations out on her. He glanced out the window again and noticed the sun had already set. Shadows darkened the room, and he turned at a shuffling in the doorway. "It's time to go, sweet pea."

Rosie's lip trembled in the waning light. "No. I want to stay here with you."

Jackson crossed the room and knelt in front of her. "That's what I want, too, but we can't. Not yet."

"Why?" Tears dripped down Rosie's cheeks.

"Because the judge said you have to stay at the O'Keefes' until. . ." He cast a glance at Miss Doyle. How much did she know?

"I don't wanna go." Rosie dashed back to her room.

Jackson sighed and stood. It was so hard to take her back when he wanted to keep her so badly. He found her on her bed and picked her up.

"No. . .I don't want to go." Rosie kicked at him and pushed against his chest. "Put me down."

Holding her tight with his jaw set, he carried her outside, not even checking to see if Miss Doyle followed. Another chunk of his heart broke off and lodged in his throat.

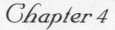

Chapter 4

The window in the stage office door rattled as the door opened. Mrs. Winningham entered, followed by three of her six boys, reminding him of a mother duck with her ducklings.

Jackson laid his pencil down and rubbed his forehead. Ben or Amanda always handled the bookwork. Trying to make all those numbers line up wasn't something he enjoyed, but it had to be done.

He stood and forced a smile in spite of the headache clawing his forehead.

The young widow Mabel Winningham had made her interest in him well known, at least to him. She wasn't especially pretty, with her hair all pinched tight in a bun and those too-big-for-her-face amber eyes and buck teeth, but she was friendly enough. "Good day, Mr. Lancaster." She smiled, batting her eyes, reminding him of an owl.

The first of her boys, a three-foot-tall blond, stopped beside her. The last two, identical twins with snow-white hair, plowed into the back of their brother.

"Hey! Stop it." The older boy spun around and shoved one of his brothers, knocking him backward into the other boy. Both landed on the floor, staring wide-eyed at their attacker. They turned in unison to look at each other, and as if they passed some silent code, both wailed at the same time.

Mrs. Winningham grabbed the shoulder of the oldest boy. "Bruce, you stop treating your brothers that way."

"They started it," he whined, sticking out his lip in a pout that would have swayed a weaker woman to his side. "They conked me in the back."

"Sit down over there." She pointed to the extra chair near the window. "Bobby, Billy, stop that caterwauling. I can't hear myself think."

Jackson pinched the bridge of his nose, thankful that the other three Winningham boys were at school and not here. How did their mother find the energy to deal with them all day after day? He couldn't help feeling sympathy for her.

"Sorry about that, Mr. Lancaster." Her lips turned up in an embarrassed smile. "But boys will be boys."

He was certain she knew all about boys. Bruce knelt in the chair, blowing steam rings on the window Jackson had just cleaned the day before. "What can I help you with, ma'am?"

She patted her head, not that a hair was out of place, what with it all being stuck down. Did women use hair oil?

"I wanted to make sure that you know my sister will be riding your stage from River Valley to here the week before Christmas. I'm concerned for her safety, what with all the robberies and, well. . .you know."

He sighed inwardly. She wasn't the first person to challenge him on a passenger's safety, and he of all people knew the danger. "I'm working on hiring an extra man to ride shotgun. Before the robberies started, we had no need for a guard."

"Well, you certainly need one now." She hiked her chin and looked at him with piercing tawny eyes.

Evidently she wasn't interested in winning his heart today. Thank goodness. He needed a wife, but he wasn't ready to take on a whole tribe. One little girl was enough for now.

Suddenly she softened her expression, and he swallowed hard.

"Ethel's not married. I was hoping you might come to dinner once she's here."

Uh-oh. Jackson glanced at the calendar on the wall. Just two weeks to find a bride. Was he that desperate? At least the sister most likely didn't have a half dozen boys.

Surely some other woman—one without six hooligan kids— would like to marry a man who owned his own business and a nice house.

"Uh. . .thanks for the invitation, but I'm pretty busy right now, running things here by myself."

Her gaze hardened. "Well, maybe after Christmas. Let's go, boys." She spun around and yanked the two toddlers up from where they were wrestling. Bruce marked a *B* inside one of the many fog circles he'd blown on the window. He pointed his finger like a gun and pretended to shoot Jackson and then jumped out of the chair.

Jackson closed the door the boy had left open and watched through the window as the Winningham tornado blew down the street. He wondered how the slight woman managed to feed and clothe all those boys, much less keep them in line. He made a mental note to go hunting and take her some meat. But maybe it would be better if he delivered it after dark, so she wouldn't know who'd brought it. He didn't want her getting the wrong idea.

Jackson sat at his desk and opened the center drawer. Mabel Winningham's name had been at the bottom of his list of prospective brides—a very short list. He licked the end of his pencil and drew a line through her name.

Elmer Limley, the town drunk, had a daughter who was a few years older than Jackson. The spinster had never married and hid herself away in her home, doing mending for a few of the town's wealthier people. He'd often felt sorry for Thelma Limley. She was as homely as a stray mutt, but she was kind. She'd be nice to Rosie, but he didn't want his niece exposed to the likes of Elmer Limley. For the time being, he left Thelma's name on the list.

He'd even penciled in Larkin Doyle's name, not that the quiet woman had ever shown any interest in him. But if he married her, he'd never be free of Mrs. O'Keefe's meddling.

He stared out the window, watching a wagon slowly move by. He'd never thought too much about getting married before but always figured he'd marry for love like Ben had. Amanda had come to town to visit a family that used to live in Prairie Flats. The first time Ben saw her, he'd acted like a schoolboy with his first crush. Jackson smiled, remembering.

Ben and Amanda had lived only five short years together, but they'd been years of love and laughter. That's what Jackson wanted. A home he looked forward all day to returning to. Not one where he'd have to hide out in the barn because he'd married a woman he had no feelings for.

But couldn't love grow out of such a situation?

For Rosie's sake, he had to do something. He had to find a bride in just two weeks.

Tapping his pencil on the desk, he thought of all the smaller towns that his stage visited. Was there a woman in one of those places willing to marry quickly—a woman who'd be a good stepmother for Rosie? His needs didn't matter so much, just as long as Rosie was back with him.

Looking up at the ceiling, he sighed. "I need some help, Lord. How do I find a wife so fast? Guide me. Show me where to look.

"Please help, Father. I can't lose Rosie."

❧

Jackson tied his two horses to the ornamental iron hitching post in front of the O'Keefes' large home. Arriving to pick up Rosie definitely felt better than returning her. Even after two weeks, she still cried and fussed when he had to leave. In fact, her fits seemed to be getting worse rather than better. He ran his hand down his duster, making sure he looked presentable, and knocked on the door.

"He's here. Uncle Jack's here." Rosie's muffled squeals on

the other side of the door made him smile. Nobody called him Jack, but early on, his niece had shortened his name to that.

The door opened, and Rosie rushed past Miss Doyle, grabbing him around one leg. He brushed his hand over her dark hair and pressed her head against his thigh. "Evening, sweet pea."

She reached her hands up to him, and he picked her up, planting a kiss on her cheek. "We going home again?"

"Not today. The sun's out in full force and there's no wind, so I thought you might like to ride Horace."

"Oh boy!" Rosie clapped her hands together and looked at Miss Doyle. "We're gonna ride hossies."

Jackson wasn't certain, given the natural pale coloring of Miss Doyle's fair skin, but he felt certain that all the blood had just rushed out of her face.

She stepped outside, closing the door behind her, and peered wide-eyed past him to the horses. "Sure now, I've never been on a horse in me whole life."

Ah, so that was the problem. Jackson flashed a reassuring smile. "It's nothing to fear. We'll just walk them."

"C'mon, Larkin. Hossies is fun."

Miss Doyle looked down at her dress. "I can't ride a horse in me dress."

Rosie giggled. "Your dress won't fit on a hossie."

A shy grin tugged at her lips. "'Twould be a funny thing to see, for sure. What I meant to say is that I can't ride since *I'm* wearing a dress."

With a smile on her face, the young woman was quite

pretty. She was always so somber and quiet around him. He'd wondered if she didn't like him for some reason.

Jackson lifted Rosie onto Horace's saddle and then offered a hand to Miss Doyle. Would she stand her ground and refuse to go? He wouldn't mind time alone with Rosie but didn't want the young woman to get in trouble with her employer. "Look, if you'd rather not go, I understand. We're not leaving town, just walking around. Rosie loves horses, and I thought she'd enjoy a short ride."

Miss Doyle darted a glance at the closed door and shook her head. "Mrs. O'Keefe says I must go, or. . ."

Jackson hated putting the young woman in such an awkward position, but since Rosie was all ready to ride, he didn't want to disappoint her. "I'll help you mount the horse, and then you can fix your skirts so they're respectable."

Green eyes stared at him as if he were a loon. "Will you be riding or leading the horses?"

"Ride with me, Uncle Jack."

He shrugged. "Guess I'm riding. But I can lead your horse if you prefer."

He could tell she didn't want to ride, but she shuffled toward the horse, stopping four feet away. His heart went out to her. Here she was being forced into another situation she didn't desire, but she wasn't complaining, and for that, he admired her.

Before she could object, Jackson scooped her up and deposited her on Maudie's back.

"Oh!" she squealed as she struggled to hide her bare calves with her skirt and cloak. That done, she glared at him.

"'Twould have been kind of you to have given me warning, Mr. Lancaster."

He grinned, enjoying her lyrical accent. She looked as ruffled as a hen being chased by a fox. "Call me Jackson—since we're seeing so much of each other."

"You can call her Larkin." Rosie smiled. "That's her name."

Jackson lifted a brow at the young woman, and she nodded. "Aye, call me by me first name."

He mounted up behind Rosie. "It's a pretty name. What does it mean?"

Glancing over his shoulder, he noticed her cheeks had reddened. "'Tis actually a man's name. Lorcan means fierce or silent."

Well, the silent part sure fit, but not the fierce. Sweet might be a better description.

"Me da liked the name. He said it reminded him of a lark. A bird." She shrugged, as if that wasn't an acceptable reason for giving a baby girl a male name.

"It's pretty and suits you." He guided the horses toward the edge of town, wanting to kick himself for complimenting her. He didn't need her to think he was happy to have her around. She was just an intruder, an interloper, distracting him from the short time he had with his niece.

Jackson tickled Rosie. She giggled and squirmed, making him forget about his silent shadow.

❧

Larkin concentrated on holding on to the saddle horn and not falling off the big horse while Jackson led it behind his mount. She'd made the mistake of peering down to the ground and didn't want to do that again. She rocked to the horse's gentle gait, relieved they weren't going any faster.

Up ahead, Rosie giggled as Jackson tickled her. Larkin admired his broad shoulders and the loose way he sat in the saddle. Not at all like her all-tensed-up gotta-hold-on-tight-so-I-don't-fall rigidness. Maudie's walk was gentle, making Larkin sway side to side a bit. Still, she didn't trust animals and kept a tight grip on the horn in case the horse decided to run away.

Larkin rubbed her gritty eyes and yawned. She'd lain awake late the previous night trying to make sense of things. Against her wishes, she liked Jackson Lancaster. His nearly black hair was almost the same color as Rosie's, and his blue eyes reminded her of the vast ocean she crossed after leaving Ireland. The man had a rugged, shaggy look, kind of like a lost pup that needed someone to care for it.

She knew he ran the stage line with his brother, who'd been killed. Perhaps it was too difficult to care for an ornery four-year-old and a business, too.

Rosie let out a squeal, and Jackson chuckled, making his shoulders bounce.

Larkin smiled, glad to see Rosie happy again. The lass was becoming more withdrawn at the O'Keefes', as if she were afraid she'd get in trouble for touching things, which she had.

Mrs. O'Keefe had little patience for a rambunctious child, especially one who accidentally broke an antique vase from

Ireland. She had ordered Larkin to take Rosie on daily walks to help the child run off some steam. They'd been to the Lancaster Stage office several times, but to Rosie's disappointment, her uncle hadn't been there.

Why had Maura wanted the child in the first place? Did she think it lifted her up in the eyes of the community to be generous to an orphan? Did it fill a hole in her heart from losing her own child so long ago?

A rogue gust of wind flipped her cloak behind her, revealing her bare calf. Two men on the boardwalk elbowed each other and grinned at her. Cheeks scorching, she hurried to grab the corner of her cloak and secured it under her leg.

Jackson had done nothing to indicate he didn't want his niece. In fact, he acted the opposite. She was beginning to think Mrs. O'Keefe had misled her. But why?

Larkin always tried to believe the best of people. But if Mrs. O'Keefe had lied about Mr. Lancaster just to get Rosie, then she'd done the man a horrible injustice.

Jackson looked over his shoulder at her. "You doing all right?"

She smiled and nodded, warmed by his concern for her. She had tried hard to remain aloof. To not like Jackson Lancaster.

But it was too late.

Looking toward heaven, she prayed, *Father God, if Mrs. O'Keefe lied to get custody of Rosie, I pray You'll make things right. Jackson loves his niece, I can tell. They're family and should be together. Please make it so.*

Chapter 5

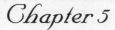

Mrs. O'Keefe peered over the top of her spectacles at Larkin. "When do you plan to accept Frank's offer for dinner?"

Larkin's heart skipped a beat. She'd hoped the subject wouldn't come up. "I'm not particularly interested in dining with him, mum."

Maura's pale blue eyes widened. "Why ever not? He's a fine-looking man and is vice president of the bank. It's more than a girl in your position should hope to find."

Her words cut like a surgeon's scalpel. A servant—that was the position she meant. As much as Larkin had hoped to become the daughter Maura always said she wanted, she knew she never would be. Maura had taken her in as a way to get free labor, and Larkin wasn't about to be tied the rest of her life to someone else who didn't love her. She twisted her hands together. "Mr. Barrett makes me nervous."

"That's the silliest thing I've ever heard. Why, he's a perfect gentleman." Maura's lips twisted, reminding Larkin of a snarling dog. "If he asks you again, you will accept. Is that clear?"

Larkin nodded, but inside she was screaming. Oh, how she wished she could leave this house and find a place of her own, but she had little money, and nobody would hire her if the mayor's wife told them not to. And how could she leave Rosie with Mrs. O'Keefe? The little girl's life would be miserable.

Maura enjoyed dressing her up and strutting the little lass around in front of friends and acquaintances, showing how generous she was to take in the waif. But at home, Maura couldn't be bothered with Rosie. She was relegated to the kitchen and Larkin's room and not allowed access to the rest of the house for fear she'd break another of Maura's valuable decorations. At least now Larkin had a cause to live for. She would tend the child she'd come to love and make sure that Rosie never knew the loneliness that she had.

Hurrying back to her room, she found Rosie sitting on the bed rubbing her eyes, her nap over. With her braids loosened, hair tousled, and cheeks red, she was as darling as ever. "Is Uncle Jack coming today?"

"Aye." A flutter of excitement tickled her stomach at the thought of seeing Jackson again. She was only happy for Rosie's sake. The lass was a different person on the days her uncle came. She was happy and not quiet and moody, like she'd recently become.

Larkin picked up the brush, undid Rosie's braids, and in quick order rewove them. She was thankful Rosie had quit asking for her mum and da but didn't like how she was starting to withdraw. The poor child had been through so much recently.

She didn't deserve to be stuck in this house where only Larkin and Wilma loved her.

"Shall we go see if Wilma baked some sugar cookies while you napped?"

Rosie smiled and nodded. Larkin helped her into her shoes and fastened them, then took her to the necessary and then into the kitchen, where they washed their hands. Rosie shinnied onto a chair and drank half the glass of milk Wilma had set out for her.

Larkin cringed when she wiped her milk mustache on her sleeve. "Use your napkin, lass, not your sleeve."

Rosie shrugged and picked up a cookie. As she ate, she stared off into space. Larkin wondered what she was thinking about as she helped herself to a cookie. After eating another cookie, Rosie took two more and wrapped them up in her cloth napkin.

Larkin lifted her brows. "What are you doin'? Have you not had enough cookies?"

"I'm saving them for Uncle Jack."

How sweet. Larkin glanced at the clock on the hearth. Jackson was later today than normal. She wondered if he was having a hard time running his business without his brother's assistance. Each time she saw Rosie's uncle, the bags under his eyes seemed larger and darker. Did he ever sleep? Was he eating properly?

"He'll be here soon," Wilma said as she added potatoes to the pot of boiling water.

Being separated from Rosie seemed to be more of a problem

to Jackson than the fact that someone was watching her for him. He should be grateful for that, at least, as busy as he was.

Larkin shook her head. Why all the worry about Jackson Lancaster? He could have kept Rosie instead of giving her to Maura. But hadn't he mentioned something about Rosie being stolen from him?

It was all so confusing that Larkin's head was swirling like a weather vane in a windstorm. Who was right? And who was wrong?

A knock at the kitchen door pulled her from her worries. Wilma dusted her hands on her apron and opened the door. Jackson had started coming to the kitchen entrance to avoid seeing Mrs. O'Keefe. It seemed to Larkin that every time the two were together, Maura enforced some new rule that only irritated the man further. Was there bad blood between the two of them?

Jackson tipped his hat to Wilma and Larkin, but his lovely blue eyes lit up when he saw Rosie at the table.

She smiled and waved to him. "I saved you some cookies."

"Did you, now? You know I like cookies." Jackson lingered in the doorway as if afraid to come in.

A frigid breeze cooled the overly warm room, stirring up the scent of wood smoke and baking chicken. Larkin's stomach growled.

"Sure smells good in here." A shy grin tugged at Jackson's lips.

"Well, don't just stand there letting in the cold air—not that it doesn't feel wonderful to me after standing in front of this stove all day." Wilma waved her stirring spoon in the air. "Have a seat at the table and eat those cookies your niece saved for you."

He hesitated a moment and looked past them. Was he making sure Mrs. O'Keefe wasn't around? Finally, he stepped inside and shut the door, then sat at the table. Rosie shoved her napkin toward him. He unfolded it and smiled. Larkin's stomach twittered at the sight of his dimples.

"Thank you for sharing with me, sweet pea." He took a bite and closed his eyes, as if he'd never tasted anything so good.

Larkin was saddened to think of him living alone and working so hard after all he'd lost. As far as she knew, Rosie was the only family he had left. His dark hair hung down over his forehead, so different from that of the many businessmen who visited the O'Keefe house, who wore their hair slicked back with smelly tonic. His cheeks bore the tan of a man who was often outside, not the paleness of men who worked in an office all day.

He caught her staring and winked. She resisted gasping and turned to find something to do. She grabbed a glass, retrieved the milk, and poured him some. When she handed it to him, his warm smile tickled her insides as if an intruding moth were fluttering at a window, seeking escape.

"I brought you a surprise." He looked at Rosie, reached into his coat pocket, and pulled out a handkerchief. He slid the bundle across the table.

Rosie clapped her hands and rose to her knees. She opened the present, revealing four perfect wooden replicas of animals. "A hossie!"

Jackson's longing as he watched his niece confused Larkin as much as his warm smile had. He didn't seem like the kind of man to abandon a child. She never wanted to like him, but she did. A lot.

"Look, Larkin, a cow. Moooo…" Rosie walked the cow and horse across the table. "Oink, oink," she said, picking up the pig.

"I think she likes them." Larkin smiled at him.

Jackson nodded and stood.

Rosie cast a worried eye in his direction but picked up the fourth animal—a sheep.

He glanced at Wilma then turned to Larkin. "I, uh. . . brought you something, too."

Larkin reached out and accepted the small wooden figure, her hands trembling and heart pounding. She'd never received a gift from anyone except at Christmas or on her birthday, and those had dwindled to next to nothing.

"It's a bird." He cleared his raspy throat. "It's not a lark, but I thought you might like it since you said your name reminded your dad of a bird."

Her throat went dry at the thoughtfulness of the gift and the time involved in making it. Larkin could only nod. She turned away, lest he see the tears burning her eyes, and poured a glass of water.

Wilma's upraised brow caught her eye. The cook grinned, something she rarely did.

Larkin swallowed another drink, wiped her eyes, and turned back around. "Thank you. I've never had such a thoughtful gift."

A shy smile tugged at his lips; then he broke her gaze.

She turned to Rosie. "Shall we go and put our lovely animals in our room so you can spend time with your uncle?"

Rosie stuck out her lip.

"Maybe she could bring one with her?" Jackson asked.

"Aye, that is a grand idea."

Larkin escorted Rosie back to their room, all the while examining her own gift. The bird, carved from a light-colored wood, more resembled a sparrow than a lark, but the fine craftsmanship and detail made even a plain sparrow exquisite. She probably shouldn't have accepted the gift, being as it was from a man, but she clutched it to her heart, knowing it was already one of her most treasured possessions.

Fifteen minutes later, Larkin and Jackson walked down the boardwalk with Rosie between them, holding their hands. To someone who didn't know them, they could be a family on their way to the mercantile or somewhere else. But as much as Larkin longed for a family of her own, she didn't dare hope it could be this one.

She didn't have the freedom to choose her own family. She'd always be grateful to Mrs. O'Keefe for taking her in when she was orphaned, but hadn't she paid her debt by working hard these seven years? Even indentured servants were freed after that long.

"I'm cold." Rosie blinked away the flakes of snow that had landed on her eyelashes.

Jackson lifted her up and wrapped his duster around her. "We'll be home soon. I've already got the fire going, so it will be warm."

Pulling her cloak to her chest to block the biting wind, Larkin quickened her pace to keep up with the long-legged man.

Though many people loved the snow that had started falling this morning, it only reminded her of the times in New York when her family had been cold, living in a drafty shanty with little food or fuel. She longed for the warmth of the sun and beautiful wildflowers.

"Afternoon, Miss Doyle."

Larkin stopped suddenly to keep from colliding into Frank Barrett. "Good day, sir." She attempted to go around him, but he sidestepped, blocking her way. At least the wind was less severe with his body shielding her, but the look in his eyes chilled away any warmth she'd gathered from his presence.

"When can I expect the privilege of your company for dinner? I'd hoped we could dine together before now."

She shivered, remembering Maura's warning. If she refused Mr. Barrett, Maura might put her out on the street, with no home and no job. But she wasn't a slave. She didn't have to dine with this man if she didn't want to. Perhaps she could put him off until another means of escape provided itself.

"Mrs. O'Keefe took in the Lancaster girl, as you know." She attempted to look around him to see if Jackson had heard her or noticed her gone, but Mr. Barrett blocked her view. "I've been quite busy caring for Rosie. 'Twould not be proper for me to dine with you and neglect me other duties. Perhaps after Christmas. . ."

"I'll talk with Maura and make sure that you have some free time. I've waited long enough for you."

His mouth pursed, and something flickered in his steely gaze that sent chills down Larkin's back, as if someone had dumped snow down her shirtwaist. "No. Please do not do such a thing."

"Why? Do you not wish to enjoy my company? I'm quite wealthy, you know." His mouth twisted into an arrogant snarl.

Larkin searched for an answer, but her mind froze.

"Excuse me, but Miss Doyle is with me at the moment."

Relief melted the chills at the sound of Jackson's voice behind Mr. Barrett. The shorter man spun around to face him.

"No one asked for your advice, Lancaster."

"The mayor's wife has instructed Miss Doyle to escort me and my niece. Do you want me to inform her that you kept her ward from her duties?"

Larkin hurried past Mr. Barrett to stand beside Jackson. He handed Rosie to her then faced Mr. Barrett again.

"Uh. . .no, I didn't mean to keep Miss Doyle from her duties." He glanced at her. A muscle ticked in his jaw. His cold gaze could have frozen hot water. "Another time, then." He pivoted around and marched down the boardwalk.

Somehow Larkin felt sure she'd be the one to pay for his displeasure.

❧

Jackson double-checked the ammunition in his Winchester. He set it on the desk, then grabbed another rifle and loaded the cartridges in it. He had a payroll for Carpenter Mills that had to get through. With Shorty driving, him riding shotgun, and

Cody Webster, a sharpshooter disguised as a city slicker, riding inside the coach, Jackson hoped to deliver the payroll without incident. His customers were getting leery of traveling on the Lancaster Stage after all that had happened.

His boots echoed on the boardwalk and down the steps. The four horses fidgeted, anxious to be on their way. Jackson handed up his rifles to Shorty then passed him a canteen filled with coffee and a small satchel that held their lunch. He walked to the front of the stage, checking harnesses and talking to the horses.

"Uncle Jack!"

He pivoted at Rosie's call, his heart jumping. He'd never minded driving the stage, but going today would mean he wouldn't be back until Thursday and would miss Wednesday evening with Rosie. Mrs. O'Keefe had been stern and refused to allow him to visit his niece on another day. No amount of sweet talk or arguing could sway her. As much as he loved Rosie, he couldn't take care of her and provide for her without his business.

Rosie ran into his arms, and he tossed her in the air. Larkin followed a few yards behind, walking demurely, her cheeks brightened by the cold wind that tugged at her dark green cloak.

"We sneaked out."

Jackson raised a brow at Larkin, and she ducked her head for a moment.

"Mrs. O'Keefe had a tea to attend with the banker's wife and some of her other friends, and Mr. O'Keefe was still sleeping. Since you'll be gone tomorrow, we thought to come and see you off." Larkin shrugged one shoulder, as if it were a small thing, but to Jackson, it meant a lot.

He smacked a kiss on Rosie's cheek, making her giggle and washing away his longing of not getting to see her. She turned her head, giving him access to the other side of her face, on which he happily planted another kiss.

"I wanna go with you." Rosie clung to his neck.

"I wish you could, sweet pea, but it's too dangerous." He wanted to say, "Maybe after we catch whoever's been robbing the stage," but didn't for fear it would make her think of her parents.

"Bring me a present."

Larkin stepped forward. "Now, Rosie, 'tisn't good manners to ask for gifts."

Jackson handed his niece to her and helped a female passenger into the coach. He checked his pocket watch as Cody winked at him and stepped inside. Jackson closed the door and looked at Shorty. "Ready to go?"

His driver nodded and turned up his collar. "Yep."

Jackson knelt in front of Rosie and hugged her. "Be good for Miss Doyle, all right?"

"Her name's Larkin."

"Be good for Larkin. . .and don't correct your elders." He hugged his niece tight, never wanting to let her go. But time was ticking. The stage needed to leave, and Christmas was drawing closer.

He stood and gazed at Larkin. She was so pretty in her dark green cloak and with her cheeks rosy from the cold air. He felt a sudden urge to pull her close and hug her but shook off that crazy thought. "Thank you."

She nodded and took Rosie's hand.

Jackson cleared the huskiness from his throat, jogged around the back of the stage, and climbed aboard.

Rosie waved.

"We'll be praying for your safety," Larkin called out. She caught his gaze then darted hers to the ground.

Shorty let off the brake and shouted a loud, "Heeyaw!"

Rosie jumped up and down from her safe spot by the office window. "Yaw. Yaw!"

Jackson grinned and waved, his heart warmed by their brief visit. He positioned his rifle on his lap, watching as they left town to see if he noticed anything out of the ordinary.

The snow had stopped, leaving a thin blanket of white all across the open prairie. His cheeks burned from the chilly wind, and he hunkered down, keeping a watchful eye. It would be hard for anyone to sneak up on them for the next five miles, since they were on open prairie.

His mind drifted to the quickly approaching Christmas Day. It was on a Saturday this year. Would he even get to see Rosie? Would he spend the day alone, remembering last year's happy Christmas with Ben and Amanda?

And how in the world was he going to find a wife in nine days? But he had to—or lose all that mattered to him in this world.

A pheasant darted upward from a nearby bush, making Jackson jump.

Shorty chuckled. "A little edgy, huh?"

"I was just thinking, that's all." Jackson refocused on his duty.

If all else failed, he could ask the Widow Winningham to marry him. He shuddered—and he knew it wasn't from the cold. The thought of being a stepfather to her six rowdy sons made him quiver as badly as being lost in a blizzard with no coat on.

And how would little Rosie fare with all those rough boys? There had to be a better answer.

He checked the landscape for intruders—anything that looked out of the ordinary—then turned his thoughts to God. *Help me, Lord. Show me what to do. I can't lose Rosie.*

Desperate, he turned to Shorty. "I don't reckon you know any women that want to get married."

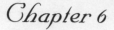

Chapter 6

Larkin sat on the edge of her bed and rocked Rosie back and forth.

The girl sniffled and huddled against Larkin's chest. "I want Uncle Jack."

Larkin stroked her hair and murmured softly. "I know, lass. He's busy with work, I'm sure of it."

As Rosie sobbed, Larkin's ire grew. How could Jackson disappoint his niece like this? Why hadn't he warned her that he'd miss two nights with her instead of just the one? She'd stirred Rosie up, thinking he was coming today, only to severely disappoint her.

Larkin rocked and prayed, hoping business had kept Jackson away rather than injury. It had been a whole week since he'd come for Rosie, but at least the child had gotten a few moments with him when they'd visited him at the stage office.

Rosie's breathing rose and fell as sleep descended. Her little body grew heavy.

Larkin tucked her in bed then softly kissed her cheek.

Caring for Rosie made her heart ache with longing. Oh, how she wanted children of her own—and, of course, a husband. But no man other than Mr. Barrett had shown an interest in her, and she had no desire to get to know him better.

She faced a dilemma similar to those of the sharecroppers in Ireland who worked the soil of the wealthy landowners. They had to give a share of their crops to these landowners and thus had barely enough to feed their families. There was no hope of a better life.

At least Maura had seen that Larkin was educated and had allowed her to attend school through the eighth grade. But she paid her no wage, only providing food, shelter, and clothing. How could she move somewhere else when she had no money? What man would want to marry a woman who was nothing more than a servant?

Jackson's blue eyes invaded her thoughts. The charming way his coffee-colored hair hung over his forehead made her want to brush it back. Would it be soft to touch, or thick and wiry?

Larkin shook her head at the foolish thought. She would never know the answer to that. Jackson Lancaster tolerated her presence only because he had to.

Dropping to her knees on the cold floor, she folded her hands and prayed, asking God to soothe Rosie, to protect Jackson—for Rosie's sake—and to provide a way for her to start a new life, outside the O'Keefes' home.

The next morning, Maura left with Rosie in tow as she went to visit the Flemings, a family with two girls a bit older than Rosie. Larkin donned her cloak and left after they were out of view. She marched down the boardwalk, her boots pounding on the weathered wood.

She'd stewed last night until she'd finally fallen into a restless sleep and then had to listen to Maura's gloating at breakfast. Maura was certain they'd seen the last visit from Jackson Lancaster. On and on she'd told Larkin and Mr. O'Keefe how much better off the child was with them.

Larkin wasn't sure if she was truly angry because Jackson had disappointed Rosie or because she had to listen to Maura's self-righteous boasting. More likely, both situations had fueled her Irish temper, one she kept in check on most days.

She knocked on the stage office door but knew by the darkness inside that nobody was there. She tried the door handle, thinking to leave Jackson a note, but found it locked.

Swirling around, she studied the town of Prairie Flats. The place lived up to its name. Located on the Illinois prairie, the town was as flat as a sheet of paper. There were few trees to block the steady winds, which was a blessing in the summer but a curse in the winter.

There was work to be done at the O'Keefes', but rarely having time to herself, Larkin wandered toward the mercantile. On occasion, Maura allowed her to purchase an item or two and charge it to the O'Keefes' account. Of course, there would be extra chores required to pay for those necessities.

Christmas was quickly approaching, and Larkin wondered what she could give the people in her life. She could make Rosie a doll, but she didn't want a new one competing with the doll the child's mother had made. Perhaps she could sew a small quilt from the scraps she'd been saving. Larkin smiled at the pleasure such a gift would surely bring the lass.

But finding something for the O'Keefes was more difficult, and the fact that it was expected took the joy out of the giving. Larkin sighed. What could she give them that they didn't already have? For just being the mayor of a small town, Mr. O'Keefe was a superb provider and often worked long hours. The O'Keefes lacked nothing.

A woman a few years older than Larkin smiled at her husband as they squeezed past in the crowded aisle. Melancholy tugged at Larkin, and she couldn't resist watching them. The husband wrapped his arm around his wife and whispered in her ear. The woman giggled and looked at him with adoration.

Larkin had never felt so lonely. Staying busy at the O'Keefes' had kept her from developing friendships, and Mr. O'Keefe, Jackson Lancaster, and Frank Barrett were the only men who actually talked to her, except an occasional guest at the big house.

The scents of spices and leather and the sweet odor of perfume that a man was testing out as a gift for his wife hung in the air. People chattered, and two children played hide-and-seek around their mother's skirt as she waited to have her purchases tallied up.

What would it be like to wake up each day next to a man you loved and to have children to tickle and hug and receive wet, sloppy kisses from?

She stopped in front of a box of colorful Christmas ornaments and picked one up. Never had she seen such elaborate decorations—or even a real Christmas tree—until she'd move in with the O'Keefes. She had vague memories of hanging holly and ivy in their small home in Ireland, and those times were the happiest she could remember. Hers was a home where a child was free to laugh and talk, not one where she had to be cautious and quiet. The faces of her parents had faded over time, but not the feeling of being loved and cherished. Would no one ever love her again?

Larkin pursed her lips. She ached for a home of her own, and at nineteen, she felt it was time to find a way to get it. Perhaps she could find a job with room and board and a small wage. It wouldn't be much more than she had now, but it would be hers and not Maura's.

Still. . .how could she leave Rosie? The child needed her.

Leaving the store and its cheery inhabitants, she plodded along the boardwalk. Her dilemma tugged at her. She crossed the street and dropped onto the empty bench in front of the stage office. Still no sign of Rosie's uncle.

In spite of her irritation with him for hurting Rosie, she couldn't help worrying about Jackson. She'd asked around and discovered he had an excellent reputation. Not at all what Maura had said. And she knew he loved Rosie.

Larkin's thoughts drifted to a vision of Jackson laughing and tossing Rosie in the air. She'd never wanted to like him—thought him an ogre for not keeping his niece. But instead of hating him, she feared the opposite was true. Her feelings had grown like the abundant wild ivy of her homeland. Did she love the man?

But what did that matter? He could never return her

feelings when she worked for his enemy. Looking heavenward, she prayed, "Please, Lord, don't let me feel these things for Jackson. And please bring him home safely."

She glanced in both directions, hoping to hear the jingling of harnesses and the pounding of horses' hooves. "Jackson, where are you?"

❧

Jackson brushed down the last of the horses and then put the tools away. Now that each horse had fresh hay and water and a measure of oats, he could go home. But where was home?

He'd tried living at the big house but hated the silence of the place. Amanda's knickknacks and utensils cried out for a woman to use them, but he was out of luck in that respect.

He'd even spent an extra two days scouring the small towns his stage stopped at to see if there was a kind woman who'd marry him. But none of the available women wanted to marry a man they didn't know so quickly, no matter that he owned his own business.

He sighed and scratched his bristly beard. He wanted to see Rosie, and it didn't matter one bit that today wasn't his day. Turning around, he headed for the O'Keefe house.

Just a hug from Rosie, and he'd know she was all right. Then maybe he could sleep.

Seeing Larkin would be a bonus. The auburn-haired sprite's name was still on his list, but he didn't dare ask her to marry him. If she said no, his visits to Rosie would be awkward and unbearable.

He'd never been friends with a woman before, except for Amanda, and she was family. Besides, though Larkin's stance toward him had softened, she'd never indicated having any affection for him. She'd been through enough in her life. She didn't need to marry a man she didn't love.

He stopped at front of the O'Keefes' kitchen door. Was he doing the right thing, coming here on a day he wasn't expected? Before he could knock, the door flew open.

Wilma stood there with a bucket of dirty water. She blinked and smiled. "Well, about time you got back. Here, save my old bones a chill and empty this on that shrub for me."

Jackson took the bucket and did as she bid, glad that she seemed happy to see him. Inside, he set the bucket by the door, taunted by the fragrant scent of baking bread and knowing there was nothing warm for him to eat at home. "I realize it isn't my day to be here, but do you think I could see Rosie?"

Wilma's lips pursed. "I wouldn't mind except that she's abed with a fever, and I don't think it's proper for you to visit her in Larkin's room."

Concern stabbed his chest. "How long has she been sick? Has the doctor seen her? Larkin's room?"

Wilma nodded and moved a pot of something to the back burner. "Rosie shares Larkin's room. Seems the madam didn't want to take a chance on her breaking something in the guest room."

Irritation battled concern. Mrs. O'Keefe had made a big deal about his place not being good enough for Rosie, but now she was living in the servants' quarters. They were probably much nicer than his room behind the office, but the thought that the mayor's wife had banned Rosie from a better room irked him. "I want to see her. Either take me to her or bring her to me."

Wilma gave him a scolding stare then softened. "I imagine it would help her to see you. Give me a minute."

Jackson removed his jacket and hung it on a chair and laid his hat on the table. He paced the kitchen, enjoying the cozy warmth but anxious to see his niece. After what seemed like hours, Larkin hurried into the room. "You're back. I was so worried."

He stopped pacing directly in front of her. "How is Rosie?"

Larkin shrugged and twisted her hands together. "She's had a fever for two days. 'Tis my fault, I fear."

"Why?" Jackson took her hands to keep them still.

Her lower lip quivered. "We built a snowman. Rosie's been wantin' to play outside, and I thought 'twould do her good to get some fresh air. I—I'm so sorry." Tears gushed from her eyes and down her cheeks.

Jackson pulled her close and patted her back, hoping to comfort her. "It's not your fault. Children catch colds and fevers."

"I shouldna have taken her outside." Larkin clung to his shirt.

She sniffled, and Jackson couldn't resist resting his head against hers, hoping she didn't mind that he was fresh off the trail.

After a moment, she seemed to gather her composure.

Wilma entered the room, and Larkin stepped back. "Sorry."

"Don't be." He smiled and wiped a remnant tear from her cheek. "I know it's not a proper thing to ask, what with her being in your room, but may I please see Rosie? Just for a minute?"

"If you want to know what I think"—Wilma glanced at them over her spectacles—"you're just what that child needs to get her back on her feet. She's pined herself into a tizzy missing you. I don't know what Mrs. O'Keefe is doing keeping you two apart."

"C'mon. I'll take you to her." Larkin took his hand and tugged on it.

He enjoyed the soft feel of her small hand in his. They passed a big closet and then entered a room that was slightly bigger than his but sparsely adorned. His gaze landed on a small lump under a colorful quilt. His throat tightened.

"The doctor says she will be fine. He left some medicine for her and said not to let her outside until Christmas."

Jackson knelt beside the bed and reached out his shaking hand to brush the hair from Rosie's overly red cheeks. Clearing his throat, he forced some words out. "Sweet pea, it's Uncle Jack."

Rosie stirred, and her eyes opened. She blinked several times; then her mouth curved upward. "Hi."

Jackson glanced at Larkin. "Can I hold her?"

Her lips tilted upward, and she nodded.

Jackson lifted one corner of the quilt, but Rosie sat and climbed into his arms. Her hot cheek warmed his. *God, please touch her. Heal her.*

"I thought you'd gone to heaven. Like Mama and Poppy."

Jackson clutched her small form as tightly as he dared. "No, precious. I told you I'd take care of you, and I mean to do that."

"Good." She snuggled in his arms and was soon fast asleep.

Larkin motioned to a chair in the corner. He took Rosie and settled down. Larkin laid the quilt over them both.

"Just let me sit here and pray a few minutes; then I'll leave." Not that he knew how he'd be able to leave her.

"If you need anything, just call out." Larkin patted Rosie's head and left the room.

It held a single bed, making him wonder how both Larkin and Rosie managed to get any sleep. Besides the chair, there was a small desk and a crate that held a stack of clothes. Two pegs hung on the wall, holding a pair of dresses, both ones that he'd seen Larkin wear. There wasn't even a fireplace. The lack of amenities stunned him, considering how fancy the rest of the house was.

The bird he'd carved sat in the middle of the windowsill. There were no pictures, no decorations of any kind. He hugged Rosie closer, his irritation with Mrs. O'Keefe growing. Had Larkin lived in near poverty her whole life? Was that what Rosie was doomed to endure if he didn't get her back—to be the mistreated servant of a selfish, wealthy woman?

A racket sounded in the kitchen and moved his way. Maura O'Keefe stormed into the room, her pale eyes colder than the winter sky outside. "What is *he* doing here?"

Larkin wrung her hands together. "He learned Rosie was

sick and wanted to sit with her a few minutes. Surely you can't deny him that."

"Oh yes, I can. The judge was clear in his orders. Put that child in her bed and leave my house this instant."

Rosie whimpered and cuddled closer. "Don't go, Uncle Jack."

Jackson clenched his jaw tight to keep from spewing out his anger on the woman. If Rosie hadn't been sick, he would have marched right out the door with her, but he couldn't risk her getting sicker. Against his wishes, he laid her on the bed.

Rosie tried to cling to him, but Larkin squeezed in between them. "No. . .don't go. . ." Rosie's wails followed him down the hall and into the kitchen.

Maura crossed her arms over her chest and frowned. "First thing in the morning, I'm going to the judge and tell him what you've done."

Jackson glared back at her and stepped closer.

Her ice blue eyes widened.

"And maybe I'll just tell the judge how you've relegated my niece to the servants' quarters, not even giving her a bed of her own. What do you think he'll say about that?"

Mrs. O'Keefe paled. "Get out and don't come back."

Jackson snatched up his jacket and stormed outside without even putting it on. How had things turned out so badly? The days were ticking away. He couldn't leave his niece in that woman's care. If he didn't find a wife soon, he'd leave his business and whisk Rosie away in the night. The two of them could start over somewhere else.

Even as his thoughts traveled that trail, he knew that wasn't the answer. God wouldn't have him react in anger, but where was He in all of this? So far his prayers had gone unanswered.

Jackson grabbed a fistful of snow, wadded it into a ball, and threw it against a tree.

Could he just walk away from the house his parents had built? And the business he and Ben had worked so hard to make a success?

And what about Larkin? Could he leave her to live out her days in that little room with no hope of a future?

He slammed the door to the office, rattling the window, and strode back to his room. If he had any hopes of getting Rosie back, he had to move into the big house and put aside his hurts.

He glanced at the calendar. Only six days to Christmas.

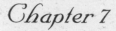

Chapter 7

H ow is your dinner, Miss Doyle?" Frank Barrett's charming smile would have won over most maidens.

"'Tis delicious. Wilma is a fine cook." Larkin avoided his gaze and glanced at Maura, who was watching them. Why did she want to push Mr. Barrett on her? Larkin had no fortune. He had nothing to gain by a union with her.

"Christmas will soon be past; then I will expect you to accept my dinner invitation." Mr. Barrett shoved a huge bite of veal into his mouth.

Larkin's heart pounded, her appetite disintegrating. She glanced across the table.

Miss Eleanor James, eldest daughter of the town's banker, glared at her. The woman had made her interest in Mr. Barrett clear, but he seemed oblivious to her wiles. Why didn't he pursue Eleanor instead of her?

On cue, Wilma touched her shoulder just before dessert was served. "Miss Rosie is ready for you to tuck her in, Miss Doyle."

Larkin dabbed her lips with her napkin. "Thank you, Wilma. I shall see to her right away."

Frank Barrett and the other men stood as she rose from her chair, but he along with Maura scowled as she left the table.

Her heart hammered, and she almost felt guilty for prearranging her escape, but the thought of spending the evening avoiding Mr. Barrett's advances and her employer's glares had set her nerves on edge. As she passed through the kitchen and entered the servants' quarters, her heart slowed and her breathing returned to normal.

Rosie sat at the kitchen table eating a late-night snack of bread with apple butter. She smiled when she saw Larkin, then yawned. Normally she was in bed an hour earlier, but Larkin had asked Wilma to keep her up as long as she didn't get in the cook's way.

"Ready for bed?"

Rosie stuffed a final bite into her mouth and nodded. She licked her fingers, then downed the last of her milk and yawned again.

"Best get that youngun to bed before she falls off that chair." Wilma sidled a glance at them as she sliced a peach pie and placed a serving on one of Maura's favorite china plates.

Larkin carried Rosie to their room and helped her into a nightgown, then tucked her in.

"Uncle Jack comes tomorrow." Rosie's eyelids rose and closed, getting heavier by the second.

"Yes, lass, tomorrow is his day to see you." Larkin hoped his work wouldn't keep him away again. There hadn't been any robberies in the past week, but with people coming to visit family for Christmas, as well as extra orders to be shipped because of the holiday, Jackson seemed busier than ever. *Please don't disappoint Rosie again.*

Larkin brushed the hair from Rosie's face, thankful for the natural warmth of her forehead and not the burning fever that had kept the child in bed the past three days. Donning her own gown, she wondered if Jackson was poring over the stage bookwork or eating a warm meal. She wasn't certain but thought that he'd lost weight since she had first gotten to know him.

Kneeling beside her bed, she shivered and prayed, "Heavenly Father, please make a way for Rosie and Jackson to be together. Also, if You could work things out so I could leave and get my own place, I'd be forever grateful. Bless Wilma and thank You for her friendship."

She scurried into bed as she murmured, "Amen," knowing she'd be both delighted if Rosie was returned to her uncle and sad to lose the little girl she'd grown to love. She'd even miss seeing Jackson regularly.

She scooted down in the covers and snuggled up next to Rosie's warm body, hoping Maura didn't come looking for her, demanding that she return to the dinner party. And how was she going to get out of dining with Mr. Barrett? Would Maura actually punish her or perhaps even turn her out if she continued avoiding the man?

Larkin nibbled the inside of her cheek, wishing she had the nerve to tell him she wasn't interested. "Lord, make me bolder."

She closed her eyes; her body relaxed. As the fog of sleep descended, it wasn't Mr. Barrett's dreary gray eyes she saw, but Jackson's somber blue ones. He carried more than his share of concerns. She longed to rub the crease from his brow—to kiss away his pain.

Larkin's eyes darted open, and she stared into the darkness. Why hadn't she noticed before? When had it happened?

Jackson Lancaster had sneaked in and stolen her heart.

❦

"D'you find a gal to marry yet?" Shorty peered out of the corner of his eyes at Jackson then refocused on the road in front of him, keeping the horses at a steady pace.

"Not yet." If no problems presented themselves, he'd be home by noon and have time to clean up and see Rosie this evening. Christmas was only three days away, and his hopes of finding a bride were diminishing.

"I talked with two women from neighboring towns. One was seven years older than me and had three children." It wasn't that he didn't like children, but he had Rosie to think about. Becoming an instant husband and father to one child was daunting enough.

"The other woman had an elderly mother who lives with her." Jackson's heart went out to them, but he just couldn't bring himself to ask the woman to marry him—not when a pair of moss green eyes kept invading his dreams. And that cinnamon hair. He longed to run his hand through it but tightened his grasp on his Winchester instead.

Suddenly a flame ignited, as if he'd been shot in his gut, making his whole body go limp. When had he developed feelings for Larkin? Why hadn't he noticed sooner?

Shorty chuckled. "Two women at once might be a bit to take on."

Numb with the realization that if Larkin were to accept his marriage proposal, he could have Rosie back by Christmas Eve and a wife he loved instead of some stranger, he turned to Shorty.

The driver shot several sideways glances at him and looked around. "What's wrong?"

The ricochet of rifle fire echoed across the barren landscape. The edge of the footboard in front of Jackson and Shorty shattered. Both men ducked.

"Heeyaw!" Shorty shook the reins and urged the team into a gallop as he hunkered down.

Jackson scoured the area, his heart thumping hard.

"There!" Shorty yelled and pointed with his stubbly chin.

Three riders charged out of the tree line, rifles aimed straight at the stage. Jackson fired, and one rider lurched backward out of his saddle. Below him, Cody shot from inside the stage.

How had anyone known about the payroll? He'd handled it personally. He fired again, knowing he had to live for Rosie's sake. The child couldn't lose another person she loved.

As if he'd been branded with a blazing hot iron, his left shoulder exploded with pain. Jackson didn't take time to look at his wound but raised his rifle to the other shoulder and shot another man.

The outlaw clutched his side but stayed in the saddle. He slowed and turned his horse around. With his two cohorts gone, the third thief swung around and raced back to the trees.

Even though the outlaw might have been responsible for Ben's death, Jackson couldn't shoot the man in the back, but Cody must have had no qualms about it. His weapon blasted, and the last man jerked and flew off his saddle.

Fighting intense pain, Jackson braced his feet and struggled to stay on the jarring seat as Shorty kept the team racing for Prairie Flats. Jackson yanked his kerchief out and shoved it under his shirt to stay the bleeding. Though only noontime, a foggy darkness descended, and Jackson felt himself falling.

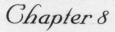

Larkin steadied Rosie's hand as she hung one of the older Christmas bulbs on the tree. Though it was still several days until Christmas, Maura had insisted the tree be up and decorated, as well as the parlor and dining rooms, before her annual December 23 dinner party. Larkin hoped the pine boughs scenting the room didn't wither before tomorrow evening.

Mistletoe hung in clumps over doorways, tied with colorful red bows. Unlit candles stood in the windows like soldiers on guard, waiting for nighttime, when they would be lit to show visitors the way. Pine boughs and red bows decorated the stairs and fireplace mantel.

Everything looked festive, but Larkin shivered at the thought of another evening with Frank Barrett. Maura had made it clear that she'd accept no excuses this time. Larkin sighed. She was expected to remain at tomorrow's dinner until all the guests left; then she was to change clothes and help Wilma clean up.

"Did you have a tree when you were little?" Rosie reached

for another of the colorful glass balls.

Larkin hurried to her side. "Let me help you. And no, I never had a Christmas tree until I came to live with the O'Keefes."

"How come?" Rosie's lower lip protruded as if she thought Larkin terribly unfortunate.

"I lived in Ireland until I was eight. There are few trees to be found there, so we decorated with holly and ivy. The holly has lovely red berries on it. At Christmas, me mother would fix bread sauce made from bread crumbs, milk, and an onion with cloves stuck in it for flavoring."

Rosie turned up her nose. "I don't like yunyuns."

Larkin smiled. She turned at the sound of quickly approaching steps.

Wilma hurried into the room, her gaze jumping from Rosie to Larkin. "I need to speak with you alone."

A fist clenched Larkin's heart at Wilma's worried expression. What was wrong? Could something have happened to Jackson? That thought made her want to crumble into a huddled mass of misery. What if he died without knowing how she felt?

Larkin took Rosie's hand, forcing the horrible thoughts from her mind. She was overreacting. Wilma's distress could be the result of a simple problem, not that she was prone to hysterics. Perhaps Mrs. O'Keefe's food order for her party hadn't arrived.

"I've made some Christmas cookies." Wilma smiled at Rosie. "I don't suppose anyone would like to help me sprinkle colored sugar on them?"

Rosie bounced up and down as they walked toward the kitchen. "Me! I can do it."

"Before you can work, you need a snack." Wilma placed a plate with three cookies in front of Rosie and then set a glass of milk on the table. "Stay here and eat while I talk to Larkin."

They hurried back to the parlor and sat on the settee together. Wilma took Larkin's hands; her brows dipped down, and her lips were pursed.

"Tell me what's wrong. You're scarin' me."

"There was a stage robbery attempt, and Mr. Lancaster has been shot."

Larkin surged to her feet. "Where is he? Oh, is he. . .alive?"

Wilma nodded. "He's at Doc Grant's and will be fine. Sit down. There's more."

Larkin hurried to obey, though all within her wanted to rush out the door and over to the doctor's office.

"It seems Mr. O'Keefe and that Frank Barrett were part of the outlaw gang that's been holding up the stages. Since Barrett worked at the bank, he was privy to information about payroll deliveries. Barrett is dead, but Mr. O'Keefe is in jail. He was shot and is singing like a songbird now."

Larkin's eyes widened. She pressed her hand against her chest. "Poor Mrs. O'Keefe. Is that why I haven't seen her all day? How is she taking the news?"

Wilma's lips twisted. "Gone. On the train this morning. She was probably neck deep in all of this. That's why she kept pushing Barrett on you. Wanted to keep things all in the family."

Larkin peered around the cheerful room, such a contrast to the horrible news she'd just heard. "What will happen to all of us?"

"We're to close up the house. I don't know after that."

Larkin wrung her hands. Where would they live?

With Mrs. O'Keefe gone and Mr. O'Keefe in jail, what would happen to Rosie? Surely the judge would allow her to go back to Jackson. He would take his niece home and have no reason to visit Larkin ever again.

Could she tell him how she felt? Was it too forward of her?

She jumped up. *Please, Father, let him live.* "I must see Jackson."

"I'll watch Rosie while you go." Wilma's expression warmed, her eyes twinkling.

⁓

As the haziness of sleep fled, Jackson glanced around. He wasn't in his own bed. Where was he?

He tried to sit up, but a sudden pain in his shoulder and a pair of strong arms pushed him back.

"Hold it, young man. You've been shot."

"Doc?"

"Yep. There was a stage holdup, but you got the rascals. They won't be bothering you anymore."

Jackson lay back, his foggy mind struggling to remember what had happened. "Shorty?"

"He's fine. Just got a few scratches."

"Gotta get out of here, Doc. Need to check on Rosie." He attempted to sit up again, but the doctor held him down.

"Lie still or I'll give you something that makes you sleep. Tomorrow will be soon enough. I've already sent word about your injury and told the folks keeping your niece that you'll be fine—providing you rest."

Jackson sighed but relaxed. Had Rosie heard about his injury? Would she be worried? Would Larkin? How was a man supposed to rest when he had all these concerns muddling his brain?

A door rattled and someone entered with a swish of skirts. He hoped the doctor would pull the curtain so nobody would see him down like he was.

The swishing moved closer, and he turned his head. Larkin!

Worry wrinkled her pretty brow, and she twisted her hands together. "H–how are you? We were so concerned."

"Rosie was?"

Larkin shook her head. "Rosie's fine. She doesn't know yet. 'Twas Wilma and meself that were worried. 'Tis a relief to know you'll be fine."

He smiled and held out his hand. She stared at it, then stepped forward and clasped it. "I'll come and see Rosie when I get out of here. Probably tomorrow. Don't tell her about me. She'll just fret."

Larkin nodded. "I suppose you'll get Rosie back now."

"Why do you say that?"

Her eyes widened. "You haven't heard?"

He shook his head, wondering what she meant.

She conveyed to him what she'd heard from Wilma, who'd been at the mercantile when the outlaws were brought in to town.

Jackson stared at the ceiling. Numb. The very people who

tried to take Rosie from him had most likely been responsible for his brother's death. Had it all been some big plan to steal Rosie? Or had Ben and Amanda just been in the wrong place at the wrong time? He'd probably never know.

His heart skittered. With Mrs. O'Keefe gone and her husband in jail, the judge would have to give Rosie back to him. He smiled, but when he looked at Larkin, his grin faltered. "What's wrong?"

Larkin glanced at him then stared at the floor. "I'm sure the judge will give Rosie back to you now. I'm truly happy for you."

"You don't look happy." Love for this woman warmed his whole body. He wanted to take her in his arms and kiss away her troubles. Why had it taken him so long to realize that he loved her?

"It's just that I shall dearly miss. . .Rosie."

Jackson bit back a smile. Glory be, the woman had feelings for him. They were written all over her lovely face. "Just Rosie?"

"Well. . .I. . ."

"Doc!"

Larkin jumped at Jackson's shout.

"What's all the caterwauling?" The doctor strode in, wiping his spectacles on the edge of his shirt. "Are you in pain?"

"No, but I need to sit up." Jackson sent him a pleading gaze.

"Sorry. Not today." He turned to leave.

"Wait. C'mon, Doc. A man can't ask a woman to marry him while he's flat on his back."

Larkin's head spun toward him, her beautiful green eyes wide. A slow smile tilted the lips he longed to kiss.

Doctor Grant chuckled. "Well. . .I suppose I *could* make an exception for that."

Jackson gritted his teeth, pushing away the pain as the doctor helped him up.

The man quickly left the room, a wide grin brightening his tired features.

Jackson reached for Larkin's hand and took a deep breath. She looked so vulnerable, almost afraid to hope. "Did you know the judge gave me until Christmas to find a bride or I'd lose Rosie for good?"

Larkin shook her head.

"I realized yesterday that I'd been searching in vain. The woman I love is right here. Will you marry me, Larkin? Help me raise Rosie?"

Her lower lip trembled, and tears made her eyes shine. She nodded.

He grinned.

"I love you, too, Jackson. 'Twould make me very happy to marry you."

That was all he needed to hear. With his good arm, he pulled her to his side and kissed her, showing her how he felt and making promises for the future—promises he was eager to fulfill.

"Don't the candles look beautiful?" Larkin tossed the kindling she used to light the parlor candles into the fireplace. "Tradition has it that they are a symbol of welcome to help Mary and Joseph find their way as they looked for shelter the night Jesus was born."

"They'll help Uncle Jack find his way." Rosie stared at the dancing shadows the flickering flames made on the walls.

"'Tis true. He and Doc Grant should be here soon. Let's go help Wilma."

In the kitchen, Wilma took the goose out of the oven. Its fragrant odors had been making Larkin's stomach growl for hours. "Thank you for cooking that tonight. Smells truly delicious."

Larkin lifted Rosie onto a stool. "There's one quaint custom in Ireland where the groom is invited to his bride's house right before the wedding and they cook a goose in his honor. 'Tis called 'Aitin' the Gander.'"

Rosie grinned. "You're the bride."

Larkin felt her cheeks warm. . .or perhaps 'twas just the heat of the kitchen. "Aye. Tomorrow your uncle Jack and I shall marry."

The thought of being Jackson's wife brought twitters to her stomach that had nothing to do with hunger. A knock sounded at the door, and she jumped. Her beloved was here.

Rosie slid off the seat, but Larkin beat her to the door, pulling it open. Jackson stood there, his arm in a sling and his jacket around his shoulders, blue eyes smiling.

"Uncle Jack!" Rosie wrapped her arms around Jackson's leg. He patted her head, but his gaze never left Larkin's face.

Larkin's heart flip-flopped. Oh, how she loved this man.

And tomorrow he'd be her husband.

Someone behind Jackson cleared his throat. "It's cold out here. Don't suppose we could go inside where it's warm so you two could stare at each other by the fire." Doc Grant peered around Jackson's shoulder, grinning.

They hurried inside, and Larkin helped Jackson with his jacket. Rosie and Doc sat at the table. Wilma set a bowl of applesauce on the table and smiled at the doctor.

"I need to talk to you in private a moment," Jackson whispered in Larkin's ear.

She nodded and led him to the parlor. He glanced around the room at all the pretty decorations. Maura's dinner party had been canceled, but the lovely room would make the perfect spot for a Christmas wedding. Their wedding.

Jackson's gaze landed on the mistletoe over the doorway. He grinned wickedly, dimples flashing, and tugged her to the parlor entrance. "In America, we have a tradition. If two people stand under mistletoe together, they have to kiss."

Larkin's whole body went limp, and if Jackson hadn't pulled her to his chest, she was sure she'd have melted into a puddle at his feet. How was it she could come to love this man so much, so fast? His lips melded against her, and all other thoughts fled. Too soon he pulled back.

"No doubts about tomorrow?"

She shook her head. "Not a one. I've prayed hard, and God has made it clear. You and Rosie are my future."

"I feel the same way. Tomorrow can't come soon enough." He stole another quick peck on her lips and led her back to the kitchen. Jackson seated her at the table and took the place next to Larkin, holding her hand.

"I'm gonna get Christmas presents like Baby Jesus did," Rosie declared to Doc Grant.

He waggled his eyebrows at Larkin and Jackson. "I heard you're getting something really special for Christmas."

Jackson chuckled and hugged her.

"I've been looking for a cook and housekeeper." Doc Grant smiled at Wilma. "Looks like I've found one."

Larkin breathed a prayer of thanks to God, knowing her friend would have a place to work. . .and maybe more, someday.

She glanced at the table, her stomach growling. Steam rose up from the mashed potatoes. Canned green beans with bits of ham awaited them, as did Wilma's shiny rolls. Only the goose was missing.

The room quieted as Wilma carried a silver platter covered with a fragrant golden brown goose to the table. She set it in front of Jackson and stared at him. "Well. . .I guess your goose is cooked."

Doc Grant's gaze darted toward Larkin and Jackson. He burst into laughter at the same moment Jackson did. "Ain't that the truth."

Larkin failed to see the humor in the situation but laughed anyway, happy that her beloved's face held lines of joy instead of sorrow.

Tomorrow she'd become Mrs. Jackson Lancaster. She uttered a silent prayer: *Thank You, Lord.*

VICKIE MCDONOUGH

Vickie, an award-winning inspirational romance author, has written twelve novels and novellas. Her stories have continually placed in prestigious contests, such as the ACFW Book of the Year and Noble Theme contests, the Inspirational Readers Choice Contest, and Heartsong Presents annual readers' contest. She is active in local and online writers' groups and enjoys mentoring new writers. Vickie has been married to her wonderful husband, Robert, for thirty-two years. They have four terrific sons and have finally evened the odds with a sweet daughter-in-law and a granddaughter. She has lived in a part of Oklahoma that used to be Indian Territory all her life, except for one exciting year when she and husband lived on a *kibbutz* in Israel. When she's not writing, Vickie loves to read, watch movies, and travel.

LITTLE DUTCH BRIDE

by Kelly Eileen Hake

Dedication

For all of us who need to be reminded of God's promise
to care and provide for His children.

Chapter 1

Willowville, Kansas, 1883

Hopeless." Jerome Sanders shook his head as he surveyed the once-proud barn, now dilapidated with age. The doors sagged on beaten hinges, wood roughened by weather and bristling with splinters for those unwary enough to brush against it. Just one more thing to be overhauled on Gramps's farm. Just one more item on a list he already couldn't afford.

He could sand out the worst of the splinters and rehang the doors easily enough; then the structure might last through the winter. If not, he'd start losing cattle, which was the last stop before losing the farm.

"Not going to happen." Jerome spoke the words aloud as he strode back toward the wagon. Gramps had left the farm to him, and he'd do whatever was necessary to honor that legacy.

For now, that meant heading to the general store for nails,

sandpaper, and varnish. He added leather oil to the list in hopes that some of the items left overlong in the barn could be restored.

The trip didn't take long, since the snow still held off. He and the mules only had to contend with wind carrying the sharp promise of a cold winter.

Jerome was grateful to enter the store, where a central stove kept the whole place toasty warm. He nodded at a few of the older men who'd set up a game of checkers nearby and helped himself to a cup of sludge. Abel's coffee was thick enough to use as mortar. Jerome eyed it for a minute before discounting the possibility.

"What'd you like?" Abel slid out from behind his long counter.

"Best get some of everythin'," one of the old-timers cautioned. "Snow's a-comin'."

"Your knees tell you that?" one of his friends scoffed.

"You know my knees don't lie!" With that, he made it to the other side of the checkerboard. "Now king me."

Jerome couldn't help but smile as he gathered the items he'd need. He tacked on some dry goods and kerosene. . .just in case Horace's knees were right.

After he'd paid for the goods, while Abel packaged every-thing in sturdy brown paper, a flyer posted on the counter caught Jerome's eye: "Town meeting tonight—urgent. Meet at the church no later than five o'clock!"

"What's the meeting about?" He tilted his head toward the notice.

"Can't rightly say, but better to be there and hear it firsthand." Abel lowered his voice. "The elders have something up their sleeves. Been whispering all day."

"I don't know whether to be interested or wary." Jerome pulled out his watch. If he grabbed a bite at Thelma's diner, he'd be just in time for the meeting.

"Don't matter much, long as you're there."

"Count on it." Jerome took his packages, walked back to the rickety town stable, and put the load in his wagon. He popped in to give the mules some supper before heading to Thelma's.

⸎

A hot meal later, he strode into the church just as the meeting began.

Clarence Ashton clanged a large cowbell to quiet the assembly. Jerome eyed the older man as he leaned back, hands folded over a healthy stomach, waiting for the undivided attention of everyone in the building. Yep. The rascally mayor was up to no good. Again.

"Good evening," Clarence boomed, the front legs of his chair crashing to the floor as he leaned forward. "The reverend will bless this town meeting, and then we will begin."

Jerome bowed his head as the reverend began a slightly long-winded and extremely enigmatic prayer. Referring to fruitfulness at the beginning of winter seemed incongruous to a farming community.

"Now. . ." Clarence rose to his feet and began to measure the length of the platform with his steps as he spoke. "I'd like everyone to take a look around. Go ahead, see the familiar faces of your neighbors and friends."

Jerome looked around, trying to shrug off thoughts that he was the new one. Not quite a stranger, since he'd spent many summers of his childhood here, but not quite a "friend," either. He nodded at a few of the men he'd grown to know through farm business and waited for Clarence to continue.

"I'd say we all know each other and that this here qualifies as a tight-knit community. Am I right?" The mayor paused as everyone agreed with chins up and smiles in place.

"You lot look pretty pleased about that." More smiles in response to Clarence's statement, but Jerome could sense a change in the wind.

"Maybe you shouldn't be." The words stunned the towns-people like a visible blow. Some blinked; some shifted in their seats; others just gaped.

Jerome paid closer attention. What could the wily old fellow be getting at?

"What I'm getting at here is that we need new blood in this community. Now there's no denying that the women of our town are some of the finest in the country." He took a pause while every man in the audience who knew what was good for him vehemently agreed. "But we need more of 'em! There are three men to every female, and that's not going to help the growth of Willowville."

One of the checker players, obviously prepped for his role, sprang to his feet to belt out the question, "What're we going to do about it?" He added a theatrical wave of his cane for good measure before plunking back down.

"I'm glad you asked. As mayor, I've come up with a plan to motivate the young men around here to find some wives and rejuvenate our community."

Jerome's gaze slid around the room, lighting on some interesting reactions. The few unmarried ladies sat straight and tall, shyly avoiding the avid stares of eager bachelors. Not-so eager bachelors all but squirmed as they braced for the announcement to come.

"The town is offering a cash incentive to any man who brings a new woman to town and ties her to Willowville by marriage." Clarence had to stop because of the dismayed gasps of the ladies and the furor of questions from the men. He held up his hands and glowered until things settled back down.

Jerome, for his part, couldn't have said a thing even if he'd wanted to after Clarence named the sum. *That'd be enough to save the farm. More than enough.*

"I ain't finished yet," Clarence barked out. "There's one more thing you have to know: You only get the money if you get the woman by the town Christmas celebration."

$$\sim\!\!\gtrsim$$

Idelia van der Zee reached out and raised the wick of her kerosene lamp to coax a little more light onto the garment she was mending. She refused to so much as glance at the large basket full of fallen hems and hole-ridden clothing also awaiting her needle.

"*Wat* ails you, *dotter*?"

"When winter comes, I think of home." Idelia smiled at her mother. "Tomorrow is Sinterklaas Eve, which makes me think of Da."

"Ah, and how he would dress as Zwarte Pieten to help Sinterklaas hand out gifts at the docks?" Mama smiled. "*Ja*, these are good memories."

"It is strange, still, to think Americans have no Black Peter to help Sinterklaas, who is called Saint Nicholas." Idelia bit off her thread and reached for another shirt. "Stranger still that he comes on Kerstmis here."

"The Americans do not separate Sinterklaas Eve and Kerstmis, Idelia. You know they celebrate them as one."

"*Ja*, though I miss the way the excitement stretched throughout the month, as Sinterklaas came twenty days before Kerstmis. Now it seems the season only lasts but a week or so."

"I, too, miss the horns at sundown, announcing the coming of Kerstmis, and the day we celebrate our Savior's birth." Mama settled her spectacles on her nose. "But we've not seen the tradition of Sinterklaas since you were but a tiny child, since we came to America."

"*Ja*." Idelia left unsaid the longing to share the traditions with her own children. Should she ever find a good man and loving marriage, she'd want her children to enjoy the full experience of Kerstdagen—as she had long ago.

Her thoughts turned to Jerome, as they had so often since the early winter storm had landed him in their boardinghouse. She'd cherished their week together, but he'd left to take over his grandfather's farm. She shut her eyes against the swell of sadness that he'd not asked her to be his wife, that he'd been able to leave her behind as he began a new life.

"You think of Jerome." Mama's voice sounded grim. "Many a man in town would offer for you should you give any sign of accepting."

"Yes, Mama." Idelia kept her answer noncommittal. Mama did not know how deeply she'd felt for Jerome, how she'd wanted a lifetime of working alongside him, seeing love in his caramel eyes as he looked at her. And it was as well she'd kept her hopes secret. Less pain when they were crushed.

"It has been two months, Idelia." Mama's hand came to rest on hers. "And still you have not let him go?"

"My heart felt a strange tug the day he came to town." Idelia pulled a handkerchief from her sleeve. "But he didn't feel the same. He made no advances, much less promises."

"Love awaits you, Idelia." Mama patted her hand once before leaning back. "It will come when you least expect it."

"Then it must be soon, *ja*? For no more do I expect it."

Chapter 2

The next morning came as any other, bearing no clue that the day before had been one of the most cherished holidays of Idelia's childhood. She hastened to the kitchen to begin breakfast before the two boarders awoke and found her mother already bustling about, the warm scent of cinnamon perfuming the air.

"*Goedemorgen.*" Mama didn't so much as look over her shoulder as she stoked the stove.

"Good morning to you, too, Mama. I must have overslept."

"*Nee*, the sun has scarce shown itself this day."

"Mama, are you making *pepernoten*?" She couldn't hide her excitement as she saw Mama add brown sugar to the flour in her mixing bowl. Cinnamon, nutmeg, and ginger sat beside it.

"When you woke up I wanted to have them ready." Mama cracked an egg into the bowl, added some water, and began to stir. "Your talk of Sinterklaas last night made me think of how you loved these."

The hard cookies, almost a crispy gingerbread candy, had

always been her favorite. She reached out to draw her mother into a hug. "*Bedankt*, Mama."

"Ah, *welkom*, Idelia."

Without another word, she set to making the morning meal for their two boarders. Mrs. Irming and Mr. Rolf had taken the two rooms of the van der Zee's humble inn and would expect breakfast to be prepared when they left their rooms.

Idelia took a deep breath of appreciation as Mama slid a pan of pepernoten into the oven, the heat spreading the fragrance throughout the kitchen. Soon enough, the sulfur of the eggs she'd make would overpower the homey aroma of the cookies. Yesterday's extra biscuits already sat atop the stove, warming, so she'd not have to do much.

The morning chores passed in a familiar rhythm, breakfast made, water pumped and brought in, until the boarders came downstairs. Idelia took a few of the pepernoten and fanned them on a china plate, setting them on the table before she joined everyone to bless the meal.

Mr. Rolf reached for the biscuits and gravy, Mrs. Irming scooped eggs onto her plate, and Mama poured coffee for their guests. Idelia wasted no time sliding the plate of pepernoten toward her, placing two of the sweet treats on her own plate before passing it along.

She crunched into the first bite, relishing the tickle of gingerbread as the cookie melted on her tongue. It tasted like all the things she loved about winter—happy memories and warm fires and the sweetness of spending time with loved ones. A small sigh of contentment escaped her.

"What're these?" Mr. Rolf poked one of the pepernoten with a blunt finger, pushing it across the plate.

"A Dutch winter treat," Idelia explained. "Kind of a hard, crispy gingerbread."

"Never liked gingerbread." Mrs. Irming sniffed. "Cookies shouldn't be so. . .spicy."

"Yurgh." Mr. Rolf swallowed and tried again. "You're missing out, then. These're good."

Mama shot Idelia an amused glance as the pepernoten vanished in minutes. Idelia smiled back, sending up a prayer of gratitude that she'd thought to put some of the cookies in the bread box. Later that night, when they took up the mending again, she'd brew some tea and bring them out.

"Gotta go." Mr. Rolf slapped his hat on his head and stomped out the door.

"I'll be leaving, as well." Mrs. Irming pressed a napkin to her lips before rising. "My son-in-law should have made a great deal of progress, thanks to the good weather. I expect you'll have a room free rather soon."

If those roof repairs were finished, it could only be a blessing to a family sure to be struggling. A new baby needed constant care, and it was good of Mrs. Irming to come to her daughter's aid.

All the same, it would cost the van der Zees. Idelia closed her eyes and tabulated the money they'd lose if Mrs. Irming moved into her daughter's house a week early. If only there were some leeway in their budget.

As it was, Idelia and Mama shared a tiny room behind the

kitchen, where the stove's warmth kept them cozy enough. They'd cut back to only one lamp at night as they mended, and the light was so insufficient they'd moved to the kitchen table to see what they worked on. The laundry they took in during the warmer months kept them afloat, but even that tapered off in winter.

"Stop fretting," Mama admonished as she began to clear the table. "The Lord has always provided for us, even if things have been more difficult since your father passed on."

"I know." Idelia forced a smile as she started to scrub the dishes. "And together, we'll find a way to make it through the winter ahead. God has a plan—it's up to us to find it."

❦

If only he could find another way—but the more Jerome thought it over, the fewer options he had. The railroad strike last spring had brought Grandpa's farm to its knees. He scarcely had enough seed corn and wheat to make a go of it the next year. Meanwhile, everything needed repairs, livestock to be butchered for winter should be replaced, and Jerome's pockets were empty.

Either he could sell half of the farm, failing his legacy, or he could take a wife before Christmas came. Both choices made his mouth dry and his palms wet. Lose the farm or gain a wife. No wiggle room in sight as he sat at his desk and was confronted with the accounts once again.

The meticulously written numbers scarcely betrayed the shake of an old hand—Grandpa hadn't let anyone know he'd lost his partner to influenza a year ago. Had been too proud to ask for help as the farm fell down around his ears. This land meant everything to him. And if Jerome let his own pride keep him from living up to his grandfather's expectations, they both would have failed.

When he came right down to it, Jerome knew the truth. There wasn't even a choice. He'd have to find a bride from out of town—and fast. Now he just had to figure out what woman would say yes, work alongside him to revitalize the property, and not drive him crazy with endless chatter.

Idelia. The name of the boardinghouse beauty whispered through his mind. When a freak storm had stopped his progress to Willowville, he'd thought to wait out the fierce rain in boredom. Cooling his heels had held no appeal. . .until he'd met the mother-daughter duo who opened their home to travelers.

The van der Zees were tall Dutch women, warmhearted ladies to the core. They'd insisted he learn their names, laughing with him until he pronounced them perfectly. Lurleen seemed absurdly young to be Idelia's mother, but the two shared fine white-blond hair and clear gray eyes. More than that, the easy affection between them made their bond obvious.

For four days he'd sat at their table, eaten their wonderful food, and had some of the best discussions of his life. The van der Zee women were remarkably well-read, intelligent, hardworking, and lovely; thus, Jerome couldn't fathom why they were left to fend for themselves.

Were the men of their town blind? True, they'd just come out of mourning for Mr. van der Zee, but Idelia hadn't mentioned a sweetheart who waited for her hand. The only way Jerome could explain it was that the men thereabouts were too awestruck—or too intimidated by a woman who could support herself—to step forward. Fools—the whole lot of them.

But perhaps Jerome could reap the benefit of their inaction. Marriage to Idelia—now that was a choice a man would be glad to make! He sat up straighter, pulled a scrap of paper toward him, and uncapped his inkwell. Now all he had to do was figure out how to make her say yes.

Wait. A letter would take too long. Today was December sixth already. A week for the letter to arrive, a week for her to respond—by then the snows would have come, making it impossible for her to come by Christmas. His brow furrowed. It'd have to be a telegram, then. And Alastair Pitt would make certain everyone in town knew he'd proposed. If Idelia refused, he'd be a laughingstock.

But if she agreed, Jerome would be the envy of every man on the prairie. He wouldn't even mind if his mother-in-law came over for the holidays and the births of their children. Lurleen would make a wonderful grandmother, after all. And he wouldn't expect Idelia to abandon her mother—not when the two of them ran a boardinghouse and took in mending to make ends meet. When the farm was a going concern, he'd be sure to send Lurleen a monthly allowance. In fact, he should be sure to mention that in the telegram. Idelia would need to know he planned to provide for both of them, or she might not be willing to leave.

The scratch of pen against paper continued long into the night, until he was satisfied with the telegram. Perfect. That ought to prove to Idelia just how serious he was.

Chapter 3

W hat a horrid joke, Clarence Billings!" Idelia scowled at the gawky lad. "No one would propose via telegram!"

"I'm tellin' ya, Miss van der Zee—if you come down to the telegraph office, you'll find a message with your name on it," the child insisted. "True as I'm standing here!"

"It must have been mistranslated." Mama shrugged. "Wires are never to be trusted. You must see if it can be made correct. The boy came through the snow to fetch us."

"All right." Idelia swung her heavy pelisse over her shoulders as Mama bundled up. "I must admit to some curiosity. I've heard of mistakes like this, where a man asks for a bridle and ends up with a bride!"

"I bet he was happy with the switch"—Clarence beamed up at Idelia—"if his woman were half as pretty as you."

"*Bedankt*, Clarence." Mama ushered them all out the door. "My daughter is a woman any man would be proud to call his own."

Not any man. Idelia shook her head to clear away thoughts of Jerome Sanders. By now he'd probably forgotten her name, no matter how they'd laughed when he learned it.

Idelia's gaze caught on the word "wife" before she read the entire message. Then she read it once more, her mouth shaping the words silently, her pulse pounding in her ears.

"Well?" Clarence puffed out his chest. "What did I tell ya?"

Mama stood as still as a stone, her head tilted slightly as she waited for the news. It was one of the things Idelia had never understood about her mother—this ability to remain calm even in the face of crippling curiosity and anticipation.

Obviously the Billings men were cut from the same cloth, as both father and son avidly took in her reaction. As tactfully as possible, Idelia led Mama to the far corner of the small shop.

"It's Jerome," she breathed. "He asks me to be his wife in Willowville." She handed her mother the message and spoke more rapidly. "He invites you, too, Mama!"

Lurleen van der Zee scrunched her brow as she tried to make out both Mr. Billings's writing and what few written English words she knew. "Wife. . .mama." She bobbed her head. "*Ja*, is truth."

"He wants us to come right away." Idelia chewed the inside of her cheek. "Would you want to go, Mama? Leave the inn and start a new life?"

"I would not send you to this place alone." Mama's brief glower softened. "We sell the house to Mr. Rolf and go together."

"But Papa built our house. All the memories of him—"

"Stay in us. I remember the love of my husband, dotter. Now is time for you to learn of yours."

"You got an answer for that fellow?" Mr. Billings shifted his weight from foot to foot. " 'Cause I'll send it right out."

"Yes." Idelia smiled.

"All right. What's the answer, then?"

"Yep!" Clarence whooped. "You can tell just by lookin' at 'em."

"Yes?" Mr. Billings ignored his son.

Idelia took a deep breath as Mama clasped both her hands. "Yes."

❧

"No." The telegraph operator rolled his eyes as he scribbled down the letters of an incoming message. "This here's to say the stage is late again—busted an axle."

"When will she be in?" Jerome slapped his hat against his knee. Idelia was supposed to arrive on the weekly stagecoach—yesterday.

"I reckon it'll be about two hours." The man raised his brows. "Your bride'll get here in plenty of time."

Now. Jerome didn't voice the unreasonable demand. Instead, he gave a curt nod and pushed through the door. Hazy sunlight lit the main street, dimming and brightening as clouds passed. Good weather to greet Idelia.

What to do for two hours until she came? The saloon held no appeal, and he'd spent yesterday afternoon playing checkers with the old loafers at the general store. . .while the stage never came. And while he didn't begrudge them their jabs about the possibility that he didn't really have a fiancée coming to town, he wasn't about to invite another round of ribbing.

Especially when he was starting to wonder if the stage would ever make an appearance.

He wandered over to the mercantile, where Sadie Straphin did everything from make orders, ring sales, mend clothes, and create frilly fussies for. . .well, whatever women used them for.

The bell strapped to the door gave a cheery tinkle as he stepped inside. Now that he had time to think on it, having a gift for his bride was a fine idea. There had to be some little gewgaw in this place that would make Idelia smile.

A hat? He paused before a wall of headgear. Idelia wore a simple bonnet outside, so maybe she'd enjoy having something fancier for church?

He plucked a straw hat off the display, looking at the yellow ribbon threaded around the brim and dangling down to tie beneath a lady's chin. A spray of fake flowers burst from the side. The yellow color wasn't as pretty as Idelia's hair, so he put it back and reached for another.

This one boasted a purple-checked ribbon ballooning around a clump of brambles. Jerome brushed at the thing, trying to dislodge it from the hat. *Must've blown in the shop and Sadie didn't notice.*

"Like the bird's nest, do you?" A voice beside him made him stop trying to brush the thing off.

"Bird's nest?" He looked closer.

"Yes." Sadie reached over to straighten the ribbon. "Very popular."

Women had been running around with birds' nests on their heads and he hadn't noticed. Jerome blinked. The mayor was right—Willowville needed more women. Preferably women with more sense.

He handed her the hat. "Not today." While she rehung the thing, he retreated to the back corner of the store. For sure he'd have to get something now since Sadie knew he didn't like her hat. No sense riling up someone who could make a good friend for Idelia. . .even if these purses were too tiny to hold anything worth toting around.

He glanced in a small bin full of thin, gauzy fabric then backed away. Stockings were undergarments—far too intimate to give his bride when she stepped off the stage.

He bumped into a spindly shelf of small jars and soaps. Soap? He shook off thoughts of Idelia rubbing it into her long hair. *Too personal.*

A few steps took him to a display of handkerchiefs. Pretty, but for sure he wasn't going to give her a present that said, "I know you're going to be crying a lot."

It was then he spotted it—the perfect gift. Something to say he'd been thinking of her, something that she could actually use, and, most important, something that wouldn't embarrass either of them.

"These." He plunked them down on Sadie's counter and asked her to wrap them in some pretty paper. Jerome pocketed the gift and left the store.

Idelia would come soon, and now he was ready.

This is it!" Idelia peered through the stagecoach's murky windows as they pulled into town. "I hope Jerome got the message that we'd be late." *I hope he'll be as excited to see me as I am to see him.*

"Is nice to be out of this coach." Mama gestured to the hard seats they'd been bouncing on. She ducked through the open door first, grasping a man's hand as he helped her down.

"Mama Lurleen?" Jerome's voice sent a flutter to Idelia's heart, but she still noticed that he seemed surprised.

"*Hallo.*" Idelia put her hand in his as she stepped out of the coach. "So sorry there were troubles." She looked up into his warm brown gaze, her breath catching when she saw the thin lines crinkling the sides of his eyes. *Ja,* he was glad to see her.

"I'm just glad you're here." He offered her his arm and belatedly offered the other to Mama. "You're both here."

"*Ja,* it was good you knew I'd never send my Idelia alone." Mama beamed up at him, and Idelia suddenly remembered another reason she'd liked Jerome—he was one of the tallest men she'd ever met. Usually she stood at most men's eye levels, but her fiancé was the perfect height for her to lean her head on his shoulder.

"You're flushed." Jerome led them to a small bench and gestured for her to sit. "You rest a moment while I fetch your luggage."

Idelia offered a small smile and a big prayer of gratitude that he didn't know why she was blushing. The idea of being so close to a man, even one as strong and kind as Jerome, made her nervous. As he easily hefted her trunk, she revised that opinion. Jerome made her *especially* nervous. But in an exhilarating, hopeful way.

"Excuse me, ladies." A short man with broad shoulders took off his hat and made an awkward bow, his eyes fixed on Mama. "I was wonderin' if you were staying in Willowville or if you were both passing through with the stage."

"Staying." Idelia looked past the man, whom she judged to be about the same age as her mother, in hopes that Jerome would come back.

"Oh, good." A wide smile spread across his face. "I'm Mayor Ashton, and on behalf of all Willowville, I want to say you're a welcome addition to our town."

"*Dank u.*" Mama pursed her lips the way she did when biting back a smile. "We are come for my *dotter* to wed."

"I wondered." The mayor rocked back on his heels. "Heard tell a Miss van der Zee would be coming soon to marry up with the Sanders boy."

"That's right." Jerome's form blocked the sun, so it was

hard for Idelia to make out his expression. "And you should know better than to frighten off my bride and her mother." He shifted so he stood beside her, his arm resting along the back of the bench and brushing against her shoulders.

"Mother?" The mayor cast another admiring glance at Mama, who'd stopped trying to suppress her smile. "Surely you mis-spoke, Sanders. These two can only be sisters!"

"I'd accuse you of blatant flattery," Jerome said, "but I thought the same thing when I first met them."

"*Dank u.*" Mama's eyes sparkled as she drank in the attention.

"Van der Zee, eh? I suppose that means you're Dutch."

"*Ja.*" Idelia had relaxed when she realized that Jerome knew the man and that he'd made her mother smile.

"Well, you'll have to tell me about some of your Christmas traditions. We have a town celebration every year—unless there's a blizzard—and we're always looking for fresh ideas."

Idelia felt a slight pressure on her elbow and realized Jerome was helping her to her feet.

Mayor Ashton wasted no time offering his arm to Mama. Her smile flagged for a moment when she stood up and he only came to her chin.

Not again. Idelia closed her eyes for a swift prayer. Hopefully the mayor wouldn't disapprove of Mama's height. Some men, she knew, felt threatened by that.

"It keeps getting better and better," Ashton said to Jerome. "Two women come to town, both as beautiful as statues but with smiles to warm a man's heart."

Mama instantly obliged him with one of those smiles, and

Idelia joined in. The mayor, it seemed, would be a great help in making Mama feel comfortable in the new town. The two fell into conversation while Jerome gently drew her a short distance away.

"Idelia, I'm so glad you came to be my wife." His words melted her heart as he reached into his pocket. Could he have a wedding band for her? "And I want to give you something to celebrate your arrival."

❧

Jerome watched her eyes widen and felt a rush of gratitude he'd thought to bring her a welcoming gift. "This is for you." He pulled the package from his coat pocket and gave it to her.

She made tiny sounds of surprise as she turned it over, carefully unfolding the paper around her gift. She went about it as though unearthing something precious. Idelia's face glowed as she finally eased the gift from its packing. "Bootlaces?" Her brow furrowed as she held them up, the paper crumpling in her hand. She turned her gray eyes toward him, her gaze a question.

Should have gotten her the bird's nest. He kicked a rock across the road.

"What bird's nest?" Though he'd thought it impossible, she looked even more confused as she repeated the words he'd not meant to speak aloud.

"Didn't mean to say that," he hastily assured her. Bootlaces and birds' nests. He wouldn't blame the woman if she hightailed it right back to that stagecoach.

"About the laces," he said, reaching for them, "I thought maybe you could use them, but it was a bad idea."

"No!" She pulled them to her chest at his gesture. "It was kind of you to think of me. I'm glad to have these."

"Well, then. . ." He couldn't take back a stupid gesture now, not when she was being so sweet and trying to thank him. Jerome shrugged and led her back to her mother. *At least she saw the meaning behind it and is staying to be my wife.*

"Wat is this?" Mama Lurleen pointed at the laces, making Jerome give a silent groan.

"A welcome from my husband-to-be." Idelia displayed the laces proudly. "To show that he will provide for even the little things that most men forget."

He clenched his fists to keep from taking her in his arms. How God had blessed him in giving him this woman as his wife—not just because she would enable him to get the money he needed to save the farm, but because she had such a generous heart.

Mama Lurleen spoke in a spate of Dutch words, and Jerome saw Idelia give her a warning glance. *Now what can that be about?*

A few minutes later, when he helped his bride-to-be into the wagon, he caught a glimpse of her feet. A trim row of buttons marched down the line of her boot.

❧

"It's a good-sized town." Idelia counted a feed store, a general store, and a mercantile as they rode down Main Street.

"Yep. Gets busy in better weather. Most folks have stocked up for the winter already and are taking care of late autumn chores." Jerome flicked the reins, redirecting a mule headed for a clump of late grass.

"Not many people now," Mama agreed, "but the mayor."

"Clarence can always be found. We'll see him at church if the good weather holds till Sunday." He turned toward Idelia. "Everyone will be there, and I hoped we could make it our wedding day."

"*Ja.*" Idelia stifled her blush. She didn't want to sound overeager, but she and Mama would be staying at Jerome's farm. It wouldn't be proper to wait, and the last thing she wanted was to have a bad reputation in a new town.

"Until then, I'll be bunking in the barn." His words mirrored her thoughts. "I won't stay in the house until there's no question in anyone's mind that it's right."

"*Nee!*" The fervor in Mama's rejection of the idea let Idelia know how much she approved of Jerome's decision.

"I won't have anybody thinking you're less than the ladies you are." He turned the wagon down a worn path. "We'll be home in a minute."

Home. Idelia leaned forward on the bench, drinking in the sight as they approached the farm. December stripped the prairie of all but the hardiest—and driest—of tall grass, coloring the landscape in browns and yellows. Come spring, the earth would burst in shades of green, but first all would be covered under a white layer of snow.

Up ahead, a two-story farmhouse stood straight and solid,

with fair-sized windows to welcome them. Yards away, a barn slumped, red paint weathered and peeling, a good-sized silo looming at the far end. Not far away stood another structure, this one in better repair. It looked to be a stable.

"For both horses and cows?"

"Yep. There are hogs and chickens, too." She read pride in the subtle straightening of his spine.

"I had not known if we'd have many animals or mostly crops." Idelia glanced to see his reaction to her use of "we."

He didn't disappoint, looking back at her and nodding. "We grow wheat and corn in the fields. My grandma had a garden long ago. There are signs of plants now, but we'll have to replant it for it to be of use."

"I'd like that." *He, too, sees us as a team.*

She put her hands on his shoulders after he pulled up before the stable and came to the side.

He swung her down but didn't take his hands from her waist immediately. "Welcome home, Idelia."

The warmth of his fingers lingered even after he moved to help her mother. She took the time to gather her thoughts and get a closer look at the farm.

From a distance, the buildings seemed solid, but as she stood near the house, Idelia recognized it wasn't only the cattle barn that needed repair.

Parched weeds pushed through slats on the porch, shutters hung at crooked angles, and the entire house could use a good scrubbing—and a few coats of whitewash. This place hadn't seen the loving touch of a woman for too long, and she'd guess

Jerome's grandfather had some trouble caring for everything in his later years.

It was good there was much to do. She and Mama would start tomorrow and work to make Jerome's farm a home they could all be proud to call theirs.

Chapter 5

Jerome woke to the sound of his rooster, which came through much louder since he was in the stable. For such a scraggly little bird, it had lusty lungs and a strut to match.

Jerome splashed himself with icy water from the pail he'd brought inside the night before. Thanks to a heap of fresh hay, the blankets he'd brought from the house, and the heat of the horses, he'd stayed comfortable through the night. When winter came, the nights would be freezing.

But I'll be back in the house with my beautiful bride come Sunday. With that in mind, he set about his morning chores. First he pitched hay from the loft to the horse stalls below, leaving the mucking for later. Next he climbed the ladder on the side of the silo, sinking into the soft silage at the top and forking loads of it below. The cows feasted on the sweet-sour mash of corncobs while he grabbed bucketfuls and slopped the hogs.

That's when things became odd. The chickens, already pecking at strewn seed, had not a single egg in the coop. *Idelia and Mama Lurleen must be up and moving.* Jerome quickened his pace back to the barn. Once he finished the milking, he'd see if the women had started breakfast.

His stomach rumbled in anticipation as he entered the barn. Both cows turned drowsy eyes toward him. He went to Maisy, a cow who'd seen many years with his grandpa but still gave milk. Not this morning.

He frowned. It was still fall—early for the cows to stop milking. Maybe the old gal had finally dried up. Jerome moved on to Netta, the younger cow he'd bought shortly after returning to the farm. Nothing.

Two cats prowled along the edges of the walls, impatient for their morning share of cream. With two milking cows, Jerome had more milk and cream than he could consume, so the hogs and mousing cats reaped the benefit.

He returned the three-legged stool and pail to their places and noticed what he hadn't before—two pails were gone. Idelia had been busy working alongside him, even if he hadn't known it. He made his way toward the house with a light step. His bride-to-be was already pitching in. And once they were wed, Mama Lurleen would return to her inn. Then he and Idelia could truly begin their life together, funded by her unexpected dowry.

The barn and stables would be repaired, the house neat and clean. The tools in the barn stable would be replaced, the crops flourishing from the new implements and the time he could spend in the fields. He envisioned the garden bursting with vegetables, the kitchen fragrant with good cooking, and Idelia smiling as he came through the door. And someday they'd have children romping around their feet.

He knocked on the kitchen door before wiping the mud from his boots and entering. The smell of frying bacon hit him before he heard the telltale sizzle of the pan on the stove. Mama Lurleen nodded to him but kept an eye on the meat while Idelia stooped to draw a pan out of the oven. It looked to be some kind of bread, the scent warm and sweet as she set it on the table.

"*Goedemorgen*, Jerome." She gestured for him to sit while she fetched the coffeepot from the stove.

"Good morning, Idelia. Mama Lurleen," he acknowledged as his future mother-in-law set a platter of hot, crispy bacon next to the pan of breakfast rolls. A pitcher of chilled fresh milk rested by his arm as they all took their seats.

He bowed his head and offered a prayer of thanks for the women's safe arrival and the food before them. Then breakfast began.

Lurleen heaped bacon onto his plate while Idelia poured drinks. A tall glass of milk sat next to a steaming cup of coffee just behind his plate. Then they passed around the breakfast rolls.

Unable to resist, Jerome picked up one of the flaky brown pastries and bit into it, warmth spreading to his stomach as he savored the flavor. Small lumps like golden raisins offered an unexpected sweetness. "These are great," he praised. "What are they called?"

"*Krentebolletjes*," Mama Lurleen told him.

"Currant buns," Idelia added, reaching for her own glass of milk. "We found a small box of the currants in your root cellar."

"I like krankyballets," he said, trying out the new word.

The women both giggled, Idelia trying again. "*Krentebolletjes*," she repeated.

"Maybe I'll just stick with currant buns," he decided, crunching into a piece of bacon. "Doesn't matter what you call them"—he swiped another from the pan—"so long as I can eat them!"

"You wouldn't want them every morning," Idelia teased as Jerome proved to have the healthy appetite she'd remembered.

"Don't be so sure about that." He took a swig of coffee. "But I wouldn't want to talk myself out of other treats!"

"It is Kerstmis season, so we usually make the traditional feast." Idelia realized she'd have more than one reason to celebrate this year. It would be her first Christmas in her own house, as a married woman.

"*Ja*." Mama began to plan out loud, "We have *speculaas*, *kerststol*, *poffertjes*, *pasteitje*, *rollade*, *kerstkrans*, and *oliebollen*."

"And *pepernoten*," Idelia added. She'd make a batch of it as soon as they'd settled in and serve it with warm spiced milk.

"I have no idea what any of that is, but I'm already looking forward to it." He slathered butter on another bun and shot a conspiratorial glance her way. Then he turned to Mama. "I'd say Mayor Ashton would love to hear about all of them.

Maybe you'll help him plan this year's town celebration of. . . Curstmiss?"

"Kerstmis, yes." Mama patted the table for emphasis. "Tradition is much important."

"And here we'll have the chance to start a few of our own." The smile he sent her made Idelia's heart beat faster.

Tomorrow. Tomorrow this man will take me as his wife before God and the community. "And what is planned today?"

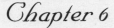

Chapter 6

"S ince you've looked around, is there anything you need from the general store?" His question made her think of his awkward gift. Jerome might believe he'd erred in his choice, but Idelia would treasure those laces forever.

"The larder is well stocked, and we brought a trunk of provisions in case we were caught in a blizzard. The only things we wondered about were if you have a springhouse and where you keep the eggs." She gestured to a basket against the wall where that morning's eggs lay waiting.

"I don't have a springhouse," he admitted. "The well is rigged with a basket so you can lower milk and such to keep it cool. The eggs I store in the root cellar."

"We didn't see them." Mama and she had explored the root cellar earlier and been delighted to find sacks of vegetables, barrels of dried apples, and even a few jars of preserves. Bushels of potatoes and sacks of walnuts rounded out the supplies.

"I'll show you." He walked over to the trapdoor, opened it, and grabbed a lantern. Once it was lit, he led them down the wooden slats serving as stairs.

"Here." He took them to the side, where they'd found the preserves, and pointed toward the stairwell. There someone had carved a low niche into the soil, and Jerome had put straw-filled crates in the space.

"We didn't look behind the stairs," Idelia confessed. "Such a clever place, too. Now we can add to the winter store until the hens stop laying."

"Right. I haven't had the time to make any butter, though there's a churn upstairs. The smokehouse is fairly well stocked, but I planned to butcher a hog this week, and soon I'll be able to go to the pond and fill the icehouse."

"We'll have ice year-round?" Idelia couldn't hide her grin. "And extra cream, it seems. I think we can plan to enjoy some ice cream next summer!"

"Mmm." Mama closed her eyes.

"If you bleed the hog, we can boil water for the scalding and then make butter while you scrape it. With the three of us, we can butcher it today, if you don't have other pressing chores."

"Sounds like a fine idea. You never know when a blizzard will blow in, so it's best to have everything ready as soon as possible. While you boil the water, I'll wrangle out the biggest hog and start things."

❧

Not many women would be more than willing to slaughter a hog the day before their wedding, and Jerome knew it. But then, only a rare woman would appreciate the thought behind so simple and plain a gift as bootlaces—especially when her boots buttoned.

How blessed I am in my bride, he praised the Lord as he grabbed his butchering kit. *I wasn't sure when I telegraphed her but knew she wouldn't come if it wasn't Your will. When she said yes, I wondered whether we'd be a good match, if we could share a lifetime together. Idelia is a beautiful, intelligent woman and a hard worker, but beauty fades and there is more than work between a man and wife. How thankful I am that she already loves this place, and her presence makes it even better.*

He made his way toward the hog pen, his eye on the big boar who'd taken a liking to shoving sows away from the trough. Slaughtering was never pleasant, but by choosing this mean fellow, he'd bring meat to the table and eliminate the problem.

Jerome grabbed a pail of slop and lured the bully from the pen. The sows had learned to let him through when grub appeared, so it was easy to get the hog around the corner of the barn. Didn't take much time to do the deed and hang the greedy pig to bleed out.

When he returned to the house, he found the women out in the yard, tending a large fire. They'd rigged a travois to hold the scalding pot, and the water was heating. Idelia saw him approach and gave a small wave before disappearing into the house.

"Will boil soon," Mama Lurleen pronounced and proved to be right.

By the time Idelia emerged from the kitchen, bearing a pail of milk and the butter churn, they had the hog in the huge pot.

When its hide softened, Jerome would scrape off the hair and the butchering would begin.

"Potatoes and onions are on the stove," Idelia reported as she spooned heavy cream from the top of the pail into the churn. "And this morning's eggs are oiled and stored in the cellar. If the hens keep laying for another week or so, we should have enough to last through winter."

"Potatoes?" Jerome wasn't sure what she was making—they'd just had breakfast and noon was hours away.

"Ja." Mama Lurleen settled herself on a log he hadn't chopped fully yet. "Boil sliced potatoes and onions, and bake with butter and cream." She pointed to the hog to make her point. "Eat with slices of fried ham for dinner."

"It takes awhile, so it's good to start now," Idelia told him as she started a second fire to boil and clean the meat. "But since we have fresh cream and ham, and we'll make the butter now, it will be delicious today."

"Sounds like it." Jerome's still-full stomach gave a small growl as he imagined it. The plan also explained why she'd only brought out one of the pails of milk—they needed both butter and cream.

And ham. He used a long stick to test the hide and found it coming along nicely. By the time they sat down to that dinner, they'd have earned something wonderful. After the past two months of brutal work followed by hard tack, cold biscuits, and old coffee, Jerome relished the prospect.

It made the hours fly by, and when the sun shone high above, Mama Lurleen had made the butter, and the potato dish baked in the stove. He'd scraped the hide and done the butchering while Idelia boiled the meat and prepared it for curing. She'd also cleansed the entrails and set them aside for later use.

After lunch they'd smoke the ribs, hocks, and sides of bacon before making sausages. But for now, the women were slicing ham and making it sizzle in the skillet. He couldn't actually hear the sound from where he stood, drawing water to wash up for the meal, but he knew that when he stepped inside, the meal would be ready.

They sank gratefully onto the chairs around the table before thanking God for His provision, the productive morning, and the food waiting to nourish them. Jerome kept his eyes shut a moment after the prayer ended, inhaling the savory fragrance of the potatoes, turned thick, golden, and bubbling from the oven.

Silence reigned as they filled their plates and dug in. Jerome speared one of the potatoes on his plate and popped it in his mouth, its rich, creamy texture and flavor melting in his mouth. He followed it up with some of the butter-fried ham, chewing slowly to enjoy it all.

Yes, Jerome decided, *God has blessed me more than I even imagined.*

Idelia woke early the next morning and rolled out of bed, careful not to disturb Mama. There were beds in only two rooms, and Idelia couldn't bring herself to sleep in Jerome's bed. The thought that after today they'd spend the night together as man and wife brought heat to her cheeks.

She threw on the dress she'd worn the day before and crept down to the kitchen, where she started to heat water. She'd dragged an old metal tub from the barn yesterday morning and stowed it in the parlor, where the door shut and the curtains were thickest. While the water heated, she lit the parlor fire for warmth and sneaked upstairs. When Idelia came back, she laid out some towels, her soap and brush, and her best dress—a light blue wool warm enough for the weather and a color that flattered her eyes.

The stove heated two large pots—not nearly so large as the scalding cauldron—at a time. She emptied the first round into the tub and put more on to heat. Snagging her cloak from a peg by the door, she fed the hens and gathered the eggs as swiftly as possible in the dark. The crisp cold of approaching winter chilled her before she came back to add more hot water to her bath. The small tub wasn't even half full, which would be enough.

Next she hurried to the barn, gratified to see that Jerome hadn't filled the trough with silage yet—she still had time. When she came back to the house, the water was ready. One more load and she'd slide into the bath. In the meantime, she started coffee, mixed batter, and took out the waffle iron.

She bathed hastily, wishing she could luxuriate in the warm comfort of the bath but knowing Mama was stirring and would like a bath herself. Besides, she still had to dry her hair and make breakfast! Idelia slipped into her chemise and petticoats before settling by the fire to towel dry and brush her hair, which hung past her waist. Luckily, the fine strands dried quickly, and she was putting it up in a soft twist when Mama came down.

"So early this morning!" Mama looked longingly at the tub while Idelia finished dressing.

"Go ahead while it's still warm, Mama," she encouraged. "I've done the morning chores and will have breakfast going."

"You could not sleep for thoughts of your wedding?" Mama knew her well. "I could not when I was about to marry your father—so much excitement."

"I wanted to have a bath this morning, too," Idelia pointed out. "And make sure everything goes smoothly."

"My *dotter* will make a fine wife." Mama reached out and cupped her cheek. "Ready and loving, you are. It will be good marriage."

"I hope so, Mama. It seems an answer to prayer." The smell of burnt coffee wisped into the room, making her head for the kitchen. Sure enough, the coffee had sat too long and was strong enough to bring any man to his knees. She sloshed it outside and set about making another pot.

While Mama took her bath, Idelia fetched the syrup and cooked up stacks of waffles. The sweet, buttery aroma filled the kitchen, chasing away the last traces of burnt coffee. On a whim, she decided to chop up some of the ham left from the day before and mix it into scrambled eggs. The large skillet sizzled, adding to the smell of a hearty breakfast.

"*Stroopwafels*!" Mama entered the kitchen with pails of the wash water, which she took outside, emptied, and brought back.

"*Ja.* I thought Jerome would like them." Idelia finished up while Mama emptied the rest of the tub.

"Smells great." Jerome came inside just in time, freshly shaven and wearing what looked to be a new shirt. He'd even polished his boots.

"*Stroopwafels*," Mama repeated.

"Waffles I know." He settled into his seat at the head of the table. "What's the other part?"

"Syrup." Idelia poured a mug full of coffee.

"That's one I can remember." He forked several onto his plate. "Stroop waffles." A large bite found its way to his mouth. "Mmm..."

"Is not *krentebolletjes*," Mama teased. "But Idelia thought you would like them."

"And she's right." Jerome dug into some of the eggs and ham. "This is mighty good."

"Better than the *krentebolletjes*?" Idelia couldn't help pressing—Jerome seemed more than willing to eat whatever she placed before him, but it was good for a wife to know her husband's favorite dishes.

"Not better." He leaned back as he chewed another bite. "Not worse. Everything you've made is wonderful."

"*Dank u.*" Idelia poured some more syrup over her waffles, just the way she liked.

"And you look beautiful this morning." His next words almost made her choke. "The men of Willowville will all be green with envy when they see how fortunate I am. . .and they haven't tried your cooking!"

"I, too, am fortunate"—Idelia met his gaze despite the blush she felt—"to have found a good man who is also handsome and kind. I will be proud to stand with you and become your wife."

❧

Jerome rushed to hitch the horses to the buckboard. Getting to church at the right moment required precise timing. Too early and men would flock around the women. That wasn't an option. Too late and they'd be embarrassed upon their first introduction to the community.

Jerome planned on a respectable entrance before the opening prayer but after everyone began settling in the pews. That way, nothing could make Idelia think twice about going through with the marriage. They'd be wedded before they left the church, and no one would be able to sweep her away.

And if he were a betting man, he'd stake everything he owned that an entire contingent of Willowville bachelors would make a play for Idelia. Though he couldn't blame them—even if there was no money attached, any man with two eyes and ears would be interested in her—he'd do everything in his power to stop them.

Of far less importance was the stir Mama Lurleen would cause. She'd obviously wed young and born Idelia soon thereafter, making his mother-in-law-to-be an attractive young widow in her own right. Keeping the men from buzzing around Lurleen van der Zee would be Clarence's problem—Mayor Ashton would have to move fast to stake his claim.

They were under way right on schedule, clipping toward the service at a comfortable pace. Jerome was so pleased by their timing he almost didn't notice Idelia fidgeting with the ribbons of her Sunday hat. Almost.

"Something wrong?"

"Just nervous," she admitted.

"About the wedding?" Cold fear clenched his gut. *What if she doesn't want to marry me?*

"Of course not." She waved away the concern as though it were no more than a pesky fly. "Meeting everyone in town."

"Oh, they're good folk for the most part." The tension in his shoulders eased. "You'll be more than welcome."

"Especially when they taste what we will make for the celebration of Kerstmis," Mama Lurleen added. "Mayor Ashton should be pleased."

"I think you could bake a brick and please the good mayor, Mama." Idelia stopped fidgeting to tease her mother.

"*Nee*, no man would eat a brick."

"A man can do worse if he's making his own meal." Jerome grimaced at the memory of a stew he'd attempted. "I once made a dinner of burnt stew with too many onions. Couldn't choke it down, and even the hogs wouldn't touch it when I added it to their slop."

"Tough choice,"—Idelia chuckled—"break your teeth on a brick or burn your belly with stew. But I meant that the mayor is so taken with Mama, it wouldn't matter what she put before him."

"He is nice man," Mama Lurleen insisted.

"Clarence can be right ornery at times, though." Jerome thought it only fair to give Mrs. van der Zee a warning. "When he gets a notion, it takes a team of mules to pull him off it."

"I like decisive man." Mama Lurleen's voice was firm as she put an end to the discussion. "And I will like this town."

Her pronouncement came just as they pulled up to the church. Sure enough, Clarence was by their side, ready to help Lurleen out of the buckboard as soon as she held out a gloved hand.

Once Jerome swung Idelia out of the wagon and onto the ground, he could sense the crowd of men gawking at his bride. It took a prayer to quell his urge to tell them to go about their business and leave him to his.

"See?" Alastair from the telegraph office pushed through to give him a sharp elbow in the side. "I told you she'd make it."

"Of course." Idelia's expression was soft as she looked at

Jerome. "I wanted to come here."

"And here she is." Jerome offered her his arm, the air crisp as he filled his lungs. *And she's mine.* He gave the other men a warning glance to make sure they knew it.

"Lucky man." Alastair looked from him to Idelia, his face a portrait of mischief. "With two whole weeks before the deadline."

Jerome fought to keep his smile as Idelia turned toward him, confusion painting her features.

"What deadline?"

Goose bumps raised along Idelia's arms as she saw Jerome's expression. Obviously something was wrong—which was not to be permitted on their wedding day.

"Idelia. . ." He placed one large, work-roughened hand over hers, his calluses rubbing her gloves as he spoke. "The mayor encouraged the bachelors of Willowville to go marry before Christmas came and winter snowed us in."

"Wise." Mama Lurleen beamed at Mayor Ashton, who hovered by her side.

"Didn't want them to wait till spring." Ashton's words confirmed Jerome's statement, but a small wrinkle of worry wavered between his brows.

"That's right." A man she hadn't met broke into the conversation. "And Jerome's a lucky rascal to have found such a pretty wife so quick."

The man who'd first approached Jerome raised his voice and gave her a meaningful look. "Especially since now he gets the wife *and* the money."

❧

"Money?" She scooted closer to Jerome and farther away from the troublemaker.

"Yep." Yet another man she didn't know butted in. "Since he got you here and is marrying you before the Christmas shindig, he gets a nice wad of cash."

"Is this true, Jerome?" She gazed up into his eyes, begging him to deny this awful accusation. Her groom wasn't a man who would send for a wife just for money. *Jerome chose me because he felt as I do.*

"It is true that if I marry by Christmas, the town council will give us a marriage gift." His eyes didn't meet hers.

"On account of the town needing fine women like yourself and your mama," Ashton placated, patting Mama's hand.

Mama, however, was not to be placated. She withdrew her hand from Ashton's at the same moment Idelia pulled free from Jerome's grasp.

"You brought me here for money?" The hurt ringing in her voice sent rage coursing through her. How dare he make a fool of her and trap her in this town! "You will be sorely disappointed, Mr. Sanders."

She turned her back to him, linked arms with Mama, who was glowering fit to scare a buzzard from a gut bucket, and marched into the church. Thoughts churning, she scarcely noticed men crowding the pews beside and around them until Jerome wedged himself at her side, displacing another fellow.

Since the other man smelled strongly of onions, Idelia took

a moment to debate whether or not she should ask Jerome to sit elsewhere. She settled for pivoting slightly, giving him her shoulder.

The opening prayer sounded like a faint drone buzzing in her ears, so she made a prayer of her own. *What am I to do now, Lord?* The words came from her heart to her lips over and over again, though she didn't give voice to them.

It was plain as day she wouldn't be marrying Jerome this afternoon. It would be a mockery of a sacred commitment between man and woman if he did not love her.

The thoughts repeated over and over as they sang hymns. Idelia stood with everyone but couldn't find her voice. Praise was the last thing she felt able to give when her dreams of love and family had wisped away in the morning mist. She was grateful to sit again and set herself to listening closely to the sermon. If ever there had been a time when she needed the guidance of the Lord, this was it.

"This morning I'm going to divert from our study of the book of Romans to address what I see as a danger lurking in our town." The reverend's words did nothing to ease the tumult in Idelia's heart, but he pressed onward.

"The town council put out an amazing proposition recently, despite my objection. Until now, no one has gotten to the point where it is an actual problem, but as of this morning, that bridge has been crossed."

Please, Lord, don't let him be talking about me! Idelia reached up and massaged the back of her neck.

"The Word tells us that whatever man finds a worthy

wife finds favor with the Lord and that a virtuous woman is a treasure. So it stands to reason that any man who finds a wife he'd be proud to call his own is blessed."

Jerome was nodding so vehemently Idelia could feel the ribbons of her hat wave in the breeze he caused. Well, he could bob his head until kingdom come for all the difference it would make.

She thought he'd sent for her because he, too, felt a special warmth. Because he'd established his home and was ready to share it and his life with her. And she'd accepted his rushed proposal because starting a family with a man like Jerome had been the cry of her heart since before Da passed on. And with him gone, her need to gather love around her, to expand their family, had intensified.

Had she been so anxious for a family of her own that she'd imposed her wishes over the Lord's plan? Her throat went dry. The telegram had seemed a perfect opportunity, the long-awaited answer to prayer.

Oh Lord, forgive my haste. I thought the path was laid before me, but I didn't seek You when the opportunity came. And now, Lord, here I am, bound to a man I cannot marry. Wedding vows are sacred, and now that I know Jerome doesn't feel that love for me, I'm trapped. Where do I go from here?

❧

Home. I just have to get her home and reason with her before all the men here descend on her like hounds after a fox.

The hairs on the back of Jerome's neck prickled. The envy in the eyes of every man in town had been replaced by speculation. There wasn't a single bachelor who didn't gape at Idelia and her mother, but until Alastair stirred up trouble, Jerome hadn't concerned himself about it.

Idelia was to be his wife, and he'd been clear about staking his claim. But now everything turned topsy-turvy as Idelia's hurt and anger simmered throughout the sermon.

Anger he understood. In fact, he was mad enough to admit she had cause to be miffed. *Why didn't I tell her about the cash in the telegram?*

The answer all but smacked him in the face. *I knew it might make her say no. At the very least I should have mentioned it once she arrived and I'd made it clear how glad I was to be marrying her. What a mess.*

He had to save Gramps's farm. To do that, he needed money. In order to get that money, he'd been told he just had to marry a woman from out of town. He'd prayed about it and it seemed the Lord placed Idelia on his mind, so why was he being villainized?

Yes, Jerome saw he should have told Idelia about her unexpected dowry so they could share the joy that they'd save the farm. Including Idelia in the planning would have been the smart thing to do, and even he could see that having some local clodpoll tell a woman on her wedding day that her groom only wanted the money would put any gal's nose out of joint. But how could he fix it?

Jerome directed his attention back to the reverend's sermon. Since he was talking about the wedding incentive, maybe the man of God would have a solution to the problem somewhere in his message.

"Now I'd like to take you to Proverbs 15:27, a verse I feel is very relevant to this situation." He began to read. " 'He that is greedy of gain troubleth his own house.' I'd say that's pretty self-explanatory."

The air left Jerome's lungs in a whoosh. The fact that the reverend was looking directly at him reinforced whom that verse was supposed to reach.

Greed? Jerome's hands clenched in denial. How could it be greedy to want to restore and preserve his family legacy—to honor his grandfather? That was a noble goal, biblical in its own right.

And yet. . .the second part certainly applied to his situation. Though things were fine when he woke up, trouble had since descended upon his household. Come to think of it, until they got this sorted out, he wouldn't even be living in his house. Until he and Idelia were wed, he'd be bunking in the barn. He could feel himself scowling at the realization and glanced at Idelia.

One look at the upset on Idelia's face gave him indigestion, which was a real shame after such a fine breakfast. Anger he could respect, but the idea that he'd hurt her. . .well, that he couldn't stomach. Jerome looked at her lovely face again and saw her blinking as though holding back tears.

And that's when he knew. In trying to fulfill his goal, worthy though it may be, he'd only thought of himself. Now his Idelia paid the price for it. And what was another word for "greed" if not *selfishness?*

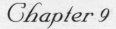

Chapter 9

If anyone asked Idelia how she'd gotten back to Jerome's farm after church, she wouldn't be able to answer. Simple fact of the matter was that everything blurred together.

One moment she was a bride entering a church with her intended. The next, a fool who wasn't wanted. Jerome was taking her in exchange for the money, almost like a punishment! And then the sermon, bringing home to her how much she needed her husband to treasure her. After that she just remembered Mama ushering her back to the wagon, pointedly ignoring everyone who tried to speak with them. Idelia didn't say a word, just kept a smile pressed tightly on her face until the farm was in sight.

The moment she saw the house, her facade crumbled. Home. *This was supposed to be home—a place where I was wanted, where Jerome and I would make happy memories to share.*

"This isn't my home." She spoke the words aloud, the finality in them sinking her heart a notch lower.

"Yes, it is." Jerome swung her out of the wagon but didn't

release her. His hands still encircling her waist, he said, "I want this to be your home, Idelia."

"I know." She squeezed her eyes shut and stepped backward, out of his grasp. "You want the money to restore this place, and you can only have it if I marry you within the next two weeks!"

"No." He reached for her, saw the glare she shot him, and shoved his hands in his pockets. "I want you here because you belong here. With me."

The honesty in his voice pulled her up short. "Why didn't you tell me about the money? That the reason you sent for me immediately wasn't because you couldn't stand to wait until spring but because you couldn't afford to?"

"I was afraid you wouldn't come." He swallowed hard. "And I was too selfish to consider what you'd think when you heard about the council's proposition."

"Proposition." Mama snorted. "Not proposal. One is love, one business. You chose business."

So true. Tears pricked behind her eyes, tiny darts whose discomfort paled in comparison to her remorse. *I chose you for love.* She wanted to fling the words at him but couldn't. Not when he'd so obviously made his choice. Not when he didn't care for her in the same way.

"I don't anymore." Jerome stepped around Mama to clasp Idelia's hands. His warmth wrapped around her fingers, his gaze penetrating her defenses. "When you came, I thought about how God had blessed me with not only the means to save the farm, but a wife to enjoy it with for a lifetime. I want to marry you, Idelia. No one else."

For a moment she believed him, ready to fall into his arms and give up her last shreds of dignity. She held back though. "Why?"

"I just said why." His brow furrowed. "You're the woman I want to spend my life with."

"Even if you didn't get so much as a dime?" She crossed her arms and awaited his answer. At the moment, she didn't know what she'd do if he had the wrong answer, but she had to know.

"Idelia,"—he took a deep breath—"I don't see why we can't have both. But the answer is yes. I want to marry you—money or no money—because of who you are."

"In that case," Idelia replied, moving to clasp hands with Mama, "you don't have long to prove it."

❧

As the two women walked into the house, Jerome resisted the urge to let loose a howl of frustration. As soon as the door shut, he snatched the hat from his head and slapped it on the ground to vent some steam.

Didn't help.

He reached down, picked up the trusty hat, patted the dust out of it, and plunked it back on his head. It wasn't his Stetson's fault he was in this mess. Jerome acknowledged that.

He turned his head at the sound of a horse riding fast and saw Clarence Ashton pounding up to the hitching post. Jerome took a savage satisfaction in blocking the mayor's path to his house. It didn't hurt that Ashton looked more than a mite disgruntled himself. Good. If he had to suffer for this whole thing, Ashton should be in the stocks alongside him.

"Mayor,"—he made a show of tipping his just-dusted hat— "what brings you here this fine afternoon?"

"Cut the garbage, Sanders." Ashton tried to sidestep him. When Jerome anticipated the move, the mayor scowled. "I told the other men in town that I'd fine 'em if they stopped by your place today, but I can't hold 'em off forever. After the stunt you pulled this mornin', Lurleen won't so much as look at me!"

"*Mrs. van der Zee*," he said, taking particular care to emphasize the proper form of address, "realizes that this whole situation is your fault. You deserve a cold shoulder for trying to rush men and women into hasty marriages like that."

"Ha!" Ashton hooked his thumbs through his suspenders. "I didn't try to rush any woman into marriage. Just encouraged you young bucks to get out there and do as the Bible says—be fruitful. The town needs women and children, and you bumps on a log weren't doin' anything about it!"

"First off, I've scarcely been here for two months," Jerome countered. "Second, you dangled money in front of our noses when you knew full well that the railroad strike last spring devastated the farmers hereabouts. There's not a man in this town who can say that a sum of cash like that wouldn't be a balm to his household. It was manipulative."

"Now see here, Sanders, I and the council did what we thought was right to encourage town growth and help some of the farms most affected by the strike—like yours. The proposition was straightforward. Everyone knew the score." The mayor worked his jaw. "Until you brought in those wonderful women and didn't see fit to tell them. And this here conversation isn't getting either of us back in their good graces."

"I asked her to marry me. She said yes. It doesn't get much simpler than that." Jerome couldn't quite meet Ashton's gaze as he said it. "But I should have told her we'd have the farm and the money, too."

"Why didn't you?"

"She might not have come."

"I'm not a lackwit, son." Ashton rolled his eyes. "I meant. . . why didn't you mention it, casual-like, once they got here? Didn't you figure some smart-mouth like Alastair Pitt would put a spoke in that wheel?"

"Nope. I just figured we'd get married, and Idelia would be my wife, and we'd set about building a life together. Guess I didn't think much beyond that."

Ashton took a step back, his brows relaxing. "So that's the way of it. It's not just for the money."

" 'Course not!"

"Don't get all het up. You wouldn't have sent for her if the council hadn't offered the incentive, and you know it. Just think about how that looks to a young gal and her tender mother."

"How could I ask a woman to marry me when the farm was failing and I wasn't in a position to provide for her?"

"Good point. Have you apologized to her yet, started to make it all up to her?"

"I told her I'd marry her without the money." Jerome

followed Ashton's gaze to the house, where a curtain twitched as though someone had been peeking out just a moment before. "And now I have to make her believe me."

"Then we're going to have to strategize." Ashton tilted his head toward the house and lowered his voice. "Because 'making' a woman do anything she isn't inclined to do is harder than coaxing a carrot from a starving mule."

Chapter 10

"Did you catch that?" Idelia glanced at Mama, who'd copied her position at the window on the other side of the door. They'd opened them to encourage a fresh breeze. When they overheard the mayor and Jerome arguing about their situation, they pressed their ears close to hear every word.

"*Nee.* Just 'strategy' and then mumbles." Mama looked as put out as Idelia felt.

"They're going to the barn now." She didn't eavesdrop often, but when the topic of discussion would decide one's fate, so to speak, it was much more difficult to resist. Idelia straightened up. "But did you hear what they said?"

"*Ja.*" Mama brightened. "They are wanting us to not be upset with them and will now court us."

"Yes, us." Idelia couldn't help but grin at Mama's enthusiasm. Obviously she returned the mayor's admiration. "Even better, Jerome knows he was wrong not to tell me and told Ashton that he'd marry me whether he got money or not. . .that he couldn't propose before he knew he could support his wife."

"Is better." Mama shoved up her sleeves. "Now we remind them why my *dotter* is reward enough alone. He has not proven worthy yet, but sweet helps to chase away the bitter."

Thank You, Lord, that Jerome isn't too stubborn to admit he erred and to try to fix things. Thank You that he cares enough to want to fix things. I begin to believe that it's not just the money, that Jerome returns my feelings in some measure. If it is Your will, I ask that You show me he is the man for me.

"We need something special. . .and quick to make." Idelia pondered for a moment. Mama's uncharacteristic silence made her raise her brows. "No ideas?"

Mama shrugged. "Is for you to choose."

"Fresh pork chops from the butchering yesterday, with crackling bread. I'll run and get the meat while you ready the Dutch oven. We'll need it and the stove oven both." Idelia scarcely waited for the nod of approval. Fresh crackling bread was a treat available only after a recent slaughter. The crisp bits of pork left after rendering the lard weren't usually in ready supply.

They got down to work—heating the Dutch oven, melting shortening, and laying the spiced chops within to bake. While the meat cooked, Idelia mixed cornmeal, flour, and baking soda in a large bowl. She stirred the batter constantly as she added the beaten eggs and buttermilk before folding in the cracklings. A few minutes later, a large roasting pan filled with the batter slid into the stove oven.

"Would you watch the ovens while I make butter?" Idelia swiped her forehead with the back of her hand.

"You made fresh butter yesterday." Mama waved toward the well, where the crock hung on a long rope to keep cool. Soon enough it would be so cold that anything put outside would freeze straight through.

"*Ja*. But cracklin' bread is best with sweet butter."

"Ah." She brushed the coals off the top of the Dutch oven, checking the pork chops inside.

At this silent agreement, Idelia hurried to scoop the morning cream into the churn, adding salt before she pumped furiously. When it began to resist, she poured in a generous measure of honey and finished churning. A quick wash and a moment in the butter press and it was on the table as Mama pulled the crackling bread from the oven.

Idelia stepped outside to ring the dinner bell, gratified to see the men rush from the barn in their haste. In the blink of an eye, they sat at the table, a succulent chop steaming on each plate.

"Dear heavenly Father," Jerome prayed, "we ask that You bless the hands that made this food, and thank You that Idelia and Mama Lurleen came to Willowville. Let them know how grateful we are. Furthermore, we ask that You help us be deserving of such bounty. Amen."

She couldn't help but give him a small smile for his efforts as she dished up hearty slices of the bread and passed around her sweet butter. Idelia watched as Mayor Ashton murmured something to Mama.

While Ashton cut into the meat first, Jerome slathered his bread with the creamy butter and bit into it with relish. His eyes widened as the flavor hit his tongue. "Cracklin' bread?"

"*Ja.*" Idelia wouldn't say more. It was up to him to make the conversation while Mama and Mayor Ashton were deep in discussion about the Christmas gathering.

"Cracklin' bread?" Ashton, apparently not as deep in conversation as it appeared, wasted no time spreading a hearty helping of butter on his own. "Mmm. . ."

Mama shot her an amused glance, and for a moment, they shared a woman's contentment at a dish well done and a plan carried through. Making a special dinner let the men know their ire wouldn't last forever and gave Jerome and Ashton an opportunity to appreciate their efforts. Fortunately, the men were making good on their part.

"This is wonderful," Jerome praised. "Every time you get in the kitchen, I'm sure the meal can't compare to the one before, but you always prove me wrong."

"It's been this good each day?" Ashton put down his fork in astonishment and picked it up again when Mama started slicing more wedges from the pan. He dug in with gusto to make up for lost time.

"Wait until you taste what we make to celebrate Kerstmis," Mama promised. "Then you will know true Dutch cooking."

"I can't wait." Jerome wiped his face with his napkin.

Neither can I. Idelia couldn't escape the smudge of doubt that clouded her thoughts. *Because it's the last day we can wed and still make the deadline.*

Three days after the scene at the church and Jerome wasn't much closer to figuring out how to prove to Idelia that he cared about her more than the money. If worse came to worst, he could just wait until after the Christmas celebration so she'd have no fears. Then Idelia would be secure, happy, and, most important, *his*.

Only problem with that was the money issue. He wanted his wife more than he wanted any sum of cash, but how would he be able to provide for her without it? If he were to be completely honest, he didn't like the notion of waiting that long until the wedding, either. A woman like his bride-to-be was temptation enough to ensure he stayed in the barn. Indefinitely.

But shouldn't he be able to think of some gesture now? Something so she didn't have to feel like this anymore? Memories of the boot lace debacle kept him rejecting whatever came to mind. Jerome warmed every time he thought of Idelia's kind understanding and honest gratitude for his efforts.

This time, it had to be special. Personal, even. And hang the potential for embarrassment. Maybe if he'd been more willing to risk his pride, he wouldn't have lost his bride. So what would Idelia like best? What would she love more than anything else?

He prayed for guidance and wracked his brain throughout the day, until he was chopping logs for winter fuel and he heard the supper bell. One last swing split the huge felled trunk he'd been working on into manageable pieces, but a smaller one stood ready for him later.

Jerome headed to the well, drew some water, and splashed it on his face. He used his bandanna to dry off and gave one last look at the woodpile. An idea started to tickle the back of his mind.

On that disastrous Sunday, hadn't Idelia and Mama Lurleen mentioned Kerstmis horns? Long, thinner logs hollowed out and rested on the lips of wells so the sound carried when someone blew into them. Idelia had grown a little wistful, saying she missed the loud welcome of Christ's birth.

He tromped back over to the woodpile and ran his hand along the smaller, thinner log he hadn't yet cut, judging its thickness to be about right. Jerome smiled and decided he'd start the project the next day. This was something meaningful that he could—and would—do for his bride.

Chapter 11

Saturday evening, Idelia and Mama made bacon-and-sausage gravy to be poured over warm biscuits. It was simple fare, but that night they had another focus. Mayor Ashton, enthusiastic about having a Dutch-influenced Kerstmis celebration, had met with some resistance at the town council meeting. It seemed the menfolk were hesitant to make the change since they'd never sampled Dutch baking.

"I have half a mind to say it's not that they're worried about the dishes being tasty enough; it's that they want to get extra treats." Idelia rolled another batch on a floured board. "*Speculaas* will either make them admit it's a good idea or make them decide further testing is required."

"With one week, the decision is made today." Mama popped another round into the Dutch oven before checking the ones baking in the stove. "And is not the only choice."

"*Ja.*" Idelia started stamping the cookies from the rolled dough. "Jerome has been kind and attentive, but I'd hoped for a clearer sign that the marriage is God's will. But time runs short, and we cannot stay here if I do not become his wife."

"You do not have to marry him." Mama stopped what she was doing. "We will find other way. Remember this."

"I will." Idelia transferred the cookies to a baking pan. "But if only—"

The long, low moan of a great horn sounded over the farm. Silence fell for a moment as she and Mama stared at each other. Then another blast resonated through the evening air.

Idelia put down the pan and rushed to the door. The sting of cold air hit her face the moment she stepped outside, but she didn't go back for her cloak. There, in the last rays of the sunset, was the sign she'd been seeking.

Jerome stood a few feet behind the well, holding the end of a horn braced against the edge of the well. He waved in greeting before blowing into the horn again. The sound repeated until the sun sank completely, and he drew the long instrument away from the well and walked toward her.

"You remembered." The words sounded choked, forced from her suddenly dry throat. "To usher in Kerstmis. You found a horn."

"Couldn't find one, so I made it." He held it up, its length made for two men to carry. "I thought I might not finish in time to use it properly."

"It's perfect." She ran her hand along the smooth-sanded surface. "The start of a tradition." Idelia sniffed at the thought.

"Someday I'll hold it in place while our son blows," Jerome agreed. "But tonight we won't make any decisions about time."

"But—"

"*Nee, dotter.*" Mama stepped forward. "Jerome is in the right. His gift tonight is just for us to enjoy."

❧

"Mayor Ashton has asked the two of you to speak with the council about your ideas for the festivities next Saturday, and he'll bring you back to the farm afterward." Jerome mentioned the plan just after church ended. He stared down two men who were making their way up the aisle, looking at Idelia with an avaricious gleam in their eyes. Only after they backed away did he register Idelia's words.

"We need to talk." She'd put her gloved hand on his arm.

"Agreed." He bolted to his feet. She couldn't make her decision yet—not before his second proof that he cared for her! "I'll see you later this afternoon, and we'll talk then."

Jerome gave her a broad grin and, seeing Ashton shepherding Lurleen toward the front, nudged Idelia to follow. Once everyone but the council and the van der Zees had cleared out of the church, he went on his way.

He made it home in record time, ready to make the most of the two things in his favor. First, Mama Lurleen knew about his plan and would do her best to keep the meeting going. Second, she'd kindly translated the recipe to English. While Jerome wasn't half the cook Idelia was, surely he could whip up a batch of her favorite cookies—*pepernoten*.

Especially since they were supposed to be hard anyway.

It wasn't long before he'd situated the horses and stood in the kitchen, laying out the ingredients. Flour, sorghum, water, an egg, and five different spices. He headed for the spice rack, holding up the recipe to check against the labels. Cinnamon he knew. Salt was easy. He spotted nutmeg easily enough, but the anise seeds and cloves were harder.

Hmm. . .the recipe said *powdered* cloves. Jerome opened the container and inhaled the aromatic spice. Smelled good to him, and it couldn't matter too much. Cloves were cloves, and everything would mix together anyway.

He grabbed the largest bowl in the kitchen and dumped the ingredients into it, then looked again at the instructions. *Knead.* Funny, he always thought women made desserts and such by stirring with a spoon or whisk.

Maybe it's a Dutch word for the same thing? Deciding that was probably it, he grabbed a whisk. He gave it some good, solid stirs and watched as everything melded together. Jerome looked at the recipe again. Oops. One egg yolk. Well, it couldn't make much difference that he put in the whole egg.

In fact, it would probably improve the mix. Since he'd been stirring it, the whole batter had gotten very stiff. *Better put in a little more water.* And while he was improving things, he might as well keep going. Those cloves were looking pretty strange, streaked and mashed into everything. Maybe if he added more of the other spices, it would even out. Strange that a cookie called pepernoten didn't have pepper in it. He added a pinch for good measure.

It's thicker. He peered at the bowl's contents. *It smells good.* So he started taking lumps and rolling the dough into balls. They weren't all the same size and some came out a little lopsided, but the recipe said to flatten them on the pan.

He squashed each one down flat then slid the first batch into the oven. They were supposed to take about twenty minutes—plenty of time for him to make the next batch. And maybe a few minutes to go and work some oil into his saddle.

Jerome returned to the house to find the oven smoking. He grabbed a dishcloth and wrenched open the door, plucking a piping hot pan of smoldering crisps out and dumping them on the stovetop. He stared at the blackened wafers for a moment before sliding in the next batch.

Okay, so he should have paid more attention to the "about" part of the instructions. Not a problem. This next lot would come out better. He wouldn't leave the kitchen until they were ready. Except to dispose of the singed ones. He gathered them up and hustled out to the hog pen, dumping the bunch into the trough and rushing back to the house.

He opened the oven door to check on the cookies. Still doughy. Jerome plunked down in a chair to wait. An eternity later, his pocket watch said it had been another five minutes. He opened the door again. Not ready yet. Mama Lurleen said they were supposed to darken. They were still pretty light.

But what if it only took a minute between just right and burnt? He checked more frequently until he thought they looked about the right color. Jerome decided to ignore that they looked like crispy, brownish-orange splats instead of cookies.

With plenty of dough left, he rolled more lopsided, flattened lumps and put them in the oven. The cooked ones had cooled, so he figured he should test one. He grabbed the closest cookie and popped it into his mouth.

That pepper sure made itself known. He grimaced as the cloves wedged between his teeth. And was it supposed to taste so. . .strong? He crunched it into shards and gave a swallow, staring at the mixing bowl in accusation.

He was just starting to pick up and hide the evidence of his failure when the door opened.

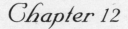

Chapter 12

No matter how long she lived, Idelia was positive she'd never forget the look on Jerome's face when she caught him with those cookies. A streak of dried dough crusted his hair, flour dusted his Sunday shirt, and his face was the very expression of consternation as he shoved a platter of his creation behind his back.

"You're home." He sidestepped toward a wall, still concealing the fruits of his labor. Jerome gave her the distinct impression that if she weren't in the doorway, he'd scuttle out of there faster than she could say, "Stop."

"Looks like you've been busy." Mama was pressing her lips together again, but it was no use. Her shoulders jerked up and down, betraying her smothered giggles. "What've you got there?"

"Nothing to be shared with another human being." He gave a pained sigh and brought the dish out. A heap of thin, dark, misshapen crisps piled atop one another, the source of the pungent smell permeating the room. "It didn't work."

"What didn't work?" Idelia looked from Mama to Jerome and back again, as they obviously knew what was going on.

"Had hard time with the *pepernoten*, did you?" Mama's words released her laughter, as well. "What went wrong?"

"You were trying to bake?" Idelia raised her brows but didn't add on the last part of her thought. *Those are supposed to be pepernoten?*

"Mama Lurleen said they were your favorite." He gave a sheepish grin and tried to run his fingers through his hair. His hand caught on the dried gunk, and he pried it loose with a glower. "I wanted to surprise you."

"You did." Idelia bit the inside of her lip to keep her chuckles muffled. Jerome had tried so hard to be thoughtful and had gone to a good deal of trouble to make this mess.

"You're always making delicious things for me, and I wanted to do the same for you." He made a hapless gesture. "Seems like baking is more of a science than I knew. Even with a recipe."

"It's not so bad." Idelia wracked her brain for something that would make him feel better. "You didn't burn them."

"Yes, I did." His shoulders hunched, and he looked gloomily at the plate still in his hands. "The first batch is in the hog trough." The "cookies" looked stranger the more she stared.

"Well, I love *pepernoten*." She took a deep breath and reached for one of his creations. She didn't move fast enough, as he jerked the plate away, causing the top one to fly up and land on his collar.

"What are you thinking?" His voice rang with reprimand. "You can't *eat* them. I'm not sure the hogs can stomach them."

"Now, Jerome." She reached around and swiped one off the plate, only to have him try to snatch it back. They both wound up with half of the thing. "You made it for me, and I'm going to try it."

"No, you're not." He made a futile grab. "No wife of mine is going to put herself in harm's way like that."

"I'm not your wife." The words stopped him in his tracks, his expression so sad she clarified immediately. "But I will be later this week." She took a decisive bite of the cookie in her hand and crunched despite the pain in her teeth. After a swallow she added, "So long as you never bake again."

"Deal."

❧

"You look beautiful." Jerome set his jaw. "Now go change."

"What?" Idelia looked down. "Why?"

"That's the dress you wore on our first wedding day. And I've already told you I'm not marrying you tonight."

"Jerome!" She clenched her teeth and let out her breath in a hiss. "Stop being so stubborn. Tonight is the Kerstmis celebration, and you have to stop digging in your heels."

"Nope." He bit back a grin. She looked so cute when she was indignant. "You'll have to wait for me like I waited for you."

"But you know I love you," she wailed. "There's no reason to wait."

If I give in, this will be our wedding night. He tamped down the temptation. "Yes, there is. No one will ever say that I married you for the money, and you'll never have cause to wonder. There will be no wedding until tomorrow."

"But I don't wonder." She drew close, smelling clean and looking so soft he had to put his hands behind his back like a military captain to keep from holding her. "And I don't care if anyone else does. We and God know that we'll mean our vows."

"I want *everyone* to know it." He watched as she came still closer, linking her hands around the back of his neck. "You are more than I deserve as it stands."

"And if marrying tonight is another blessing?" She laid her head against his chest, her hair tickling his chin. "We can't let it go to waste."

"You've heard my reasons." He took her hands from around his neck and stepped back. "And you must honor my decision."

"I don't want to be the reason you lose the farm, Jerome." Tears sparkled in her eyes. "That, I couldn't bear. Not when we can settle everything tonight."

"God brought us together, and He'll provide for our needs." He stooped a bit to meet her gaze. "I sent for you for the wrong reasons, Idelia. But I'm keeping you for the right ones."

"I'll honor your decision, as I would the decision of my husband." Idelia drew a shaky breath. "And I'll consider it practice for our marriage to come."

"So we understand each other? No more trying to change my mind?"

"Not as long as you don't make me change." She managed a small smile. "Mama will never forgive me if we make her late."

"That's right." Mama Lurleen bustled into the room.

"Everything is in the wagon but us. Let us go!"

It took more time than usual to get to the church, where torches and tables had been set up for an evening party. Jerome took special care not to jostle all the food Idelia and Lurleen had baked for the occasion.

They'd told him all the names and what they were, but he couldn't keep it all straight. And even if he could, he wasn't sure he'd want to. A little bit of knowledge in the kitchen could cause a whole lot of trouble.

As soon as they pulled up, Ashton was there to help carry everything to the tables. Though the other townswomen had brought gracious plenty, one table stood empty just for the Dutch desserts. It took the four of them two trips to transfer everything, and then the evening really began.

"Attention!" Ashton stood in front of the food and bellowed until everyone minded him. "Tonight is our celebration of the birth of Christ, God's own Son born as man to bring us salvation. So before we get to eat all this wonderful food"—he cast a glance at the dessert table—"we're going to have two special events."

Murmurs overtook the crowd at this development.

"First, the reverend is going to read to us from the book of Luke so we can remember the joy of that night long ago. It's not actually Christmas Eve, but that's what we're celebrating and that should come before anything else."

"What's the other event?" Alastair demanded.

"That"—a smile spread across Ashton's face as he stared at Mama Lurleen, who beamed back—"is a wedding."

Chapter 13

I delia's gaze flew to Jerome, but he looked as mystified as she. So he still hadn't come to his senses. She could have gotten lost in her upset over that, but she realized Mama was moving toward the mayor.

"Mrs. van der Zee has given me the honor of her hand in marriage," Ashton declared when Mama reached him. "And we'd like to have this celebration double as our wedding."

Cheers met this pronouncement, but Idelia stood stock-still. Mama was getting married tonight? But what about the deadline? She looked up at Ashton suspiciously. If he was taking advantage of her mother for the money, the man would pay dearly.

"I want to remind you all that, as the mayor, I'm not eligible for the bride-by-Christmas offer." His hand found her mother's and held it tight, easing the tension in Idelia's chest. "Lurleen and I are both of an age where we just don't see the sense in putting off the good things in life."

At that comment, Idelia gave Jerome a pointed glance, but

he kept his gaze fixed forward. Ashton and Mama blended back into the crowd as the reverend gave thanks for all the people in attendance and proceeded to read from Luke.

The familiar words brought peace to her heart. Reading of how the Son of God had humbled Himself to be born as a man to later die for those who killed Him never failed to stir her. Easter was a mix of sadness and victory, but Kerstmis...ah, Kerstmis, as the beginning of any wonderful story, brought pure joy.

Just as Jerome's telegram had brought the excitement of possibilities and love, Christ's birth was a promise of God's provision. Look how He'd brought Mama a new husband and used a foolish plot by a wily mayor to show Idelia how much her husband cared for her.

As she stood beside her mother during the impromptu ceremony, Idelia released her worry. Mama would do well as the mayor's wife, and Idelia would begin a family of her own with Jerome. No one was leaving; no one was sacrificing.

Thank You for the goodness You've given us, Lord. I know now that Jerome made the right decision in postponing our wedding and trusting that You will provide. She watched as Mama and Ashton were proclaimed man and wife. *You always do.*

❧

"You were right." Idelia spoke so softly Jerome almost missed the words. "Waiting is not just a pledge to each other, but a mark of our faith in the Lord."

"I knew you'd understand." He reached out and cupped her

cheek with his palm. "And that you were willing to honor my decision even before you agreed with it showed just how strong our union will be."

"Yes." She pulled away. "But for now, let's enjoy the food before it's all gone. Mama will be hurt if you don't try some of her *kerstkrans*."

"Cursed grans?" It didn't sound too good to him. Especially if it was anything like the *pepernoten*.

"No." Idelia laughed at his expression. It's a round cake with sweet almond paste. There's a hole in the middle where we light a candle to celebrate the birth of Christ. We made more than one this year so everyone could have some, but it's so delicious we can't wait too long."

"Sounds good to me." Jerome followed as she piled a plate full of meat, vegetables, and pastry for him before choosing smaller amounts for herself. They found a large stump where they sat and ate in comfortable silence until Mama Lurleen and Mayor Ashton found them.

"Why didn't you tell me, Mama?" Idelia couldn't quite hide her confusion. "I would have been happy for you."

"We didn't decide until this evening." Mama Lurleen smiled and tucked her hand into Ashton's.

"I'm glad you wed." Jerome picked up his piece of the rounded cake and took a bite. "May your marriage be as heavenly as this dessert."

"And nothing like Jerome's *pepernoten*," Idelia added.

"I won't move to Clarence's house until after your wedding tomorrow," Mama Lurleen assured them. "Not that I don't trust you to be a gentleman, Jerome, but we must be certain the proprieties are observed."

"Absolutely." His smile was genuine. With Mama Lurleen gone to Ashton's place after the wedding, he and Idelia would have the entire house to themselves.

"Yeah, yeah." Ashton seemed a good deal less happy about the delay, so Jerome wiped the grin from his face.

Reveling in his own good fortune was one thing; celebrating another man's sacrifice was another. And he wasn't about to cross his new father-in-law. Clarence Ashton and Mama Lurleen were a duo no sane man would care to cross.

The night flew by in a haze of laughter, celebration, and more good food than Jerome would have guessed his stomach could hold. When he fell into bed, he sent up a short prayer of thanks.

Tomorrow I'll wed Idelia.

"Are you ready?" Jerome pulled Idelia aside the next morning. "Because if you've changed your mind, this is your last chance to tell me." He looked so earnest, she wanted to hug him. "Once we're in that church, I'm not letting you go."

"I wouldn't want you to." She leaned over and gave him a peck on the cheek, stifling a blush as she did it.

He helped her out of the wagon and left to take his place in front of the church, where he'd wait for her to come to him.

Idelia smoothed the skirt of Mama's wedding dress, smiling at the memory of how Jerome had been worried about her gown the night before. She didn't hold to any superstition about the groom seeing the bride on the day of the wedding. The Lord brought them here, and a yard or two of satin couldn't ruin it.

"It's time." Ashton offered her his arm, having graciously offered to give her away. He kept his gaze fixed on Mama, though, who proudly marched in ahead of them.

Idelia didn't really pay attention to the blur of faces turned toward her as she made her way down the aisle. She'd begun a few friendships in the short time since she'd come to Willowville, but her focus was all for the man who watched her every step as she moved toward him.

The moment Ashton laid her hand in Jerome's, her breath caught, and Idelia could have sworn her heart didn't beat again until they'd both pledged to love, honor, and cherish each other for a lifetime. Of course, just as she drew in a deep breath, Jerome kissed her, and she felt faint all over again.

"I love you." His words pulled her back from the pleasurable dizziness swirling in her head.

"I love you, too."

Together they made their way back up the aisle, only to be stopped when Mayor Ashton cleared his throat. . .loudly. Several times. "Before the happy couple gets on their way," he bellowed, "the town council has an announcement to make."

They both stopped then turned to listen. If there was one thing Idelia had been quick to learn about the way things worked in Willowville, it was that Mayor Ashton's announcements were never dull.

"Now we all know that Mr. and Mrs. Sanders didn't meet

the deadline, so they won't be getting the cash incentive for their wedding." The words put a slight damper on Idelia's happiness until she shook it off.

"The Lord will provide," she whispered to Jerome, who squeezed her hand in acknowledgment.

"But the council and I talked it over this morning, and it seems to us that the bride-by-Christmas offer did result in one valid marriage before the end of last night's celebration."

"I thought you said you couldn't get the money 'cause you're the mayor!" Alastair sounded outraged, and Idelia wondered why the man so hated to see others happy.

"And I hold to that." Ashton gave a simmer-down glare and waited for everyone to be silent. "But the rules of the whole thing said that the money would go to any man who could bring a new woman to town and bind her here by marriage by the Christmas celebration."

"He can't mean—" Jerome sucked in a sharp breath.

"Yes, I do mean that Jerome Sanders brought Lurleen van der Zee to Willowville, and she was bound here by marriage by the deadline. And that means Mr. Sanders is eligible for the reward. If the second-happiest newlyweds in town would come back up here, we'd be happy to give you your wedding present."

KELLY EILEEN HAKE

Kelly's dual careers as English teacher and author give her the opportunity to explore and share her love of the written word. A CBA bestselling author and dedicated member of American Christian Fiction Writers, she's been privileged to earn numerous Heartsong Presents Readers' Choice Awards—including Favorite New Author 2005, Top 5 Favorite Historical Novel 2005, and Top 5 Favorite Author Overall 2006—in addition to winning the runner-up Favorite Historical Novel 2006. Currently she's pursuing a Master's Degree in Writing Popular Fiction and loves to hear from her readers. Visit KellyEileenHake.com for more information.

AN ENGLISH BRIDE GOES WEST

by Therese Stenzel

Chapter 1

Kennedale, Kansas, December 1884

Katherine Wiltshire gazed at the bewildering number of horses, wagons, and cowboys besetting the Kansas town she had promised Papa to come to. Her mouth went dry. How would she choose a husband from among them?

An ear-piercing shriek filled the air. Katherine startled. Savage Indians? Her father had warned her they were everywhere in the American West. At the chug and the hiss of the train departing, she let out the breath she'd been holding.

A chill shook her body, and her teeth chattered. Was it the December air or the fever that had plagued her for the last two days? Her stomach churned, threatening to undo her peculiar breakfast of grits and fried beaver. She needed to find the sheriff.

A whiskered man in a sullied shirt and waistcoat pointed

at her personal belongings. "Where'd you like your baggage delivered to, miss?"

She glanced around. Somewhere in this hamlet was the land Papa had purchased before he died, but where was the deed? If she could find the property, how did one build a house? "My baggage? Please take me to your nearest hotel."

"That's some accent." The whiskered man lifted his dented hat. "Where you from?"

"Cambridge, England."

"Boy howdy, I've never met anyone from way over yonder. Welcome to Kennedale."

Kennedale. The town that was meant to bring a new start for her and Papa. How wrong he had been. "Once I'm settled in a hotel, I would like to speak with the sheriff."

The man snatched up her bags. "I'm afraid there's no hotel. The Grisford brothers' gang burnt it to the ground."

A gang of outlaws? Kate shuddered. Sweltering underneath her warm wool dress and cape, she removed her gloves. On her fourth finger lay Papa's cross ring. A reminder of his strong faith and his belief that God's plan was for them to move to America. Now all was lost. That notion twisted over and over in her heart until a steel band formed.

God was not to be trusted.

She reached in her reticule to collect a coin, but the man carrying her bags had left her standing all alone. He was now across the street and tromping down a wooden walkway.

Woolsack. Swallowing hard, she lifted her skirts and paced after him, up a set of steep steps and down a boardwalk to the front of a brick building.

With a thump, he dropped her bags and peered in a window. "Sheriff's not here."

"I'll wait." Her breath came in gasps. "Thank you most kindly for your assistance."

As she wilted onto a wooden bench, her hat slipped off and fluttered to the ground. Folding her shaking hands, she hoped the sheriff would arrive before it was too late.

⁂

Charlie Landing pinned his newly polished tin star back onto his vest before taking a warm loaf of bread from the preacher's wife.

"Now that I've cleaned your badge, you can wear it proudly." Mrs. Gleason nodded, her white hair as neat as her crisp dress. "I'm just so pleased that Judge Ridgley sent you, a young buck of twenty-five, to protect us from that frightful gang of outlaws."

Charlie picked up his well-worn Bible from the table and gripped it. *Lord, help me to be a good sheriff.* "Thank you, ma'am. I need to get back to the jail, but tell Rev. Gleason I enjoyed our talk." He nodded good-bye and slunk out of the parsonage into a blast of brisk December air. If she only knew the truth behind why his uncle, the judge, had sent him.

It was either Kennedale or jail.

"Sheriff!"

Charlie looked up to see blond-haired, gray-eyed Miss Ida Leemore running toward him at a full gallop, clutching her elaborate floral hat. "I'm so glad I found you."

With one hand, he steadied her, keeping her at arm's length before releasing her. Now a Christian, for the first time in his life, he wanted to keep tongues from wagging. "What's the problem?"

She batted her sparse eyelashes and giggled, seemingly anxious for his undivided attention. Her wide grin revealed the large gap in her front teeth. "Well, it appears there's an English lady asleep at your office door."

Pivoting around, he shot a glance down the long row of shops and offices. He could just make out a woman in a burgundy dress, sitting with her head resting against the wall. A few people waited beside her.

His mind flitted through his list of former clients. Had he ever sold his goods to an Englishman? Sometimes the womenfolk didn't take a liking to the source of his supplies. He straightened his posture, hoping it appeared sheriff-like.

Ida's lingering gaze unnerved him. He shoved the bread into her hands. "Thanks."

Ignoring her further chatter, he strode down the wooden walkway. Even from a distance, this lady appeared so ashen he feared the worst. *Lord, help me.* A sizable crowd had gathered by the time he reached her. "Stand back."

Murmurs dropped off and the townsfolk immediately receded.

Unease coiled around Charlie. After only a month on the job, they respected his authority. Respect he didn't deserve. "Let me take a look at her."

The woman whimpered and gestured oddly.

A cold gust of air sliced through his unbuttoned jacket. Charlie handed his Bible and his keys to young Ben Watson, whipped off his coat, and laid it across her. She had the silkiest brown hair he'd ever seen.

"Unlock the jail. I need to get her out of this wind." Charlie lifted the woman into his arms. "Make way, make way."

The cell door creaked as Ben jerked it open.

Charlie laid her on a cot. His jacket fell off of her, and he couldn't avoid noticing her trim figure and soft-looking skin.

The townspeople filled the stark chamber behind him.

"English girls are mighty pale."

"I wonder if she's ever seen the queen?"

"Such a young thing. Where's her family?"

Ben poked Charlie. "Word is she came in on the train from Topeka alone. Want me to send a telegram to the sheriff there?" At fifteen years of age, he had been Charlie's shadow since he'd arrived in Kennedale.

"Good idea." Charlie stood and glanced at the folks who stared back at him expectantly, as if he were some kind of hero. Determination gripped him. He'd prove to them he was a good man. And an upright lawman. Surely, in such a small town, the details of his former ways wouldn't come to light and he could maintain his respectable identity.

"Therefore if any man be in Christ, he is a new creature." He clung to that scripture like a drowning man to driftwood.

"That's all, ladies and gentleman." He waved his hand. "Go about your business."

Mrs. Gleason wiggled her way through the crowd. "Can I be of assistance?"

"Water?" the young woman mumbled.

The reverend's wife procured a tin cup and filled it with water from a pitcher on his desk. She offered the refreshment to the young woman then leaned toward Charlie. "You probably won't hear from Topeka today. Would you like the reverend and I to look after her? Surely jail is no place to keep a lady."

The tension that knotted his shoulders released its grip. He had no idea what to do with the lone gal. "You, my dear Mrs. Gleason, are a gift straight from heaven."

"Oh, I do declare," she protested, but there was a twinkle in her kind eyes.

He reached into his vest pocket and handed her the few coins he had left. "This'll cover any expenses."

"Oh no, I could never—"

"I know money's scarce. I insist."

The young lady passed the cup back to Charlie and struggled to sit up further. "I daresay I have created a w—wretched commotion."

A sympathetic ache pierced his guarded exterior. He was well acquainted with being alone in strange places. Perching on the edge of the cot, he slipped his hand under her arm to assist her to a more comfortable position. She averted her glazed eyes and smoothed back her brown hair streaked with ribbons of blond.

"What's your name, miss?"

"Katherine Wiltshire. . .I mean. . .please call me Kate." Her face was as white as a lone cloud against a Kansas sky.

A million questions sprang to his mind, but Mrs. Gleason was leaning over his shoulder. "From?"

"England." Her head dipped, and some of her curls escaped and trickled down her long, graceful neck. "Papa and I . . ." She fanned her flushed cheeks with her hand. "W—we stopped in Topeka. He was ill. I didn't know how to care for him." She leaned forward, as if to tell Charlie a secret, and collapsed into his arms.

He caught her and eased her back onto the bed. The heat coming off of her frame told him clearly this lady might not make it to tomorrow.

❧

A rumble of a clearing throat, followed by a polite cough, woke Charlie.

Rev. and Mrs. Gleason stood in his office doorway, the sunlight shimmering behind them as if they were a vision from heaven.

Charlie's breath slammed down his throat. He yanked his feet off his desk and stood. "Good morning."

Mrs. Gleason smiled as if she held a wonderful secret and nodded toward the bright midday sun. "I believe it is afternoon."

The reverend perched in a chair by Charlie's desk. "We've come to talk to you about the English lady, Miss Wiltshire."

"Is she better?" Charlie sat down, snatched his uncle's letter, and shoved it under his Bible. He rubbed the look of concern from his face and blinked hard, trying to wake up. All night he'd been cutting leather for his friend Diego Muntavo, best silver-decorated saddle maker in the West, to try to make a little money before payday.

"After a week of much prayer and Mrs. Gleason's tender care, she's much improved." The reverend removed his hat. "The Lord must have great plans for her because I've seen this ague before and people often don't recover."

"I should have stopped by. . ." Charlie's voice trailed off at the sight of Mrs. Gleason's white-knuckled grip on the back of Rev. Gleason's chair. Odd.

Charlie cleared his throat. "But I'm sure you've heard about the four drunken arrests, and then Mr. Heelin caught a petty thief in his shop, which was followed by a fistfight over a horse. And then the missing Daley boy who was later found sleeping in the rafters of the flour mill."

"You should—"

The reverend blew a "Shh" to silence his wife.

What were they up to? Charlie shot a glance between the two. "Like I said, I should have—"

"We wanted to come and speak to you today about a serious matter." The reverend twisted his hat in his hands.

"We have an idea regarding Miss Wiltshire." Mrs. Gleason's bright eyes glistened. "You should marry her."

A bolt of alarm whipped through Charlie. A gunshot would have been kinder. He snapped to his feet. "Surely sheriffs aren't required to marry for the sake of the town?"

"Not at all." Rev. Gleason waved his hand. "Now sit down

and hear us out. Katherine—"

"Kate," his wife corrected. She leaned in toward Charlie. "The dear girl wants to be called by a more American-sounding name."

"Kate is all alone. Her father recently died and made her promise to settle the Kennedale land he'd bought while still in England. Most likely fearing for her safety, he urged her to find a good man who loved the Lord and wed by Christmas."

"And we don't want her marrying some sweet-talking, two-bit scoundrel." Mrs. Gleason clucked her tongue with disapproval. "She's such a pretty young thing and is in desperate need of the protection of a good man. An honest man like you."

Charlie froze at their pleading expressions. He needed time to redeem himself, to prove he was a good person. He cleared his throat. "I—I'm not the right man." *My sins are too great.* "There must be others—men who are well thought of—who could marry this lady."

The preacher leaned forward. "I'm certainly no matchmaker, but she is a docile, God-fearing girl. A good wife can bring comfort to a man." Insight glimmered from the pastor's old eyes, making him look like a shepherd who'd herded many a lost sheep back into the fold. "She might help you find your way. Furthermore, Kate believes the Kennedale land her father purchased is located near town and is most likely worth a lot of money. You might do all right with her."

The word "No" formed on Charlie's lips until the edge of the letter he'd hidden caught his eye. Judge Ridgley was coming in five days.

The morning Charlie had been caught stealing guns, a severe snowstorm hit. His uncle, a judge, took him into his home and, over the two-day blizzard, shared the gospel with Charlie. Instead of a jail sentence, his shrewd uncle gave his newly redeemed nephew a second chance. . .but with certain requirements. Charlie had to fill the vacant position as sheriff of Kennedale, a town plagued by gun-toting outlaws, and show he had settled down into a respectable life.

A genteel, Christian wife, who was, by her manner and dress, a cultured woman, would certainly prove to his uncle that he was a changed man. And it didn't hurt that she was an attractive gal who needed his help. "Marry her?" Charlie rubbed his day-old whiskers, trying not to appear too agreeable. "I might consider it."

Mrs. Gleason beamed with pleasure. "She's waiting for you in our guest room."

As Charlie stood, his legs wobbled. And when he went to put his guns in his holster, it only took him five tries.

"Oh, I really don't think you'll need a weapon to persuade her." Mrs. Gleason pressed her lips as if restraining her mirth.

"You don't know my history with women."

Chapter 2

The shock of icy air rushing in from the open window invigorated Kate's clouded mind as she shifted to sit up farther on her pillows. Of all the outlandish, preposterous, nonsensical situations to find herself in. Marriage to a stranger? What could Papa have been thinking to suggest such a thing?

A wave of weariness claimed her like a sultry day. This past week, lethargy had undermined her every move and thought. Because she was normally passionate and strong-minded, her father often called her his whirling dervish.

But when he knew he wouldn't live much longer, he warned her, "My dear Kate, the West can be appallingly uncivilized. Cutthroat Indians everywhere. Please, I implore you, find a good man who loves the Lord, and try to marry quickly. . .by Christmas."

By Christmas? The notion was as foolish then as it was now. If only her normal strength would return. She would leap up from this bed, dress in a mad dash, and take the first train back

East, far away from any scalping Indians. Instead, here she sat with foolish tears welling in her eyes.

Rev. and Mrs. Gleason had tended to her and prayed with her regarding her circumstances. Such kindness had rekindled her childhood faith. Could God truly help her out of this dreadful muddle?

Following the Gleasons' counsel that the sheriff was a good man of strong faith, she agreed to consider marrying him. But how could she make such a decision in her weakened condition? She yanked off her nightcap. "Lord, if You truly care about me, please tell me what to do."

Once she recovered, she would find Papa's land and build a home in memory of him—of that she felt quite confident. Perhaps a husband could be of assistance. She didn't even know what supplies were needed. Whom did one hire?

She studied her trunks that had come in from Topeka. They were filled with her mother's handmade linens, draperies, and bits and pieces, which Kate planned to use in her new home one day. Hope billowed in her heart. *Home.* It had a nice ring to it. How she wished she could be settled by Christmas. Of course, sadness tinged her thoughts. There would be no gifts from her family this year.

"Katherine."

A deep baritone voice startled her, leaving her as weak as a giddy schoolgirl. She clutched the bed covers to her chin and stared at the man waiting in the doorway. With his hat in his hand, she could see that his wavy chestnut hair matched the depth and warmth of his dark coffee-colored eyes. Seeing that he was tall with wide shoulders, she imagined him to be a very strong man.

Her cheeks flamed. Words clogged in her throat. "I—I believe I owe you an enormous debt of gratitude for aiding me in my sickly state and bringing me to the Gleasons'."

He leaned on the doorframe and folded his arms. "Just doing my job, miss."

"They have advised me that you are a good man and a brave sheriff and that I should speak with you"—every inch of her respectable breeding protested the need to admit she knew why he was here—"regarding my situation."

His head dipped for a moment, as if bowed in prayer. "Rev. and Mrs. Gleason are two of the most God-fearing people I know." His gaze pierced her. "And I agree with their concerns."

The sound of a throat being cleared let her know her guardians waited on the other side of the wall, but this knowledge did not deter her heart from fluttering. Maybe this wasn't such a clever idea. Although the reverend had assured her of Charlie's salvation, she needed more time to consider his character. "Please call me Kate. My father thought it sounded more. . .American."

He took a chair from a corner of the room and set it down a discreet distance away from the bed. "They think you need a man's protection and his name."

"My father wanted me to. . . I mean to say, he thought it important that I—"

"Will you marry me, Kate?"

Her stomach flipped. Was it the fever, or did her insides quiver at the kindness in his voice? "Why do you wish to wed a stranger?"

The warmth in his mahogany eyes receded. "I have my reasons."

Her heart couldn't thump any harder. What would Papa say? Convinced she knew his answer, she replied, "Yes." It came out in a whisper.

"In about two weeks, a Christmas Eve wedding, then?"

Christmas? A rush of pleasure consumed her. Just what Papa wanted. Visions of a home decorated with fragrant ivy, garland laced with golden ornaments, cards, lavishly printed, set on a fireplace mantel—

Thunderous sounds of gunshots split the air.

Charlie leaped up and stuck his head out the window. "Not good."

"What is it?"

"The Grisford brothers' gang."

❧

Charlie narrowed his gaze as he halted in the dead center of Main Street. The explosions of shots fired in the air and the gang's wild screeches only added to the tension in his gut.

With a burning resolve, Charlie stood tall, legs wide apart, hands next to his holstered guns, and watched the row of brothers on horses thundering his way.

When his uncle told him he'd have to become the sheriff of Kennedale if he wanted to stay out of jail, Charlie agreed and was determined to show how committed he was to the Lord. Now, staring death in the face, atoning for his sins this way didn't seem like such a smart notion.

The bitter wind sent a chill up Charlie's spine, but he continued his firm stand. Once they noticed him, the band of five brothers, Gage, Gary, Gilroy, Glen, and George, silenced their hooting and hollering.

Charlie flexed his hands on each side of his weapons. Although the brothers' brains were a few bottles short of a case, their unruly grins did not bode well for the townsfolk.

As they came to within a wagon's length of him, Charlie recognized Gage, the oldest brother of the gang. Over the last five years, Charlie had sold guns and ammunition he'd stolen from various forts around Kansas to the brothers and other outlaws. More slippery than a greased pig, Gage had once offered Charlie a box of just-born puppies in exchange for some pistols.

Charlie spat and wiped his hand across his mouth. "I'm ordering you boys," he shouted out in a low guttural voice, "to leave this town."

Gage slid from his horse. His exaggerated swagger and twirling gun read like a dime-store novel. "You're a lawman?" He laughed, revealing his yellowed teeth. "I can't believe Gun-Toting Charlie is wearing a badge."

Charlie shifted his stance. Could any of the townsfolk hear him?

George, the youngest of the brothers, called out, "Did they tell you what we did to the last tin star man that tried to stop us?"

Charlie's uncle had left out that bit of information. His stomach twisted. Miss Wiltshire's words, "brave sheriff," mocked him.

Gage leaned forward. "He ain't here no more. And if you get in our way, you won't be, neither."

"I thought you said he moved to Cleveland," Gilroy called out.

"Of all the flea-brained brothers—don't tell." Gage threw down his hat.

By Gage's odor, Charlie assumed the brothers had been drinking, the only way they could muster the courage to continually steal from innocent people. Despite Charlie's familiarity with them, his anger remained. The folks in this town had put their trust in him as sheriff, Kate among them, and he wasn't going to let them down.

He hoped.

Charlie's jaw clenched. He eased a gun from his holster and cocked it. "Leave or you'll face your Maker today."

Gilroy pushed his hat back and swiped his forehead. "Gage, didn't you say the Maker ain't too happy with us?"

"We're here for more of Diego's fancy saddles." Dirt filled the creases of Gage's swarthy face.

Charlie gripped his gun so hard his hand hurt. The town's economy had been struggling to make it. Diego's saddles were bringing in orders from all over the Midwest, but he could barely keep up with the work, much less afford to have them stolen.

"And if we don't get what we want," Gage said, gesturing around the town, "we're gonna burn another building down.

Which will it be this time, *Sheriff*? The schoolhouse?"

"As the law, I'm telling you you're done here."

"We like this place." Gage grinned back at his brothers, who sat on a row of horses sporting silver-studded saddles. "It's been very. . .profitable."

"I said. . .get out now!"

"One day you sell us guns, and the next you tell us where and what we can do?" George laughed. "You ain't nothing but a two-bit gun thief."

❦

Kate edged over to the open window. At first, when she'd heard shooting guns and the odious yells, she feared Charlie was wrong and Indians had come. Now all was quiet.

Kneeling down, she peeked over the ledge of the window to see what Sheriff Landing was doing. Sure enough, there was a group of gun-laden men on horses. The sheriff stood in front of the swarthy-looking fellows with his gun drawn. His voice rose loudly, but the wind muffled the words. How courageous of him not to back down. But why didn't he simply ask them to leave? Wasn't the lawman in the American West the final authority?

A filthy raven-haired man yelled back at the sheriff. Curiosity compelled her forward—what was he saying?

The words "two-bit gun thief" floated up to her.

She jerked back. What an impertinent thing to say. Although she didn't know him well, Sheriff Charlie was certainly no outlaw.

She peeked again. The sheriff kept looking up and down the walkway at the storefronts, probably to make sure all the townsfolk were safe. What an admirable gentleman. Rev. Gleason must have been right—Charlie Landing was a good man.

Weakness overcame her limbs. Praying for his safety, she crawled back into bed.

~~~

Charlie glanced from side to side. Would the townspeople, hidden behind closed doors, find out he knew the Grisford brothers?

His mind raced with possible options, but before he could speak, a little girl, about age three, toddled out just behind the brothers and headed toward them.

The sight tore at Charlie's insides. He shouted, "Go back."

Gary slipped from his horse, ran over, and snatched up the child by the arm. He flashed a triumphant grin that stood out against his dark beard. "Whaddya think, Gage? She'd make good firewood?"

But when the little girl started to cry, Gary's smile dropped. He gave the girl a little shake. "Aw, now, don't do that."

Gage folded his arms. "I'll make you a deal, Sheriff. You trade me her life for more of them fancy saddles."

Bile rose in Charlie's throat. This was all his fault. The past he so desperately wanted to escape had followed him here. Now an innocent child would pay for his sins.

The screams of a hysterical mother only deepened his misery. "Bethany! Bethany!" Two men, one in an apron, the other with a drooping mustache, dragged the woman back into the mercantile.

Gage looked back at the scene and laughed.

A surge of fury bolted through Charlie. He lunged for Gage then seized him by the collar. He pressed his Colt .45 to the outlaw's head. "Let go of your gun. And tell your brother to release the child if you want to live."

Gage growled but soon dropped his shooter. He nodded toward his brother, who lowered the squirming toddler to the ground.

Still gripping the outlaw, Charlie signaled with a jerk of his head toward the faint figures peering through the mercantile windows to come and fetch the child. No one dared. The little blond girl plopped down in the street, howling.

Guilt churned in Charlie's gut. In his selfishness, he'd never thought about what those embezzled guns would do to defenseless people. His sin mocked his new life and his commitment to the Lord.

God, help me. Bolstered by hope, Charlie shifted his captive toward his brothers. "If you get outta here and never come back, I'll release him after sunset."

The men grumbled among themselves.

The child's crying reached an ear-splitting peak.

Sweat dripped down Charlie's back as he clenched Gage tighter.

Gage struggled for a moment then held up his hand. "Go on, ya hear?"

The brothers inched their horses around and headed out of town.

Within ten minutes, Charlie had the toddler returned to the tearful mother, the outlaw locked in jail, and the whole town patting him on the back.

Charlie felt lower than a rattlesnake being grilled on an open fire by the devil himself.

Chapter 3

Woolsack. What had she done? In the morning chill, Kate paced the boardwalk outside the sheriff's office. She'd slept on and off for the last five days and was finally feeling like herself—well enough to regret her hasty decision. And well enough to do something about it.

She simply could not marry a man she did not love. And what had possessed her to agree to make such an exceedingly important decision in her deplorable state? Her heart pounded in anticipation of her conversation with a man who obviously had no character. A man who would prey on her momentary weakness.

Although the Gleasons had encouraged the arrangement, this was all the sheriff's fault. How could he presume on their kind hearts and ask an ill woman to become his wife? Now that she had returned to her normal sensibilities, she'd simply have to set him straight.

A babble of conversation drew her gaze. Sheriff Landing was striding toward her down the wooden walkway surrounded by an appallingly large group of wide-eyed women. For a moment, Kate suppressed a laugh at his stiff mouth and sagging shoulders as he endured their high-pitched chatter.

"Ladies, I'll look into your concerns." He cast a desperate look at Kate. "Now please excuse me."

The prattling didn't stop.

He tipped his hat in Kate's direction. A slow grin tugged across his lips as he passed by. "Morning. . .darlin'."

The women ceased talking.

Darling? Kate bristled. If he expected her to cling to his side in adoration like these other prairie women just because he had deftly rescued the town from some gun-toting ruffians, he was in for a dire disappointment. "May I have a word with you?"

◈

Frigid air fanned across Charlie's face as they stepped into his chilled office and he shut the door. By Miss Wiltshire's determined stride, he knew the room's icy temperature was due to more than just the fact that the potbellied stove needed stoking.

She whirled around. "I have made a grave error in agreeing to wed you. I don't know you, and I'm sure I could never make you happy. Could we. . . I mean, would you. . .release me from this betrothal?"

A fierce punch hit him in the gut. He tossed his hat onto a rack a few feet away. He had written to his uncle about the engagement and he was arriving tonight. Charlie had to have a compliant fiancée.

The fact that she had a fancy way of talking and a real ladylike manner made his situation look even better. He folded his arms. She wasn't even twenty, a foreigner in a strange country, and she thought she could survive on her own? She needed him as much as a lost sheep needed a shepherd. "I thought you wanted my help."

She marched to his desk and picked up a book. "I was not myself when you proposed to me. And I think it's improper of you to take advantage of me in that way."

"Take advantage? You said your father wanted—"

"Do not bring my dear papa into this."

"Listen, lady"—he clenched his jaw—"I got a lot more on my mind than marriage to some flighty, pretentious English—"

"Flighty?"

He paced over and stood nose to nose with her. "I agreed to marry you to protect you."

"Protect me? So I'm some waif you've taken in?"

"Well, it wasn't because I won you in a card game."

She slammed the book down on his desk. "I wouldn't marry you if you were the last man in Kansas!"

Charlie rubbed his whiskers. Those blazing green eyes of hers and that pink flush on her cheeks sure made an appealing sight. *But right now, cowboy, you'd better win her back.* His head dipped. "I'm sorry. Forgive me. I thought you were all alone in the world. The Gleasons said that you needed my help and that it was your father's idea for you to marry."

Her shoulders wilted. "It was. I promised him I would wed by Christmas."

"Anyone else asking for your hand?"

"No, but I'm certain that—"

"Today is December thirteenth." Hope rising in his chest, he pointed toward a calendar.

She smoothed out the fitted bodice of her dark plum dress and gracefully tucked a loose curl behind her ear. "This has all been most overwhelming."

He shifted his gaze away from her to keep his thoughts upright. God had given him a new heart, and he planned to keep it that way.

Although he'd witnessed her determined personality, fear lurked in her eyes. She needed security and someone to watch over her. And the more he saw of her, the more he was growing used to the idea of being that man. "I can provide for you, lend a hand with finding your father's land, make a home for us."

She quieted down as if weighing his words. Was that a good sign?

He cocked his head. "I did ask nicely."

A tentative smile broke through her reserve. "Oh, I'm dreadfully sorry. My temper does get the best of me at times." She pulled off her hat and twisted it round and round. "As it was what Papa wanted. . ." As if she suddenly smelled a skunk, her dainty nose tilted regally. "Of course, I would only consider this if it was a marriage in name only."

He ran his fingers through his hair. But at the sight of her slight shoulders and young face, he realized she probably wasn't being snooty—just likely scared. "Sure." *For now.*

"I suppose I must honor my promise. Shall we seal it with a handshake?"

He grinned at her formal nature, but when he allowed his grip to linger, she flushed and paced over to the calendar. Touching the thirteenth day circled in red, she asked, "Is today important?"

His heart thumped once. Hard. "My life depends on it."

       ❦

Long after the sun had set over the Kansas prairie, Kate admired the parsonage table, with its soft glowing candles surrounded by fragrant pine boughs, and the glistening bone china. It reminded her of formal dinners at home in England. A life destroyed by false accusations against her father. If there was one thing she could not abide, it was untruth.

She glanced over at Charlie as he conversed with Rev. Gleason in the front room. Charlie sported a dark ruby waistcoat with a notched collar. A crisp white shirt, a black string tie, and his lack of holster and guns completed the engaging picture.

And yet her nerves were getting the best of her. The Gleasons were hosting the dinner so she could meet Charlie's uncle. Would Charlie be pleased by her manner and dress? Would she meet his uncle's approval?

With Charlie's dark chestnut hair neatly combed and his face freshly shaved, she found his rugged good looks very. . .compelling. Even if this wasn't a true marriage, at least he was pleasant to look upon.

Mrs. Gleason came into the dining room with her customary bright smile. "I have a surprise for you." She lifted a cover off a dish and held up a pastry. The tangy smell of ginger, cloves, and cinnamon filled the air.

Flush with delight, Kate hugged the older woman. "My mother made mincemeat pie every Christmas."

"One of my dear friends had the recipe. I thought you might like a taste of home."

Tears brimmed in Kate's eyes. It wasn't so much that she missed England but that she missed the feeling of family and security. And for some reason, the thought of no trifle, no small present from someone who truly loved her, dimmed her anticipation of the upcoming holy day. She chided herself for such nonsense and quickly dabbed her eyes lest she spoil Mrs. Gleason's thoughtfulness.

Just then, Charlie and his uncle walked into the dining room. Charlie's face looked flushed. Was he nervous, too?

"Judge Ridgley, I'd like you to have the pleasure of meeting my beautiful fiancée, Katherine Wiltshire."

Kate smiled at such gallant praise. Maybe marriage would be better than she hoped. She shook the silver-haired gentleman's hand. "Lovely to make your acquaintance. Please call me Kate."

"An English lady?" Judge Ridgley sneaked an approving glance at his nephew. "I am very glad to meet you. And yes, Charlie's mother was my sister, but everyone calls me Judge, *especially* Charlie."

Charlie swallowed hard and let his gaze flit to the table.

As Mrs. Gleason refilled the judge's glass and asked about friends who lived in his town, Charlie leaned in toward Kate. His warm breath fanned her neck, and the manly smells of pine, outdoors, and soap consumed her.

Optimism welled in her heart. Could she grow to have affection for this man someday? Looking up into his warm mahogany eyes, she rested her hand on his arm. Surely he wouldn't try to kiss her?

"I need you to appear as if we are in love in front of my uncle," Charlie whispered.

A pang of disappointment welled in her chest. Kate released her grip and adjusted her white, high-necked blouse. What daft notion had taken hold of her? How could his attentions so easily woo her? He was merely playing his part of the lovesick fiancé. With her cheeks flaming, she lifted her chin and resolved to better *his* performance. She'd act absolutely besotted by him. "Of course."

The judge looked between the both of them, his one brow arched as if scrutinizing every move. He glanced above their heads. "Well, would you look at that."

Kate flashed a peek upward at the ball of mistletoe trimmed with evergreen and ribbons hanging over her and Charlie. Heat crept into her face.

Mrs. Gleason clapped her hands. "Kate told me that in England it's called a kissing ball."

Nodding, Judge Ridgley gestured toward Charlie. "Well, aren't you going to kiss her?"

Kate's breath fluttered.

Charlie's eyes widened. "Kiss her?"

She stiffened. The man wasn't in love with her, but he didn't have to act as if kissing her was the last—

Charlie's strong arms wrapped her tight against him. His warm lips smothered her gasp.

It was, for a fleeting moment, as if the world had disappeared. Her heart soared. Her breathing escalated when she returned his embrace with an ardor she hadn't known she possessed.

When Charlie pulled back, her legs felt as weak as buttered toast. Her determination to appear infatuated with him had surely muddled her emotions.

A tender expression filled his gaze before he pulled away. She swallowed. Was it hope? Pining? Shock at her responsiveness? Dazed, she watched as he strutted over to the judge, acting as if he'd just passed some test. Why was the judge's approval so important?

A tinkle of music filled the next room. Mrs. Gleason peered over the piano. "I have another surprise for Kate before dinner."

The tune of "God Rest Ye Merry, Gentlemen" filled the air.

Kate smoothed out her favorite periwinkle blue bodice and nodded at the English carol.

"Kate, will you sing it for us?"

Her mouth dropped open. She couldn't hold a tune even if the Archbishop of Canterbury offered her a basket to carry it in. Her mother had a beautiful voice and had often participated in church choirs, but Kate had always bemoaned her tone deafness. A flaw she was anxious to hide from Charlie. "I–I'm not sure—"

"Oh, forgive me." Mrs. Gleason flipped through her sheet music. "I'm sure this is a difficult time for you. Let's sing an American carol, 'O Little Town of Bethlehem.'"

As Kate mouthed the words, she stole glances at Charlie. His rich tenor voice rang out above the others'. She had many things to learn about this man. At the end of the singing, Rev. Gleason led everyone back into the dining room.

Judge Ridgley gripped Kate's hand and smiled. "I'm mighty glad to meet you, Kath—Kitty—Karen—"

"Kate," Mrs. Gleason and Charlie simultaneously interjected.

The judge nodded. "Kate. The woman who is going to marry my nephew. I just can't believe you agreed to take this scoundrel on."

Kate blinked. *Scoundrel?*

harlie stiffened. His hands clenched. Would his uncle betray him? Just when he was sure the jig was up, the judge's roaring laughter filled the dining room. Heaving out a long sigh, Charlie tugged on his tight collar and glanced around the room. How long would he have to dread someone discovering his past? How could he keep Kate believing he was worthy of her hand?

The judge slapped Charlie on his back. "Actually, I very much admire Charlie's strong commitment to the Lord, and although his life hasn't always been easy, I'm sure he'll make an exceptional husband. And I hope, for his sake, those Grisford brothers never come back."

"A hearty amen to that. Now let's eat." Rev. Gleason pulled out a chair for his wife.

The dapper judge also moved out a seat for Kate before sitting beside her.

Sweat beaded Charlie's forehead. Dread still clutched at his insides, until Kate patted the empty seat next to her. "Charlie, dearest, will you sit by me?"

Her smile and twinkling spring green eyes were like a drink of cold water to a parched man. If they hadn't been surrounded by people, he would have been tempted to kiss her again.

"I think we've seen the last of those bumbling bandits," Charlie crowed as he sat, bolstered by Kate's attention.

All those gathered around the table murmured approval and bowed to give thanks for the bountiful table. Soon the aroma of baked chicken and the hum of pleasant conversation passed around.

Charlie leaned back in his chair and enjoyed the savory meal, the lively exchange, and the eye-catching woman next to him. As he had imagined, Rev. Gleason and Judge Ridgley launched into an in-depth biblical discussion. And Mrs. Gleason beamed as Kate threw sweet glances Charlie's way. Touched by Kate's efforts to act the part of an adoring wife-to-be, he held her hand under the table.

She didn't pull away.

After dinner, they all moved to the parlor, and Kate offered everyone a hot cup of her mother's age-old recipe for wassail. Charlie savored its spicy apple cider–like flavor.

A roaring fire heated the room, but what warmed him most was Kate's friendliness during dinner and while they sat on the couch together. She'd touch his hand or lean her shoulder against his. She laughed at everything he said and even complimented his deep red vest.

Judge Ridgley stood in front of the fireplace. "I heard your friend's saddle business has been quite a boon to the economy in Kennedale."

Charlie sipped his drink. "If only we could find more men willing to learn the craft of saddle making to keep up with the orders. Sure would help this town to grow."

"Now that you're the sheriff," Kate said, "surely a town with a reputation for peace and quiet will draw more families here."

Charlie's chest swelled with pride. Maybe the gang of brothers wouldn't come back. Maybe his past would stay in the past. "I've got Diego convinced to stay here for now, but if more craftsmen aren't trained, he may have to move to a larger town."

"You're a smart man, Charlie. You'll come up with a plan." The judge smiled at Kate. "Tell me, dear, what was it about my nephew that made you say yes so quickly to marrying him?"

Kate bit her lower lip as if searching for the right words. "Rev. and Mrs. Gleason told me of his character and what a faithful believer he was. And of course, he so bravely dismissed those dreadful outlaws, and"—she smiled into her cup—"I find him very handsome."

Charlie shifted in his seat. Did the parlor shrink, or had he grown in stature? Never had he heard a woman speak so kindheartedly of him. His mother had been a weak-willed woman, her life consumed by the bottle. He knew Kate was just pretending, but it pleased him that she tried so hard to act the part of a trusting sweetheart.

The judge nodded across the room. "And you, Charlie?"

His mouth went dry. Kate? Memories of her rolled through

his mind. Her creamy skin, the brown curls that had slipped loose and lay around her slender neck, the pink flush of her cheeks when she scolded him for asking her to marry him, her trim figure in the prettiest dress he'd ever seen. . . His heart thumped as he realized what a prize she was. A prize that could be easily lost. He'd never tell her about his former life. She'd be so ashamed. "She'll do."

He squirmed in his seat. Was that the best he could come up with? Sneaking a glance at Kate, whose lips were parted in shock, he resisted the urge to punch something. Not good.

～～～

"She'll do?" Kate's throat tightened as she got up from her place next to Charlie and strode to the window, his words playing over in her mind. Her body erect, she stared out at the glittering stars against a sooty sky. Of course, this engagement was nothing more than a practical union of two believing strangers. Her eyes stung with tears. Why had she even considered that it could be something more? A marriage of convenience was all she needed to fulfill her promise to her father. She'd been addled to hope for more.

She took in a deep breath to control her displeasure and the urge to throttle Charlie Landing. Now that she was going to be a wife, she needed to rein in her unruly nature. Her mother had been the model of demure graciousness, but alas, Kate had inherited her grandfather's quick temper. Smoothing back her hair, she turned to face the hushed group and fixed a smile on her lips, determined not to reveal her injured feelings.

"When you get your deed, Kate, what will you and Charlie do?" Mrs. Gleason changed the subject as she handed Kate and Charlie plates of mincemeat pie.

Charlie rubbed the back of his neck. "We should get a return telegram from the land office in Boston tomorrow."

Kate took the plate and sat down, far from Charlie. A tingle of pleasure replaced her earlier disappointment. "I am most anxious to start building a home. Also, I am an avid gardener, and although I've never grown my own vegetables, I am sure flowers and vegetables like the same treatment. I also enjoy decorating, but I feel furniture should always be comfortable and not too formal. We will have horses and a stable and—" She pressed her hand to her lips. "Forgive my blathering."

Judge Ridgley slapped Charlie on the back. "How are you going to pay for these things for your new bride?"

Charlie cleared his throat. "I suppose I'll have to sell some of the land to raise the money."

Kate's fork clattered onto her plate. One thing she would not abide was *his* making decisions about Papa's land. "Sell? Oh no, I couldn't part with one blade of grass. I'm not sure how much property he bought, but it can't be a great deal. And I must have enough for a house and a barn and a paddock."

The room and its occupants fell silent. All that was heard was the ticking of a mantel clock and the crackling and hissing of the fire.

Charlie's eyes narrowed in warning. He set down his plate and pulled Kate to her feet. "If you don't mind, I want to show Kate the new hymnbooks that just arrived at the schoolhouse.

I know how much you love to sing, don't you, my dear?"

His insult jabbed at her. Was he making fun of her inability to carry a tune? Her hand trembled as she placed her unfinished pie on the side table. By his insensitivity, obviously he didn't care one whit about her.

Her voice rang as sweet as sugar. "Why, I couldn't think of anything better." She snatched up her wool cloak and stormed outside. The fierce wind made it nearly impossible to open the door to the schoolhouse that also doubled as the church on Sundays. The icy air pierced her cloak, only adding to her cross temper, but once through its double doors and out of the biting current, she found the temperature tolerable.

A rattling shudder echoed throughout the vaulted ceiling. Kate looked upward, alarm heightening her senses. "What is that appalling noise?"

"It sounds rather ominous, but it's just the strong winds blowing through the rafters. I guess this school's pretty old." Charlie leaned back against the closed doors. "Kate, I've agreed to marry you, but I'll not be controlled by you."

She strode up toward the front by the teacher's desk and spun around with arms folded. How could she make him see her land was the last link she had with her family? And that finding it and building a house consumed her every thought? She needed roots, a place to call home. And she wanted to blend into her new country. Why couldn't he understand that? The light of a full moon cast a stark beam of light through a row of upper windows, illuminating his broad shoulders and the square cut of his jaw. What was he thinking? And why did she care?

A slow suspicion stole over her. Was that a guilty look on his face? She'd stake the Queen's bonnet this was all just a business arrangement to him. Most likely, he knew about her land and reasoned it could bring a tidy profit, and that was why he wanted to marry her. A choking sense of betrayal made her head throb. "That is my father's property and I plan on living on it as soon as a house is built."

"After we are married, we might have to leave town. Who knows what might come up? A—and then we might want to have cash on hand to. . ." He ran his fingers through his hair as if struggling to tell her something. "The property and what we do with it will be ours to decide."

Her breathing quickened. Was he threatening her? What would he do if she refused? Did she know him well enough to marry him? She grabbed a candlestick from a table, needing to grip something to control her growing frustration. "Ours? My father bequeathed that land to me before we even met, and I will not part with any of it."

Charlie paced in front of the doors as if wrestling with his conscience. In one breath, he spat out, "The-woman-I-marry-will-just-have-to-trust-me."

She muttered under her breath, "How could I have ever thought he would make a fine husband?" All her hopes and plans were unraveling before her eyes. Bitter disappointment swirled around her. How dare he demean Papa's hopes and dreams. "I am not your wife yet."

"According to your father's wishes, you soon will be."

Her temper flared. "Not if I can help it."

She lobbed the candlestick across the room, and an explosive crash resonated around them.

Kate's mouth opened. She cut a hard look at the other candlestick, still sitting on the table. "What are those made of?"

Suddenly the doors behind Charlie banged open, sending him crashing into the back of a wooden bench.

Five Grisford brothers burst into the room in a gust of wintry air, boots slamming on the planked floors, their guns held high.

Her heart hammering, Kate dashed behind the desk and peeked out.

The shortest of the five brothers strode over and jerked Charlie to his feet. "Sheriff, we got a bone to pick with you."

❧

Warm blood dripped from Charlie's nose. He swiped it with his sleeve and frantically searched for Kate. He had to protect her. He reached for his guns, only to realize he'd left them at the jail. Not good.

Hands balled into fists, he flew into Gary and knocked him to the ground. Even as he wrestled the outlaw, all he could think about was Kate's beautiful face. And if they laid a finger on her—

A gun fired behind him.

Kate's scream filled the room.

A guttural sound filled Charlie's throat. The need to shield her engulfed him. He threw Gary to the ground and charged toward her cry. Grabbing Kate by the waist, he pulled her into the safety of his arms. "Are you hurt?"

"No." Her hair spilled around her shoulders, and even now, its clean smell captured him. She clung to him and trembled.

"What do you men want?" Charlie panted to catch his breath.

Gage strolled toward them, casually gesturing with his weapon. "I see Mr. Lawman's found a fine-looking woman."

Charlie's gut clenched. Kate would hear about his former life. *Don't say it. Don't say it.* "I thought I told you boys never to come back."

Gilroy nodded. "Gage, he did ask nicely."

"So that badge gives you courage?" Gage waved his gun. "You didn't used to be so upright and honest. You're nothing but a thief and an outlaw."

Dread grabbed Charlie by the throat. *Please, please, Kate, don't believe his words.* Kate's grip tightened. "Don't be afraid; I'll protect you," he whispered.

But to his astonishment, Kate squirmed loose, marched a few steps away, and shook her finger in Gage's face. "How dare you insult Sheriff Landing. He is one of the bravest, most honorable men I've become acquainted with. I'm sure you don't even know the meaning of the word *honor*. He is true, industrious, thoughtful, kind, and I'll not stand by and let you demean his character. He asked you to leave, and I suggest you obey or—"

Charlie grabbed Kate, pulling her behind his back. Sweat ran down the sides of his face. This woman would be the end of him.

Surprised by the tongue-lashing they'd received from a

female with a British accent, the band of brothers stood with guns drooping.

Suddenly a slam thundered though the building like the sound of boots pounding on the roof. Several of the brothers gasped, their jaws hanging open as they surveyed the shadows in the darkened room.

"I'm warning you." Charlie glanced up. "Sounds like the whole town is headed this way. You'd better leave while you have a chance."

Another series of shudders racked the air. Glen's Adam's apple bobbed several times in a row. "Maybe he's right. Maybe we'd better go—"

Gilroy pushed his way through the group. "Before we burn this place down, let's take that purty girl with us."

George leaned back against the far wall, arms folded. "That was my idea," he shouted. "No one ever listens to me."

Ignoring George's words, three of the brothers advanced toward Kate.

Desperation spiraled inside of Charlie. His breath heaved in his chest. Suddenly Kate yanked away from his hold. What was that English wildcat up to now?

An inkwell flew through the air and headed straight for George. The smash reverberated off the vaulted ceiling. Black ink covered the gangly teen's head as he slid unconscious to the floor. A pewter pitcher was next, followed by a tumbler.

Without waiting to see what else Kate would do, Charlie snatched her by her hand, burst through the back door, and slammed it shut.

His boots slipped around on the ice, and the tip of his nose burned with cold as he dragged three wooden barrels in front of the door. Moving carefully, he peered around the edge of the building and watched the darkened shapes drape one of the brothers on a waiting horse. As he watched them climb onto their horses and race out of town, relief caused him to release the breath he'd been holding. They were gone. For now.

Kate slid to the ground.

He fell to his knees beside her, gripping her by her arms. "What were you thinking, woman?"

"Thinking?" Her breath blew white. "I was trying to protect you."

"Protect me? I was handling the situation just fine."

"That detestable man had a gun pointed at both of us." Her teeth chattered. "You call that fine?"

"Well, what were you doing?" He helped her to her feet.

"I was negotiating." She struggled to stand and stumbled forward.

He caught her and drew her close, burying his face in her soft hair. Her sweet scent and warm body stirred up feelings he knew he needed to rein in. "You call throwing things negotiating?"

She didn't move away. "Why did he call you a thief and an outlaw?" Her frame shivered as she laid her head on his chest. "I'm sure he was just trying to make you cross. Had you met him before?"

"No, yes. . ." Her nearness was making it hard to form words. His mind whirled. Was she as attracted to him as he was to her? "I've seen him and his brothers before, but that's all over now." His body tensed, hoping she wouldn't ask any more questions. He took her hands and warmed them in his. "The most important thing is that you're safe."

Her quizzical look disappeared, and her eyes filled with tears. "I was so scared."

He took her into his arms again, savoring the satisfaction of protecting her. "That was scared? I'd hate to see you terrified."

"You were very brave." She wrapped her arms around him. "I just let my temper get away from me occasionally. You know, Papa used to call me his whirling dervish."

He grinned, enjoying the feel of her so close. "Sometimes that dervish side of you comes in handy."

"Oh, I'll have to make a very large donation to Rev. Gleason to pay for the things I've broken."

"I'm sure he'll be glad you saved the schoolhouse from that gang of thieves."

She looked up and smiled. "I think I like you, Charlie Landing."

A rush of affection for this English wildcat flooded his chest. *A gift from God.* The words hit him. God had arranged this marriage as a blessing. But as much as he could see himself falling hard for this lady, he'd have to break the news to her soon. With what the Grisford brothers knew about his past, Kennedale couldn't be home for long.

As soon as they were married, they'd have to leave town.

Chapter 5

Kate sat nestled on the church pew beside Mrs. Gleason and shared a hymnal with Charlie. She couldn't help but smile as his robust voice sounded in her ears. The words to her new favorite hymn, "'Tis So Sweet to Trust in Jesus," challenged her faith. She needed to do what the song said and trust in Jesus more.

Charlie's finger accidentally brushed against hers, and she lost her place in the hymnal. She found it again and continued mouthing the words to the song, as she didn't want her ill-toned voice to distract Charlie from his love of praising the Lord.

She managed a glance behind her and flinched at the ink stain on the wall. But last night, after bandaging Charlie's chin, Mrs. Gleason assured her that Rev. Gleason was not the least bit upset at the damage. In his view, Kate had rescued the building from being burned down by that dreadful gang. A small comfort to her guilty conscience when one of the candlesticks on the table next to the pulpit leaned to one side like a tree in a stiff wind.

The singing over, Rev. Gleason took the pulpit as the congregation sat. He opened his Bible and read, " 'They that trust in the Lord shall be as mount Zion which cannot be removed, but abideth for ever.' " He closed the good book. "Many of you are not aware that the hymn we sang, ' 'Tis So Sweet to Trust in Jesus,' was written two years ago by an Englishwoman, Mrs. Louisa M. R. Stead."

Kate grinned. No wonder she loved that song so much.

"Mrs. Stead wrote it after she watched her husband drown."

Kate's throat clogged with sympathy; she understood the pain of losing someone dear. She pulled a handkerchief from her reticule and dabbed her eyes. Instead of relying on God more after Papa died, she had maintained a distance. And although observing the Gleasons living out their faith had encouraged hers, had she truly learned the meaning of trusting God with her life?

She stole a glance at Charlie. With his daily Bible reading, surely he relied on God to lead him. Charlie's handsome profile sent a tingle down her spine. He would be her husband in a mere week and a half. She swallowed hard. Of course, theirs would be a marriage in name only. Was that best?

She did desire to have children. Panic shot through her— did Charlie want children? She had never asked him that important question. And she still hadn't convinced him of her determination to stay in Kennedale. Anxiety gnawed at her peace until her nerves twisted into a ball of yarn.

Rev. Gleason's words permeated her dark thoughts, convicting her of not paying attention. "Trusting God is never easy, but when you do as scripture encourages you, with all your heart, you'll find He will direct your path."

Kate gripped her hands in her lap. Now that Papa was gone, she would need her heavenly Father's direction even more. *No matter what, Lord, I promise to trust in You with all my heart.*

The congregation stood to sing the final hymn. But just as the music of the piano filled the church, a back door banged opened.

"Fire!"

All heads swiveled to see Ben Watson gasping for air, his face blackened with soot. "My house. Help!" was all he managed before falling to his knees and surrendering to a flood of coughing.

Charlie shouted instructions as he made his way to the door. "Mr. Heelin, bring us some gunny sacks from your store. Mr. Larson, we'll need your ironwork tools to break the ice on Caper Pond. Miss Leemore, bring some of your mother's salve. We'll need it for burns. And everyone, please wear gloves to keep from frostbite."

As he tore out the door, all the menfolk in the church clamored behind him.

Mrs. Gleason clutched Kate's arm. "Has the Grisford Gang struck our town again?"

Kate's throat tightened. Would Charlie be all right?

God was already testing her resolve to trust Him.

Charlie bit back frustration as yet another hole froze over and the gathering crowd had to wait a few anxious moments while Mr. Larson, the blacksmith, smashed a new opening in the ice. This was Charlie's chance to prove to the townsfolk and himself that he was a good man. In minutes, buckets of frigid water resumed passing from hand to hand, but to Charlie's horror, the blaze roared on.

The Watson homestead was larger than most, as Tim Watson had added many small additions to the original structure. Now raging flames engulfed the entire back of the house, all because of a grease fire.

Mrs. Watson tended to her three small daughters some distance away, their wailing undiminished by the pile of water-damaged goods piled at their feet. The oldest one's smock was covered in soot.

"It's gone." Ben slumped to the ground near Charlie.

The acrid taste of burning timber permeated Charlie's mouth as he passed the next bucket. Compassion caused a lump to form in his throat. "Just part of the house is damaged. Come on, we're still fighting the blaze. We won't give up."

"Sheriff, quick," Diego said.

Charlie handed off the pail of water and ran to the rear of the homestead.

Pointing to the first tree in a row of towering pines, Diego shouted over the roar of the fire, "Sparks drifting upward from the back of the house must've lit the top of that tree. I'm worried. Sap can ignite like a powder keg."

Flames leaped into the air, giving off ominous blue-black smoke. Charlie's gaze searched through the tools lying on the ground that the men from the church had brought. He sorted through the pile of picks and shovels until he found an ax.

Gripping the hatchet in his hand, he swung at the base of the flaming pine. He had to get this tree down before the flames scurried like rats to the other ones. But even with gloves, his hands felt raw from the icy water that had soaked them. After a few minutes, he could hardly keep his painful grip steady.

Ben and the men who were helping gathered behind Charlie.

"Be careful where you send this tree," Albert Heelin called out. "Maybe I should—"

"I got it." Charlie shrugged off the warning. He'd run off the Grisford brothers. Now he would save this home, finally proving his worth. Heaving the ax, he kept one eye out for live embers as the tree burned brightly. Finally, a creak sounded.

"Timber!" someone shouted.

For a breathless moment, the tree swayed and then leaned away from the house. But another splintering of wood caused it to shift.

"Look out!" Charlie yanked Albert out of the way. With a *swoosh*, the forty-foot Ponderosa fell in a shower of sparks. Not backward as Charlie had planned, but to the side, slamming against the earth.

A high-pitched scream split the air.

Charlie rushed toward the sound, with Ben on his heels, to find Ben's little sister, Molly, trapped by one of the yet unburned branches. Panic seized Charlie. Because of the gust of air from the fall, the tree now burned with a sinister intensity.

His heart thumping, Charlie and Ben tried to wrench the screaming child free, but her dress had snagged on a branch. The flames of fire licked the limbs nearest her.

Mrs. Watson seized Charlie's arm. "What've you done?" Her hysterical words were barely discernable. "Y–you must save her."

Guilt engulfed Charlie like a sudden rainstorm. He'd been a curse to this town ever since he'd come. And now another child was paying for his sins. Adrenaline surged though his body. He lifted the smoldering end of the tree. Hot pain scorched through his gloves. The taste of burning flesh filled his mouth.

Ben snatched Molly from a fiery death and returned her to the safety of her mother's arms.

Charlie let go and stumbled backward on legs as weak as twigs. He landed on the frozen ground, hot agony piercing his hands.

"You all right?" Ben called between panting breaths.

Charlie winced at the raw blisters covering his palms where the flames had eaten through his gloves. Maybe he wasn't the man he thought he was. "Not good."

~⚬∾⚬~

Kate paused her sewing to savor the heavenly scents of cinnamon, cranberry, and apple tarts filling the Gleasons' parlor. The last three days, Ida Leemore's twice-daily visits to Charlie had tempered her enjoyment of adding English touches to the holidays.

Ida's mother, known for her doctoring, had died, but Ida continued the tradition of using her mother's secret healing salve. A recipe she refused to share even with the town's doctor, Neal Hadley.

In the last couple of years, the title of town spinster had been given to Ida. Although somewhat manly and in possession of a rather forward nature, she wasn't dreadful to look upon. The mole on her chin wasn't that large, and the gap in her front teeth was not as wide as the Kansas River, even if Ben Watson claimed it to be true. Was it the look of desperation in Ida's eyes? Or her overt flirting, as if frantic for a husband, that had earned her the ruinous title?

Kate threaded her needle with another strand. How she'd like to write her name on Charlie's forehead so Miss Leemore could clearly see to whom he belonged. Another high-pitched giggle sounded from the Gleasons' dining room—the room that was hard to see from the parlor—where Ida brought her salve to use on Charlie.

Charlie's low voice rumbled back in friendly banter, but Kate couldn't quite make it out. Her efforts to ward off a jealous spirit melted like wax on a candle. She heaved out a sigh as she ripped out the stitches she'd just sewn across the table runner instead of along the edge.

"There, there, dear, pay no mind to her." Mrs. Gleason patted Kate's hand. "In a few days she'll be done with her doctoring and you'll be wed to Charlie."

A wave of trepidation rippled through Kate. Was she truly prepared to do this? Since Charlie had gotten hurt, all the conversations she'd planned to have with him had been put off, as he was in too much pain. She tried as hard as she could to commit to Rev. Gleason's sermon and trust God with all her heart. But now a handsome man was pulling on her emotions, straining her trust that God had everything neat and tidy.

"Kate," Charlie called from the other room.

A giddy sense of happiness filled her as she bounded up from her chair and flitted into the dining room. Her breath caught in her throat at the sight of his chiseled jaw and mahogany-colored eyes. His gaze seemed to swallow her. Was it just her, or had the room become overly warm?

Ida's gaze was riveted to Charlie's hands.

But Charlie held his arms stiffly out from his body. "Miss Leemore tells me—"

"Charlie, please call me Ida. We're friends now."

Kate swept her hands behind her back and made two fists. Her determination to leave her temper behind was already failing. *Lord, please help me hold my tongue.*

"Ida has offered to sing at our wedding." He turned his attention back to Kate as a slow grin spread across his lips.

Kate swallowed hard. His inspection of her made her cheeks flush.

"Ida sings like a bird," he said.

A wave of inadequacy stole Kate's felicity. Was he attracted to Ida? With her broad shoulders and square frame, she certainly was a hard worker.

"When he begged, I couldn't say no. Never have been able to resist the charms of a lawman." Ida's laugh trilled.

Kate's ire loomed.

As if to prove her worth, Ida sang a little song as she tied a cloth around Charlie's palms, leaving his fingers free. A touch that lingered too long as far as Kate could see.

"There, all better." Ida smiled with a gap as wide as the Kansas River.

Charlie stood up, holding his bandaged palms close to his chest. "Thanks, Ida. You sure have a way with hurting people."

A lump formed in Kate's throat. What about the cups of coffee, the baked treats, and the extra pillow tucked at his head she'd provided for him? Surely he was merely trying to behave gentlemanly toward Ida. But indeed, did he have to try so earnestly?

"Just don't know what I'd do without your help, Ida."

Kate bit back a retort. *I know what I'd do with her.* She winced at her unkind thought. *Sorry, God.*

The blond girl stood and took a longing glance at Charlie. She shoved her things in a satchel and, with a defiant glance in Kate's direction, dropped an extra bandage to the floor.

"Let me get that." He knelt to retrieve it.

Ida fell beside him, her shoulder brushing his. "Please allow me. I can't let you hurt yourself. Then I'd have to keep coming back, and I have many other fellows. . .oh, I mean *things* to occupy my time."

"I'm sure you do." As he walked Ida to the door, he gave Kate's arm a squeeze.

Kate paced the floor. By all that's royal, why had he called her in there except to wax eloquent over Ida's talents and abilities? Abilities she didn't have. She wrestled with wanting to share with Charlie how much she'd been drawn to him in deeper ways and yet wanting to storm out and refuse to marry him. But her wedding veil, resting on the buffet table, reminded her that soon she would be Charlie's wife.

The thought made her blush.

And gave her a brilliant idea.

She strode through the kitchen to the front door. Ida and Charlie were still talking. Ida's hand touched his arm.

Anger forced its way past all propriety, and Kate bristled. The nerve of that woman. As soon as Kate threaded her arm through Charlie's, Ida pulled her hand back and her chatter ceased.

Heat flooding her cheeks, Kate stood on tiptoe and planted a kiss on Charlie's warm cheek. "Thank you, Ida, for helping his hands heal in time for our wedding."

Charlie turned his head, but not before she saw him bite back a grin.

Kate set a smile on her lips. "Good day, Ida."

Ida scowled. "Good day, Charlie. Katherine."

"Kate," Kate said, holding her smile until it hurt.

Ida huffed and left, tromping down the road toward home.

With her heart pounding, Kate made her way back to the dining room, picked up her wedding veil, and studied the intricate detail. She heard footsteps behind her.

"What was all that about?" His manly voice sounded firm but amused.

She swung around and allowed her brows to rise. "Pardon?"

A smile played about his lips. "You know what I mean."

"I daresay I have no idea—oh, you mean the kiss?" Her face scorched hot. *Woolsack.* She had to learn to control her temper.

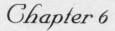

Chapter 6

"Leave Kennedale?"

Charlie flinched at the disappointment in Kate's voice. He crinkled the wax paper that held the sandwich she had brought by his office. Sweet Kate. With each act of kindness, he realized more and more the blessing she would be as a wife.

He grinned at the memory of the way Kate reacted to Ida yesterday. Kate sure was a wildcat, but when it came to telling the truth, she'd injure herself before telling a lie. She'd been hurt enough by deceit. He had to get out of Kennedale. It was only a matter of time before the Grisford brothers came back, and who knew what they would reveal this time?

There were just too many reminders of his previous sins in Kansas. His stomach churned at the thought of Kate being disappointed in him. Did she know how much he couldn't stop thinking about her? He never tired of gazing at her green eyes, the lushness of her hair, or the soft skin on her throat.

"Tell me again, why do you want to leave?"

He stood up from his desk and paced the room. "Not until after we are wed, of course. But I've always wanted to see Texas, and if we got a good price for your father's land..."

Kate's expression fell.

He hated to see the color drain from her face. This was hard for her to hear, especially since they'd just got the deed in the mail and realized it was prime land just on the edge of town, but he had to protect her good opinion of him.

"I—I thought you agreed to my suggestion that we rent the rooms above Diego's workshop until our house was built," Kate said. "The people of this town admire you. You ran off the Grisford Gang. You helped save most of the Watson homestead. You've made this place peaceful and safe."

If she only knew. Charlie folded his arms as he stared out the barred window that overlooked Main Street and watched the townsfolk going about their business.

He'd never had a home. His mother lived her life for the next drink and often left her children to fend for themselves. By age twelve, he'd run away to Topeka where he did odd jobs, stole food, even spent a few nights in jail. It wasn't until he got in with a couple of men who had a contact at a military fort that he began stealing guns and ammunition. Turned out selling stolen guns was very profitable.

For once, he'd had a decent roof over his head, three hot meals a day, and occasionally was able to bring food to his younger siblings. Although guilt gnawed at him, at the time he was determined to do whatever it took to survive. Kate with her fine ways would never understand that. "I don't want to be a lawman my whole life."

"What do you want to do?"

"I'd like to open a mercantile. I'm good at selling things." He fought a smile at the irony of that statement.

"Why can't you open a store here?"

"Al Heelin. I can't compete with him."

"I'd stake the Queen's bonnet—"

"I think we need to move, and that's that."

"Who's moving?" Ida Leemore stuck her head in his office door.

Kate scowled.

He swallowed a grin at Kate's inability to hide her feelings.

As Ida closed the door, a flurry of white flew in behind her. "I hear down at the mercantile, because of the severe weather we've had, the train from Topeka is expected to be closed till after Christmas."

"Come by the stove and get warm." Charlie pulled out a chair with his foot.

"Oh, thank you." Ida swished her skirt and fiddled with her cloak tie. "Oh, I can't get it undone. Charlie, would you be willing to help a woman in distress?"

A laugh welled in his throat as he felt icy daggers shooting from Kate's gaze, and he didn't blame her. Ida sure was putting on quite a show. He grappled with the frozen strings and they untangled within a second.

Kate rubbed her arms and looked out the window. "In England, we don't get this much snow. How long will it last?"

"A couple of months." Charlie sat in front of Ida.

Ida pulled out her salve and bandaging supplies from her reticule. "Kate, have you ever thought of moving back to England?"

Kate's lips went white, a sure sign her hackles were raised. "I'd love to bring Charlie and our children to England one day, but we have no plans to go back presently."

Children? A bolt of alarm rang through him. Sweat broke out on his forehead. He shoved his bandaged palms at Ida, desperate to shift his thoughts. "My hands are feeling much better."

"That's because hometown gals know how to take care of hometown men." The steely desperation in Ida's gray eyes unnerved him. "Oh, I nearly forgot." Ida dug in her satchel. "When I told Mr. Heelin I was headed this way, he asked me to bring you this letter." She squinted at the cursive writing. "Oh, it's for Katherine—Kate—from an Ernest Ridgley."

Kate took the missive and looked at Charlie.

Charlie stilled. Why would his uncle be writing to Kate? Surely he would never reveal any details about his past. A sense of foreboding swept over him. His mouth felt as dry as tumbleweed.

Both women stared at him.

A sudden chuckle flew out of his mouth. He snatched the letter from Kate's hand with his fingertips. "It's a wedding gift, of course." He ripped the envelope open and a piece of paper slid to the floor.

As Kate retrieved the sheet, it flipped open. The legal document had CHARGES DISMISSED stamped in red. Kate's brow furrowed.

The inquiring look Charlie had long dreaded passed over her face.

"What charges?" she finally asked.

He had to get her out of Kennedale. . .fast.

❧

Kate's punch glass dribbled a few scarlet drops onto the wooden floor at the church Christmas potluck dinner. Two days until the wedding, and she was as nervous as a fox in a foxhunt. Although the tempting aromas of fried chicken, biscuits, and peach cobbler filled the room, her nervousness would never allow her to eat. She dabbed the spill with her handkerchief as her gaze searched anxiously for Charlie.

He'd said very little to her after he'd opened that letter, except that he had some praying to do and that she shouldn't believe everything she read. Of course, the correspondence was from his uncle, Judge Ridgley, a good man, but what had Charlie so perturbed?

There were so many things to discuss before the wedding. Surely if they could talk tonight, she could make him see the benefits of staying in Kennedale, he could explain that document, and she could share with him that she didn't want this marriage to be in name only. Before she lost her nerve. Moisture broke out on her forehead just thinking about it.

After much prayer, she knew in her heart that marrying Charlie was the right decision. But these unresolved issues still nagged at her. She hummed a few bars of " 'Tis So Sweet to Trust in Jesus." That was exactly what she needed to do—

entrust her worries to the Lord.

If only Papa could have seen how well things had turned out. . . Her gaze drifted over to Mrs. Gleason, who was teaching a little girl how to play the piano. The tinkle of "Jingle Bells" rang through the church. Ben Watson chatted with one of the Heelin girls, and Rev. Gleason laid his hand on Tim Watson's shoulder as the two men prayed.

How could Charlie consider leaving these wonderful people? And where was he? She'd knitted him a scarf as a Christmas present and was anxious to give it to him.

A flash of blond caught her eye. Ida Leemore was pulling Charlie from the church entrance to a supply room. Charlie followed behind her, pulling off his hat and gloves.

Setting her punch down, Kate maneuvered in the direction of their voices. She pressed her back to the wall and leaned toward the open door. Eavesdropping wasn't exactly a ladylike pursuit, but if she was going to be Charlie's wife, wasn't it a good idea to know everything about him? Their low murmurs were hard to hear. What would Ida have to confide in Charlie? Or was it the other way round? Either way, she wasn't budging.

❧

Ida set her candle down and took Charlie's hands in hers. "I just wanted to see my fine work."

Her touch felt like a firebrand. Charlie stepped back. "I don't think it's appropriate—"

"It's just that I had pinned my hopes on you."

Panic swirled in Charlie's gut. "Me? For what?"

"A husband."

The small room, not much more than a closet, felt as if it was closing in. He'd come here tonight to talk to Kate. While he wasn't ready to divulge his past to her—probably never would be—he needed to let her know he was falling in love with her. To him, this was no longer a marriage of convenience.

But now this poor ungainly girl, who had run off every man who showed the slightest interest in her by her brash disposition, had her sights set on him? Not good. "Look, you don't know what you're saying."

"Surely you're fond of me. I've seen how you gaze at me. How complimentary you've been about my treatments."

"I—I've praised your work. I appreciate how you've tended—"

"Exactly. I can look after your needs. That English girl doesn't understand life on the prairie. You need me."

A sick feeling twisted in his gut. He cut a glance at the open door, hoping no one overheard this awkward conversation. Millions of words defending his sweet Kate sprang to his lips, but what good would it do to throw them in Ida's face? "I'm glad you think so highly of me, but my mind's made up about her."

"It is? Well, how'd you like me to tell that English snippet the truth about who you really are?" She leaned in and whispered, "Gun-Toting Charlie."

Shock bolted through him. "How did you—"

"It doesn't matter." Her hands gripped his arms. "I've admired you for so long. I know I could be a good wife to you. I can sing and mend people and work real hard. That English missy won't have anything to do with you once she finds out you-know-what." She drew closer and lowered her voice. "I know how to keep secrets."

His mouth went dry. She was right about Kate. His stomach tightened, and his thoughts whirled. The closet had become so hot and stuffy he could hardly breathe. He had to get out of there. "I should go."

"I'm tired of waiting. I don't want to be known as the Spinster of Kennedale. I'm only thirty-two. Please, Charlie, I know I could make you happy."

He headed for the open door but whipped around. "Don't speak of this to anyone." *Especially Kate.*

"Will you. . .marry me?"

His heart pounded. "I'll think about it."

What is there to think about? Kate's breath caught in her throat. She had been looking forward to telling Charlie how much she'd grown to care for him. Now she wanted to throttle the man.

Not wanting to hear more, she scurried away from the door, her body trembling with emotion. Confused more than ever, she needed to get away from the church gathering to pray. As she slipped on her cloak, the tears flooding her eyes made it difficult to fasten the buttons.

Hot betrayal prickled her scalp. How could Charlie do this to her? How could he even consider marrying another woman? Her head throbbed with turmoil. Charlie cared for her, didn't he? "Oh Lord, I thought You wanted me to marry him."

She stepped out into the frigid air, the cold cooling her racing thoughts. Her steps crunched on the heavy snow that had blown onto the wooden boardwalk. She had to seek the Lord so she could sort out what to do next. As she walked with only the moonlight for company, a dark shadow scurried across the street. Followed by another, then another. Must be the Heelin boys playing around.

As she stood in front of Doc Hadley's storefront, a freezing wind gusted past her. Shivering, she pulled up the collar on her wool cloak and shoved her hat farther down over her ears. A fuming heat flushed her face. If she could just get her hands on Charlie—

A scuffle of footsteps sounded behind her. If that was Charlie coming to apologize—

A leathery hand clamped over her mouth. Her heart raced. "It's the purty girl." A man lifted her off her feet and dragged her into a snow-filled alleyway. She'd bet the Queen's bonnet it was the Grisford brothers.

❧

His palms sweaty, Charlie washed down another swig of teeth-jarring, oversweet punch. His gaze, hungry for the sight of Kate, roved over the folks gathered at the church. He'd grown to love his English wildcat. Where was she? He had to find her before she got wind of his failings.

Before he'd come to the party, he'd spoken again with Rev. Gleason, who assured him all men had pasts they were ashamed of but God buried their sins as far as the east is from the west. Never having been east, Charlie took comfort in how far away that was. But even after they prayed together, he couldn't shake the notion that he needed to redeem his mistakes before he could ask God to completely forgive him.

He kept trying to shove down his remorse. He desperately

wanted to please Kate. Live on her father's small parcel of land. Approach Mr. Heelin, who was getting on in years, and maybe buy out his store. But Ida's icy words came back to haunt him. *"That English missy won't have anything to do with you."*

It was gut-twistingly true.

His jaw clenched, he set down his drink. Time to find Kate. Time to tell her the truth—even if it killed him. When she broke off their wedding plans, it surely would. Maybe then he could finally rid himself of this condemnation.

As he dug for his gloves in his pockets and found them missing, he noticed Ida Leemore surrounded by a passel of women in rabid conversation. In a desperate move to keep from hurting her, he'd told her he'd consider her proposal, but as quickly as he'd said it, he'd told her no. He wasn't a man to wed at gunpoint.

Had Ida already told the women his secrets?

The women giggled.

Ida returned his gaze with a triumphant glare.

The jig was up.

Kate looked up at the four Grisford brothers. "If you hurt me, I'll scream."

The tall one leaned in and squinted at her. "Yup, she's the sheriff's woman."

Kate struggled to stand, her nerves tightening into a knot. Would they take out their hatred for Charlie on her? She was in a grievous situation. Her very life could be at stake. She pressed her eyes shut. *Lord, I know I'm not very good at trusting You, but if You help me—*

"Look, missy, we ain't here to pester you. You know who we are. I'm Gage, and this here is Gilroy, Glen, and George. We got a brother, Gary, who's been throwing up, and now he's fevered and acting confused-like. He needs fixin', and we don't know how to do that."

A bubble of hysterical laughter rose in her throat. She wanted to exclaim neither did she but thought better of it. Her mind raced. Surely if she delayed long enough, someone would come looking for her. "I'm Miss Katherine Wiltshire."

She wanted to tell them she was far from the sheriff's woman but pressed her lips shut. Perhaps not the best time to bring up his name. "You'll have to tell me your brother's symptoms in great detail."

Gilroy snatched off his hat and offered her a wide grin. "Well, ma'am, he's got sunken eyes and won't drink nothing."

George elbowed his way in front of his brother. "And he complains a lot."

The brothers groaned.

"What?" George stuck his thumbs in his gun holster. "She asked for his symptoms."

Kate glanced around to see if anyone was coming to her aid. "Oh yes," she stalled, "complaining can be a wretched problem. What does he complain about?"

"Well"—George blew on his hands—"his headaches, my cooking, and his cold hands and feet—"

"Shut your trap." Glen punched his brother's arm. "We're

wasting our time. Let's mount up and get outta here."

"We don't get to burn no building? I like fire." Gilroy snickered.

Firm steps sounded down the walkway.

Hope lodged in Kate's throat. Charlie?

Gage pulled out his gun.

Before she could scream a warning, Glen clapped his hand on her mouth and dragged her through the snow and out the rear of the alley.

A row of five horses tied to a stand waited patiently. They forced her onto a horse and led her away, Kennedale disappearing behind her like a mist.

After about fifteen minutes of hard riding, they came upon a house made out of sod. Snowdrifts nearly covered one side. A glow from a fire inside revealed a long moaning form wrapped in a blanket.

Kate's toes curled up in her boots. Her nursing abilities were appalling. She couldn't even save her own papa.

Gage pointed a finger in her face. "Now get to fixin' him. If he dies, we'll have to kill you."

"Now, Gage"—Gilroy slapped his hat on his knee—"that ain't nice-like. This is a proper lady you're talking to."

Terror tightened her throat. She pulled back on the foul blanket wrapped around the sick man. His face lay as white as the snow on the ground outside, and the gray tinge about his lips hinted at the shadow of death. She pinched his cheek. The skin didn't go back in place. *Oh Lord, please don't let him die.*

With no idea what to do, she rummaged through their

few stores of goods and sprinkled a bit of sugar and salt into a canteen of water, something her mother used to do when Kate had been ill. She took the flask and held it to the man's lips. At first he refused; then he drank greedily, until it dribbled down the sides of his cheeks. She waited a few minutes and gave him more.

The psalm she'd read this morning flitted through her mind. How did it end? *"Surely goodness and mercy shall follow me all the days of my life. . . ."*

Kate sighed as she offered the man more liquid. Charlie wished to marry another woman, and now her existence was in peril. *Lord, if You think this is goodness and mercy—*

"Aren't you gonna do something fancy for him?" George asked.

"Quiet, please, I'm praying." *Lord, I fear I may meet You soon if You do not aid me.* The words " 'Tis so sweet to trust in Jesus. . . ." rang in her spirit. Desperation balled her hands into fists. She set her hands on her hips. "I am trying to, Lord."

"You're trying to what?" Glen asked.

Kate startled. "I'm. . ." She snatched the canteen and leaned in to give the sick man more water. "I was asking God for help."

George's gaze fell. "He don't hear too well out here."

Gilroy nodded. "Gage says we've made Him too mad."

"Oh, God is always listening, and He loves you." Kate fixed the cap on the canteen.

Gage spit on the ground. "No one ain't loved us since our ma died."

"I'm sorry. But all you need is to get to know your heavenly Father. One just has to. . ." A light dawned in her mind. The words to her favorite hymn played in her head. "You have to 'rest upon His promise.'"

"What promise?" Gilroy asked.

What she had been missing all along. "That His grace, and not your own, will see you through." She stood.

"Huh?" Gilroy scratched his head.

Kate gazed at her captors. Each one appeared riveted to her words. The fear-etched lines on their faces, slumped shoulders, and dark circles under their eyes told of their desperate need for a Savior.

She took in a fortifying breath. "We will pray together. Repeat after me."

"Repeat after me," Gilroy said.

Gage hit him on the head. "Not yet. She ain't started yet. Continue on, miss."

"To know God, you must first ask Jesus into your heart."

"Our ma taught us that when we was children," Glen said.

They continued to stare. She nervously licked her dry lips. "Then it appears you need to repent of your wretched ways and ask Him to forgive you."

The brothers took off their cowboy hats and nodded for her to start.

Clutching her hands to keep them from shaking, Kate led them in a prayer of repentance.

Once they finished, Glen knelt down and checked on Gary. "He shore is sleeping peacefully. I guess the Lord did hear us."

Kate bent over, noticing that Gary's face looked brighter. A rush of gratitude flooded her heart. *Thank You, Lord. Now if You could work on that maddening Charlie Landing. . .*

Gilroy scratched his head and set his cowboy hat back in place. "I know we said we'd return her, but if she was agreeable, she could marry one of us."

Kate straightened up. By the childlike expressions on their faces, she knew she had to be careful with their fragile faith. She wagged a finger. "Thank you for your kind offer, but I must decline. Now that you're Christians, you lads must live in ways that please God. No more riding into town and shooting your guns."

The brothers groaned.

"No more burning down buildings."

A grumble rolled through the air.

"No more drinking."

"Our ma'd never let us drink," Gilroy said. "Gage just splashes it on himself to smell mean."

"Don't tell." Gage threw his hat on the ground.

"And you must become men of your word, which means you must take me back to town." She bit her lip, hoping her boldness would convince them.

"But what are we gonna do? Stealing guns and selling them to the Indians is all we've ever known." Gage snatched up his hat from the dirt-covered floor.

Kate's stomach clenched. "Indians? Around here?"

"Pawnee and Osage mostly." Glen shrugged. "Just over yonder beyond the ridge we passed on our way in. I stopped and asked Great Wolf to come to see if he could help Gary."

"I don't think we need Indians, really. I'm sure prayer and more water. . ." Her voice died at the sight of three savages standing in the opening to the sod house.

The light of the flickering fire revealed their partially shaved heads that boasted narrow ridges of hair down the middle. Their beaded earrings and some sort of quills weaved into their animal skin garments took on an ominous glow.

Kate's legs gave way, and she wilted neatly to the ground.

❧

Charlie paced down the snow-covered walkway, his gut raw with emotion. He wiped off some snow on the bench outside the jail and folded onto it. The spot where he first laid eyes on Kate.

His breath came out in white puffs against the cold air. The bitter wind only added to his misery. He held his head in his hands. What was he doing thinking he could live an ordinary life? Marry such a fine girl? It was wrong. All wrong. He didn't deserve such happiness.

"Sheriff?"

Charlie looked up to see Ben Watson. Yet another person he'd let down. "What are you doing here?"

"I came by to tell you Miss Leemore's telling everyone at the church supper some mighty wild tales about you that I know aren't true."

"Well, how do you know they aren't?" His voice came out sharper than he'd intended. For the first time in a long time, moisture dampened his eyes.

Ben shifted his feet. "I just. . . My father says you can tell a lot about a man's character by the way he worships on a Sunday."

"Your father's wrong." Charlie stood, pulled off his badge, and pinned it on Ben. "Go back to the church and tell him they're all true."

With resignation like two sacks of wheat settling onto his shoulders, Charlie trudged into his dark office, lit a lamp, and quickly scribbled two notes. One to Rev. Gleason, explaining why he was leaving. And one to Kate, telling her the truth about his past. It was time he faced up to his charges. He would pin the notes to the church door and then go back to Topeka to turn himself in.

Chapter 8

"Thank you kindly." Kate took Gage's outstretched hand and slid off the horse in front of the church. Her numb fingers touched the rag tied around her forehead. "You were most kind to help stop the bleeding."

"Great Wolf shore was gentle with you when you fainted and clonked your head." Gage slid off his hat.

Kate swallowed hard and smoothed her hair once again, ensuring it was still there. Great Wolf's men had been exceedingly kind. And when she complimented their eardrops, she'd bet the Queen's bonnet they blushed. "Do continue to give Gary the special water I mixed up. God will pull him through." *Like He pulled me through. Thank You, Lord.*

The burden of facing Charlie and possibly calling off their wedding lay as heavy as a blanket of ice and snow. *Lord, now what do I do?* She closed her eyes as the presence of God comforted her with a reminder that His grace would see her through. When she opened her eyes, the Grisford brothers stood around her as if unsure what to do.

She blinked at the lights still streaming from the sanctuary windows. It was surely past eight o'clock, and the Christmas dinner was still going on? Her stomach fluttering, she hastened toward the church doors. "I'll see you next Sunday in church."

Gage stepped forward, his hat gripped in his hands. "You think the reverend will allow us to come?"

She paused. "There may need to be some restitution for the hotel you burnt down, but I'm sure Rev. Gleason and the whole town will welcome you to your new way of life."

"Well, thank you, ma'am. . .er, Miss Katherine."

"Now that we are friends, I prefer to be called Kate."

"Me and my brothers," George said, standing next to Gage, "we've talked about your idea about us learning the saddle-making trade, and we think it's a mighty fine notion."

"That will be lovely. I'll inform Mr. Muntavo to expect you on Monday morning."

The brothers climbed onto their horses and tipped their hats in a gentlemanly manner as they left. Pleased but exhausted, she yawned. She couldn't take one more misfortune. As she turned back toward the church and went through the first set of doors, two pieces of paper pinned to the door fluttered away in a gust of wind into the darkness. She pulled open the second door but halted at the sounds of shouting. In the middle of the room stood Rev. Gleason, Mr. Watson, Mr. Larson, Mr. and Mrs. Heelin, Ben Watson, and Ida Leemore, all speaking at the same time.

"Now we know the truth about why he came here." Mr. Larson's bushy white eyebrows furrowed in anger.

"I'm glad he left town. We don't need any outlaws hiding among us." Ida pulled on her wool cape.

"But he was a good sheriff." Ben stomped his boot.

"He helped save our home," Mr. Watson said.

Rev. Gleason held up his hand to silence the room. "All I know is Charlie Landing is a forgiven man. Let him who is without sin cast the first stone."

Kate pushed her way through the gathering. "What do you mean? What has Charlie done?"

Ben scurried up to her. "Miss Katherine—"

"Kate," the church members chimed in.

"Oh dear, no need to do that," Kate protested.

Rev. Gleason stood beside her. "You're one of us now, and we'll call you by your American name."

Ben nodded. "Kate, what happened to your head?"

"It's nothing. What happened to Charlie?" Kate pulled off the cloth wrapped around her forehead.

Ida's lips puckered with satisfaction. "He's gone back to Topeka. Concerned about the safety of our town, I told everyone what I'd learned—that he used to steal guns and sell them to the Grisford brothers. That's why they kept coming back here."

"No, it can't be." Kate's thoughts spun. The words "two-bit gun thief" floated back to her. But Charlie would never hide the truth from her. Untruths had destroyed her and her father's lives. A bitter sense of treachery welled in her throat.

Ida sniffed with a look of smug satisfaction.

Kate stared back at her. "You wanted Charlie to marry you.

You begged him to. I heard you ask him in the church closet."

Ida's face blanched. "I—I didn't know. . . You were there?"

Mrs. Gleason patted Kate's arm. "My dear, understandably you're upset."

Kate shot a glance between Ida and Mrs. Gleason. "No, I heard her ask him, and he agreed to consider it."

"Agreed? That two-faced scoundrel changed his mind as soon as he said it." Ida flushed. "I mean—"

"Charlie's gone to turn himself in." Mrs. Gleason's gaze fell. "I'm afraid the charges on that document from Judge Ridgley were true."

Kate's jaw dropped open. "And he left without telling me?"

Mrs. Gleason leaned in. "You'll just have to make your home with us."

Home. The word still filled Kate with longing. But a longing for what? Her father's land? Four walls? Without Charlie, it meant nothing.

"Perhaps we'd better head back to the parsonage, dear." Rev. Gleason gestured toward the door.

Mr. Heelin stopped in front of Kate. "Now I know why he was so anxious for me to buy your father's land. He wanted money to get out of town. 'Course, I couldn't buy it. I'm retiring soon."

Kate's mind clicked with revelations faster than a telegraph machine. Papa's land. Charlie wanting to leave Kennedale. His dedication to reading his Bible. His love of hymn singing. His love of her. She stepped away from the group, wanting to sort out her thoughts.

Charlie was a redeemed man still burdened by his past.

She spun around. "While he may not have revealed all of his history to me, I know that he is a good man." A glimpse of the Bible resting on the pulpit caught Kate's eye. "Reverend, you said, in your sermon this Sunday past, " 'They that trust in the Lord shall be as mount Zion which cannot be removed, but abideth forever.'"

He nodded.

"I'll not be moved. My place is with Charlie." A warm glow filled her. *I love him.*

Ben rubbed his hand over his mouth. "But the train. . . snow's closed the rails to Topeka. They'll not open till next week."

"Then I'll have to find someone who can take me," Kate said.

Mrs. Gleason touched her shoulder. "Be reasonable, dear."

Ida folded her arms. "Someone would have to be a fool to travel in this weather."

Lifting her chin, Kate replied, "I know just who to ask."

Chapter 9

"You want to go where?" Gilroy Grisford's morning mug of coffee tumbled out of his hand and nearly put out the campfire.

"Topeka. Now please rouse some of your brothers and take me." She stood outside the sod house and gestured behind her. "I have a wagon and fresh horses. It can't be that far."

Gilroy scratched his head. "In heavy snow it's near impossible to find the trail."

"Maybe Great Wolf can lend a hand." Gary stood behind his brother and pulled his blanket around his shoulders.

"Gary, you're better." A warm sense of relief eased the tension in her shoulders.

"Yes, ma'am." A slow smile spread across his face. "Better in body and soul. Now about my Indian friend..."

"Indians? Again?" Kate swallowed, her nerves returning.

"They're the only ones who can follow a route in this weather."

"Woolsack."

249

Charlie paced in front of the smoky fireplace in his uncle's guest room. "I don't understand. How can the court claim insufficient evidence? I'll give them all the evidence they need."

His uncle grinned. "It's the way the law works. I'm sorry, Charlie, but you're a free man. That's why I sent that document to your wife-to-be. All along, I assumed you'd told her. I thought it would be a relief to her."

Charlie swallowed the bitter taste of smoldering wood in his mouth. Sweet Kate. What would she do now? Who would protect her? Even the thought of another man standing beside her sent daggers of pain into his chest. He slammed his fist on the table. "You don't understand how my sin weighs on me."

"We're all sinners."

"Innocent people have been hurt by my deeds."

"God has given you a free gift of forgiveness. Accept it."

Misery stole over Charlie like a cold draft. He understood what his uncle was saying, but he couldn't let go. The swindling, the stealing, the lying, the greed that loomed over him like a shadow. . ."I can't."

"You mean won't."

"Won't?"

"Jesus paid an awfully high price for you to toss it aside." His uncle opened the door. "You'd better think on that, son."

An opening and shutting of doors and raised voices sounded downstairs. Uncle Ridgley had sent a message to his pastor to come, but Charlie wasn't in the mood for more words. Steps alerted him to someone coming up the stairs.

He stared at his clenched fists. "Go away."

"If you think I'm leaving, Charlie Landing, you have yet to understand British women."

Kate. Feelings of hope, joy, and relief fought for space in his chest. His mouth opened, but no words came out. He shot to his feet and flung open the door. "What are you doing here?"

"We have a wedding to attend to."

"A wedding?" For a moment, his mind went blank.

"Our wedding? Christmas Eve? My promise to my father?"

Guilt snatched his fleeting happiness away. "He didn't want you to marry an outlaw."

Kate strode into the room. "According to your uncle, the court has declared you innocent."

"I'm not innocent." Charlie ran a hand over his lips. "And I no longer have a job or a town to call home."

"But the people of Kennedale love you."

"Hah. I couldn't save the Watsons' home. Diego was counting on me to find more men to learn saddle making, and now you know why the Grisford brothers kept coming back, and they will continue until—"

"It's all taken care of."

"What's taken care of?"

"Mr. Heelin is retiring so you can open your store, and I've spent time with the Grisford brothers and they are new men."

This woman would be the end of him. "If those bandits hurt you in any way—"

"They've repented and accepted God's forgiveness, and

they want to learn the saddle-making trade—all five of them. Now if I could just get them to bathe."

Charlie ran his fingers through his hair. "You told the Grisford brothers about God? Did they come into town?"

"No, they kidnapped me."

He startled. "Kidnapped?"

"Their brother was very ill, and they wanted my help. So I mixed up a special drink for Gary and told them all about their need for repentance. They readily accepted God's grace."

Grace. A light seeped into his being. God had redeemed the five brothers. Why couldn't he accept it, too? "They didn't hurt you?"

"No, and they brought me here along with Rev. and Mrs. Gleason and three of their Indian friends."

"I thought you were terrified of Indians."

"I was until I decided to trust in Jesus. Did you know there is a large group of people downstairs waiting for us?"

"For what?"

"To get married."

His condemned heart lay heavy with guilt. He shook his head. Although not wanted by the law, he was an outlaw and a thief, and he'd not ruin her life by giving her his name. "I've changed my mind."

She flinched. "Deplorable situation you've gotten yourself into, but you've promised to marry me."

Dread weighed his gut. "I'm no good for you."

Her quivering lower lip betrayed her ramrod-straight posture. "But, Charlie. . ."

"Please leave." He led her to the door and shut it behind her. Desolation clutched at his insides as he rested his head on the door. Tears welled. He'd just closed the door on the most wonderful woman. His gift from God. But he wasn't worthy enough to receive it.

My grace. The words floated across his mind. He ran his trembling hand over his mouth, trying to swallow back his engulfing emotions.

Suddenly a warbling sound, akin to two cats fighting, rang out behind his door.

> *'Tis so sweet to trust in Jesus,*
> *Just to take Him at His word.*

The voice screeched and squawked, fluctuating up and down.

> *Just to rest upon His promise*
> *And to know, "Thus saith the Lord."*

Who was making that awful noise? He jerked open the door. Kate's eyes were clamped shut, her head thrown back, her mouth wide open.

> *Jesus, Jesus, how I trust Him!*
> *How I've proved Him o'er and o'er.*
> *Jesus, Jesus, precious Jesus!*
> *Oh, for grace to trust Him more!*

Grace. The word tugged again at his heart. His love for Kate overwhelmed him, and he pulled her into his arms as sobs racked his body. "I want to, sweet Kate. I want to."

She wrapped her arms around him. "Can't you accept God's unearned favor like the Grisford brothers have?"

Charlie crumpled to the floor, his face buried in his hands with Kate beside him. "I don't deserve it."

"None of us do. It's a gift." She laid her cheek against his arm.

Hope flickered in his heart. "Lord, I need You," was all he could manage. He sat up and held Kate's face. Several moments passed in silence as he worked to collect himself. "It's His grace, isn't it," he said, his voice trembling, "that helps a man forgive himself?"

"Yes."

He kissed her lips. Her broad smile warmed his heart.

Lord, I've been a fool. Thank You for Your grace that throws my sins as far as the east is from the west. And thank You for Kate, my sweet Kate.

"Does this mean you'll marry me before the sun sets?" Kate blurted out.

He studied the messy curls sprung loose from her bun and the look of tired excitement in her green eyes. He loved her. His English wildcat. "Yes, my sweet Kate."

❧

Christmas Eve night had come, and through the parlor window, stars flickered like candles in the night sky. Light snow fell like clumps of soft sugar, and the pleasant harmony of carolers walking the streets rang in the air.

Kate smiled with warmth at those who gathered in the room, witnessing her and Charlie's vows. Rev. and Mrs. Gleason, four swarthy brothers, one still pale brother who had insisted on coming, three Indians, a local pastor and his wife, and one uncle.

Charlie leaned in. His eyes shone vibrantly as only a redeemed man's can. "I guess this means we're staying in Kennedale."

Joy welled in her throat. She glanced at Uncle Ridgley, who'd just finished preaching the wedding sermon. She couldn't believe all that God had done for her. More than just finding a husband, she had found a home.

Charlie nudged her.

"Oh, I do," she said.

The judge smiled. "I pronounce you man and wife. Charlie, you may kiss Katherine—"

Charlie held up his hand. "If you don't mind, I'd like to kiss Kate, my bride and now my wife."

He pressed his lips to hers.

Her heart welling with joy, Kate responded, delighted with her Christmas gift from God.

Therese Stenzel

Therese is graduate of Oral Roberts University. She is a stay-at-home mom of three and a writer—when she can fit it in between her children's cheerleading, basketball games, and guitar lessons. She has coauthored the book, *God's Little Devotional Book for Grandparents* and has been published in *Women's Day*, *Family Fun*, and *Tulsa Kids* magazines. In addition to being the American Christian Fiction Writers Southwest Zone Director, she is also the "Head Wench" of His Writers—a group of European historical authors, and she is the founder of British Missives, a newsletter for those who love to read or write British novels. Obsessed with English history, English tea, and reading historical novels, she is currently working on her fifth historical manuscript. She and her husband, Neal, keep busy raising their three children and serving in their church, Believer's Church. Her Web site is www.theresestenzel.com.

THE COSSACK BRIDE

by Linda Goodnight

Chapter 1

Flat Rock, Kansas, 1878

Getting married was a matter of life and death. Hers.

Anna Federov hitched the tail of her green taffeta skirt above a lovely pair of kid boots to cross the mud-bogged main street of Flat Rock, Kansas. For all its progress, Flat Rock still suffered the outrageous misfortune of having herds of cattle stampede down the main thoroughfare on any given day. Add three days of cold December rain and the result was six inches of gummy mud.

Not that the mud mattered one whit to Miss Anna, late of Matilda Bellingham's Academy for Young Ladies in St. Louis. Mud had little effect upon a woman running for her life.

At the moment, neither of her conniving male relatives knew her whereabouts, and she prayed they would not find her before the deed was done. Otherwise, *she* would be done.

Anna loved the Lord with all her heart, but she wasn't quite ready to join Him in paradise. And she was also quite certain murder was not in His divine plans.

Murder. Her limbs trembled at the prospect. Her own blood relatives wished her dead. All because of a fortune she hadn't known she possessed.

Oh, they'd been kindly enough after the lawyer contacted them in regard to her inheritance. So kindly they'd insisted she marry Cousin Rupert so that he might handle her substantial wealth.

Frankly, she preferred death. And she'd told them so.

If she was going to marry, Anna preferred a groom of her own choosing. Someone meek and gentle who would allow her to control her own life—and fortune.

With a hurried gait that would have horrified Miss Bellingham, Anna stepped daintily onto the boardwalk, her boots destroyed by the red slime, and into the newspaper office. The rich scents of ink and paper, enhanced by the damp weather, assailed her.

"I beg your pardon for the mess," she said to the man behind the counter. Mud dripped in slithery globs onto the plank floor.

"Quite all right. Messy day out there. Don't hardly feel like Christmas with rain 'stead of snow." He left his leather stool to lean on the rough-hewn counter. A green visor pressed his wrinkled forehead into something resembling freshly plowed corn rows. "Bartholomew Winchell at your service, miss."

"Anastasia Federov." With her best ladies' academy smile, she extended a gloved hand. "A pleasure to make your acquaintance, Mr. Winchell. I'd like to place an advertisement, if you don't mind."

"Federov?" The man studied her with interest. "I used to know a feller by that name. Owned a nice piece of land a few miles up Turkey Creek. Heard he passed on, though. Some kind of mining accident out in Colorado."

At the sharp stab of grief, the paper in Anna's hand trembled. "Leo Federov was my father."

"I'm mighty sorry, miss."

Anna clenched her fist against the trembling. Papa was gone. He and her Cossack grandmother, Baba Lily, had taught her to be strong. Right now, strength and determination were all she had. If she took the time to succumb to self-pity, Rupert would swoop down like a vulture and snap her up.

"Thank you, Mr. Winchell. You're very kind. Now, if you don't mind, the advertisement? I've written up a piece that should do nicely." She handed it over.

He bent his visored head to read. The furrows in his brow deepened. "Are you sure you want me to run this?"

Anna stifled a blush. As humiliating as it was, she had little choice. "Absolutely."

"A woman like you running an ad like this. Don't seem right to me."

Anna was afraid to ask what he meant by 'a woman like her.' She had no qualms about her lack of physical attributes. Passable, that's all she was. Ordinary. With brown hair, hazel eyes, and skin a shade too dark to be fashionable, though she wore a hat just as Miss Bellingham had instructed. That is, when she remembered to wear one. But she did have excellent posture. And she could write a tidy hand and sew lovely stitches. Though not a beauty, she had enough qualities to make some Kansan a fine wife.

The newspaperman pushed at his visor. "I hope you know what you're doing, Miss Federov."

She was trying to stay alive. That's what she was doing.

Determined not to be dissuaded by the journalist's concern, Anna opened her string purse and handed him several coins. "Will this cover the cost?"

He hesitated before accepting the payment. "Yes, ma'am. Newspaper comes out tomorrow morning."

Uncertainty pushed at her chest, but she resisted. She must do this. She must. Tomorrow could not come soon enough. If Cousin Rupert discovered her whereabouts before she found an agreeable husband. . .

But no. He would not.

As if Miss Bellingham herself had run a hand down her backbone and commanded her to stand up straight and be of good courage, Anastasia stiffened her spine. The Lord was with her, and she had covered her trail as well as she could. Rupert would not find her until she was happily, or at least safely, married. "Thank you, Mr. Winchell. Good day."

Fully satisfied that on the female-lonely prairie, she'd have her choice of suitors in no time, Anna exited the office, the hotel in her sights. Tea and a bit of rest were called for after such a momentous undertaking as putting oneself on the marriage market.

Head down, mind churning with what was to come, she

hurried toward the hotel, her muddied heels tapping a hollow rhythm on the boardwalk. A north wind had picked up, and the overcast sky had darkened. She huddled into the warmth of her cape, heedless of anything but the irregular boards beneath her feet and the worry in her heart.

A tall, muscular form rounded the corner and slammed full-force into her. In a grapple for purchase, they both stumbled, executing a precarious dance along the edge of the boardwalk. Any moment Anna expected to plunge ingloriously into the nasty, dung-littered mud. The man, who smelled of leather and sage, abandoned attempts at acceptable behavior and instead yanked her flailing body against his.

Flushing seven shades of red, Anna pushed at an oak-hard chest. "Unhand me, sir."

A chuckle rumbled from his chest to her ear, a sound as warm and welcome as a fire on Christmas Eve. "I beg your pardon, miss." Though he sounded not the least bit sorry, he dropped his hold. Anna stumbled backward. One boot already slick with mud slid off the boardwalk. She had one foot off and one foot on in a most unladylike stance. When she tried to correct the problem, her boot stuck fast in the bog.

"If I may," the man said and dared to touch her again, this time taking liberty with her knee. With two large, powerful hands he grasped her leg just above the boot top and pulled.

Mortified, Anna slapped at his hands. "I'm quite all right. Thank you."

With a tilt of his dark head, the man stepped back to watch.

White teeth flashed in a handsome sun-bronzed face while Anna battled the treacherous mud. When it became clear that she could not correct the problem without tumbling into the street, she thrust out a palm. "Your hand, please, sir."

"But you just told me to *un*hand you."

"I changed my mind."

The man raised one very black eyebrow.

Anna's face and neck flamed hotter than an iron kettle. She was making a fool of herself and prayed that every unattached male in Flat Rock didn't observe her distress. "Well," she said.

"Say please."

With Cossack blood stronger than all the years of Miss Bellingham's constant instruction, Anna had to bite back the urge to say far more. "Please," she managed, though the word tasted like gall.

Again that chuckle, but a sturdy hand was extended, palm up. *Clean, strong but gentle, and not a stranger to work.* All three thoughts flashed quickly through Anna's head. She laid her fingers in his, squelched the rather pleasant tingle of awareness, and pulled. The mud did not give up without a fight. Splatters accompanied a loud sucking noise as her boot came free.

"All right now?" the man asked, gazing down at her with an amused look that both annoyed and charmed. He was quite handsome, really, and he seemed to know it. She couldn't help noticing the stretch of a brown wool jacket across broad shoulders and the dark, dancing eyes, almost liquid with amusement.

"Yes, I'm fine. Thank you very much."

The rough strength of his hand was both exciting and frightening. She tugged. He held on. Men always had the upper hand, not only in the physical sense, but according to the law.

"If you would release me, please."

"And if I don't?"

"Then I shall have to remove the pistol secreted in my skirt pocket and shoot your kneecaps." Not that she owned a gun, but the threat worked.

The surprised man released her. He thumbed the brim of his hat and stepped back with a tilt of his head.

With as much dignity as she could muster in mud-caked, squishing boots, Anna lifted her skirt tail and stalked across the street toward the safety of her hotel to await the morrow.

❧

Captain Jace Brackett grinned after the little brown sparrow who had just flogged him. A spirited little sparrow, she was, though he didn't recognize her. He thought he knew everyone in Flat Rock, a town his family had called home since before the Civil War.

He watched her pick her way across the muddy street and disappear into the Peabody Hotel. Still chuckling, he went inside the newspaper office.

" 'Morning, Bartholomew."

"Captain Brackett." Old Bart nodded. "What can I do for you?"

"An advertisement. We need a housekeeper at the farm."

"What happened to Effie Ringworst?"

Jace leaned an elbow on the rough green counter. "Sweet Effie was not happy living with, as she so delicately put it, three ruffians who had no hope of ever finding wives, much less eternal salvation."

"And all three of you laughed your heads off at that one, I daresay."

"You'd say right, my friend. Wives are nothing but trouble. The only one of us Bracketts who hitched his wagon to a woman can't even belch in his own house."

Bartholomew wagged his generous head with true sympathy. "Right shame, I'm thinking."

"Brilliant man that you are." Jace took a pad and scribbled the same ad he and his two brothers ran at least three times a year. Sometimes more often.

He liked women. Enjoyed teasing them and making them blush, like the lady in the mud. Women were a heap of fun, but he'd learned the hard way not to trust any of them. If Ma had lived, he'd have trusted her, but even she had abandoned the Bracketts, for death was a kind of abandonment to his way of thinking.

Then when Miss Merilee Simpkins eloped with that hog farmer over in Morris County, all while Jace was riding for the U.S. Calvary, he'd sworn off anything more permanent than a howdy do. Even now, eight years later, Merilee's "Dear Jace" letter was seared into his heart like the brand on his cows. He'd been a soldier, sworn to keep the peace on the frontier and fully expecting to come home to the woman who loved him. Instead, he came home with a musket ball in his arm to a houseful of siblings and a run-down ranch that demanded every bit of effort he had left in him.

Out of habit, he rotated the shoulder. The old wound acted up on rainy days. Fact of the matter, it had been paining him something fierce since Tuesday when the winter rains moved in.

"I seen you bump into the lady outside. Do you know her?"

Jace tore off the paper he'd been writing on and handed it over. "Newcomer, I reckon. Never seen her before."

"Name's Federov. Her pa farmed a homestead up Turkey Creek. If I remember right, he took to the gold fields a few years back. Died there."

Jace turned toward the door. A buckboard loaded with feed sacks slogged down the muddy street, but the woman was out of sight. "She here to take over her pa's farm?"

"Can't say, but she's a feisty one, if you ask me, putting an advertisement like this in the newspaper. No telling what she might get."

Jace's eyes narrowed with interest. "What kind of ad?"

"Looking for a husband."

Jace laughed. He couldn't help himself. "Figure she needs a man to work her farm?"

"Why not take on a hired hand? Or better yet, sell out and go back where she came from instead of husband hunting. Don't make no sense to me."

"Well, if it's a husband she's after, she'll find one out here." Cowboys and ranch hands and sod farmers from miles around were starving for refined female company. Even though the lady on the boardwalk was a spitfire, she was also refined. Citified, even.

"That's what I was thinking, but no telling what she might get. Pretty little gal could find a heap of trouble." He shook his wrinkled head, fretting. "You're an honorable man for all your nonsense. Maybe *you* should talk to her."

Jace shrank back in horror. "I'm not applying to be any woman's husband."

The newspaperman slapped the counter and chortled. "I know that, but you need a housekeeper. A lady such as her could be a fine influence on that sister of yours."

Jace bristled. "You saying my sister needs refinement?"

"Now, Cap'n, don't get your back up. You said yourself Rachel knows more about cows than about being a girl."

The defensive breath Jace was holding eked out. Bart was right. Rachel had spent all of her twelve years in the company of three brothers, a horde of ranch hands, and an ever-changing parade of housekeepers who took no interest in her at all. She was a good girl, but she didn't know the first thing about woman skills. "True enough."

"Wouldn't hurt to ask the lady. She might be willing to work for you until the right feller comes along. And you could kinda look out for her, so to speak."

Old Bart had a soft spot for gentle ladies.

Though Jace wasn't sure how gentle this one was. She had threatened to remove his kneecaps. But she also appeared educated in the social graces, something Rachel desperately needed.

Jace glanced toward the hotel again. He was curious, too. Why was the little brown sparrow with the pistol in her pocket so all-fired desperate for a husband?

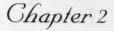

Chapter 2

A gentleman caller? Already?

Anna thanked the hotel proprietor who carried the news that a Captain Jace Brackett wanted to see her in the hotel parlor. A captain, no less. A man of honor and courage who had served his country would certainly be man enough to ward off her greedy relatives. But would he be malleable? That was the question. Still, his name alone raised goose bumps on her arms. *Captain Jace Brackett.* Yes indeed. She would give him an opportunity to convince her of his sincerity.

Anna crossed to the cheval mirror, patted her upswept hair, and pinched her cheeks before descending the stairs to the parlor. Rounding the staircase, a smile on her face, she opened the French doors to the parlor and froze. The smile slipped away. Her stomach fluttered in a most disconcerting manner.

Standing with his back to the fireplace, hat in hand, was the tall, handsome, troublesome man from the boardwalk. Captain Jace Brackett. Oh my.

She touched the brooch at her throat, glad she was more presentable now than she'd been at their first meeting. The man unsettled her. So much for her lovely but fleeting dreams of a malleable military man. "Captain Brackett, I presume?"

He stepped forward, his expression as sincere as Sunday morning. "I've come about your advertisement."

Though surprised to see this particular man, Anna decided to make the best of the situation. The newspaper ad had not even come out and already she was entertaining a candidate for her husband. Not that she had expected this one, but she might as well give him a chance. He was here. And he was strong, handsome, and soldier-brave. "Shall we sit down, then?"

As his head tilted in agreement, Anna swept her freshly donned blue skirt to the side and settled on a blood red settee in front of the cheerful stone hearth. The snapping fire bathed the room in both heat and golden light, making the parlor a cozy respite from the cold, blustery Kansas outdoors.

"Would you care for tea?" she asked.

"I ordered coffee if that's all right."

"Of course." Contrary to her first impression, he wasn't completely lacking in social graces. She offered a hand. "I'm Anastasia Federov."

"I know. I'm Jace Brackett. I own a ranch a mile outside of town."

A landowner. Good. He wouldn't be after her fortune.

The brief conversation came to a halt when the waitress brought a tray containing two stoneware cups steaming with hot, fragrant coffee.

Anna waited until the woman departed before clearing her throat. She had little enough time to waste. "So, Captain, you're in the market for a wife, then?"

His disarming smile turned to a glower. His hand froze above the sugar bowl. "No, ma'am. I am not the least bit interested in marrying you."

Anna gasped. She pressed a hand to her fluttering heart.

The astonishment and hurt she felt must have been obvious, for he hurried on: "Not that there's a thing wrong with you, Miss Federov. I just don't intend to ever be hitched to any woman's wagon. Not now, not ever."

Somehow his vehement discourse on marriage did not mollify. "Then why are you here about my advertisement?"

"I'm in need of a housekeeper. Thought you might be interested."

"I advertised for a husband, not a job."

His shoulders twitched in annoyance. "Do you have any idea what you're getting yourself into, placing a crazy fool ad like that? You'll have every lonely cowpoke for twenty miles sniffing around your door."

"A good thing under the circumstances."

"Not necessarily. Not every man who comes around will be a gentleman. You could be in danger, if you get my drift. I figure you need a protector as badly as I need a housekeeper."

She touched her fingers to her lips. Danger? To her virtue? To her reputation? "I hadn't thought of that. But I'm in a hurry, Captain. A big hurry. I must find a husband by Christmas at the latest."

His eyes dropped to her tiny, cinched waistline. "Mind if I ask why?"

Her spine stiffened. "It's nothing like you're imagining." After a glance around the parlor to make sure no one else heard, Anna said softly, "You see, Captain, I'm already in danger. Someone wants to kill me."

Jace's head snapped back. "Kill you? Come now, surely you're exaggerating."

"Perhaps. But I don't think so, and frankly, I'd rather not take the chance."

He nodded. "I see your point." He poured a hearty helping of cream into his coffee and stirred. "Would you care to explain?"

She sipped at her unsweetened drink, glad for the bracing bitterness. "It seems I am a very rich woman, Captain. Although I didn't even know it."

"And someone wants to relieve you of your fortune?"

To her great despair. Using the white damask napkin, she dabbed at her lips. "My aunt and uncle were my guardians while I attended the ladies' academy in St. Louis and while Papa was gone to the gold fields. They claimed he sent only a small allowance for my education."

"A lie?"

She tilted her head. "Sadly, yes. Then one night after Papa's death, I overhead them discussing what they planned to do about my inheritance."

"And?"

"I contacted Mr. Goldbloom, my father's lawyer who apprised me of the situation. Papa owned controlling interest in several mines and had amassed a rather stunning fortune. All of which belongs to me, either upon my marriage or at the age of majority."

"I'm afraid I don't see the problem."

"My aunt and uncle intend to have my inheritance one way or another. I am betrothed, without my consent, to Cousin Rupert, their son. A Christmas wedding is already planned, again without my consent or input."

"A nasty business, I'm sure, but a wedding doesn't involve murder."

"Oh, but it does. Both my cousin and my uncle have made veiled threats, and I've listened in on more than one conversation in which my aunt and uncle have discussed ways to be rid of the 'problem,' as they call me. Should I not attend the Christmas wedding or find a husband before my birthday, I fear what may become of me."

He set aside his coffee mug and nodded. "I'm beginning to understand. If you marry someone of your own choosing before this planned Christmas wedding to your cousin, your chosen husband will then take control of all your worldly goods, including your inheritance. Then your greedy relatives will be out of luck."

The man was astute as well as sinfully handsome. Too bad he wasn't in the market for a wife. She had a strong feeling that her relatives would not be able to stand up to a man like this.

"Exactly. Oh, Captain Brackett, it's such a relief to tell someone. When I realized what my own blood relatives had planned, I ran for my life, though I fear they will find me before

I find the right man. So you see? Even though my advertisement is rather unorthodox, it's a necessity."

"You aren't going to tell every suitor that answers the ad about the fortune, are you?"

"I. . ." She blinked rapidly. He was right. "Of course not. I have a nice dowry in the homestead. That should be enough to attract someone suitable, don't you think?"

She looked so uncertain, Jace softened. He'd never heard such a tomfool story in his life, but he knew human nature. Many a man lay beneath the sod because of greed. If the woman was telling the truth, she *was* in danger, both from her cousin and from a dozen unknown cowboys who would descend like locusts as soon as they read tomorrow's paper. "I think you need to come home with me."

She lowered her cup with a clank. "I thought you understood the dilemma, Captain. I need a husband, but you are not looking for a wife. Going to your ranch will not solve the problem."

"No. But I think we can help each other. My family and I need a housekeeper. You need a protector, both from your cousin Rupert and from overzealous suitors."

There was that. His comment that all applicants for husband would not be gentlemen had her stomach in a knot. "You don't even know if I can cook."

"Can you?"

"Quite well, thank you. But I could only work for you temporarily. A few weeks at most."

"Until Christmas. That should give me time to find another housekeeper. Ours left quite suddenly." He wasn't going to mention the goat in the kitchen or the fact that he hadn't had a decent meal in three days.

"Even if I agreed, I'd need plenty of time off for interviewing applicants."

Jace stifled a laugh. "You're looking for a husband, not a hired hand."

A rose blush tinged her cheekbones. She had pretty cheekbones, like a doll he'd seen in a catalog once.

"You're right. I really don't know how to go about this. I just want to find a nice, agreeable husband who will let me run my own life."

"A milksop?"

"I do not wish anyone to be in charge of my life. Other than myself and the Lord, of course."

Jace hadn't thought much about the Lord since before Ma died. And he sure wasn't willing to let God or anyone else control his life. After all he'd been through, he could handle anything. And right now, he felt the ridiculous need to protect this little sparrow from her unscrupulous relatives. If Rachel were in this situation, he'd want someone to look out for her.

"I have a younger sister. She's twelve years old and doesn't know the first thing about being a lady. You'd be doing me a favor to spend some time with her. Maybe teach her to cook and look after the place."

"A sister?" Her eyes glazed over with an enchanted expression. She obviously hadn't met Rachel.

"I also have two rowdy, ornery brothers, but they know their manners around a lady. With the three of us on hand, Cousin

Rupert can't get near you."

"Bodyguards," she mused softly. "I like the sound of that."

"So you'll come to work for us?"

She gazed solemnly into the fire for several long seconds while Jace wondered why her agreement had suddenly become so important to him. Then she turned those worried eyes to him and nodded.

"Yes, Captain, I'll be your housekeeper if you will serve as my bodyguard. And I sincerely pray that my presence doesn't bring trouble down upon your head."

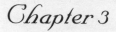

Chapter 3

The Brackett Ranch sprawled for miles, its center-piece a blue and white two-story house, complete with an enormous porch that literally took Anna's breath away.

"What a beautiful home." All the years in St. Louis had not dulled her love for the Kansas prairie. Even in bleak, gray winter, this was home—and she'd been homesick for a long time. "It will be lovely decorated for Christmas."

Beside her on the buggy, Jace tugged the reins and brought the big bay gelding to a halt beside the porch steps. He gave her a mild look as though she spoke a foreign language.

She turned toward him on the seat, thankful for the covering above her head. "Don't you decorate?"

"Haven't since Mama died."

"What a shame." And one she would remedy. The Lord's birth was something to be heralded with great joy. Was the captain not a believer?

Before she could ask, a young girl opened the wooden door

and peered through the screen. Even in a worn riding skirt and scuffed boots, dark-eyed, dark-haired Rachel Brackett was a beauty in the making.

"Is she the new housekeeper?" the child asked.

"Rachel, meet Anna Federov. She'll be helping out around here for a while." He helped Anna alight and then reached for her carpetbag. "Show her in."

Rachel did as she was told, holding the door while Anna entered. A short hall led around a gracefully curving staircase which was probably lovely beneath the litter of jackets and horse tack. Beyond this was a long rose-papered room where a fire crackled behind an ash-strewn hearth and dust had accumulated on rosewood furnishings. A musty smell of burned food hung in the air.

Oh dear. The outside was lovely, but the inside was sorely in need of attention.

"How long are you planning to stay?" Something in the defensive way the girl asked tugged at Anna.

Gently, she said, "Not long, dear. Perhaps until Christmas. Regardless of the length of my term, you and I shall have a wonderful time."

"I don't know anything about silly girl stuff."

Anna whipped off her hat with a smile. "Would you care to learn?"

The question caught the child off guard. Eyes as dark and liquid as her brother's blinked in bewilderment. "I don't know. No one ever asked me that before."

Anna touched Rachel's arm. "It's almost Christmas. We'll

decorate and bake cookies. Just wait. We're going to have such fun."

"The kitchen's this way," Jace interrupted, leading the way through the big house. "Sorry it's a mess."

An understatement. Dishes were piled on the table. Pots containing an odd assortment of unrecognizable foodstuffs dotted the stove, no doubt the source of the odor.

Rachel opened the back door. A large shaggy dog barreled inside.

"Rachel, put him outside."

Rachel paid her brother no mind. "This is Silas."

"Oh," Anna said. "He's wonderful. I had a dog once." She stooped to rub the wide head. "When Baba Lily and I lived on the homestead, we kept a dog. He used to ride on the back of my pony everywhere I went."

"Be careful. Silas gets excited and—"

Before Rachel could finish, Silas reared, placed broad paws on each of Anna's shoulders, and slurped her cheek. Anna tumbled backward, landing on the hardwood floor. She laughed. The dog reacted with joyful wiggles, wags, and more licks before Jace caught him by the scruff and guided him back outside.

"Are you angry?" Rachel asked, hands on her hips in a defiant gesture Anna did not understand.

"Angry at such an exuberant welcome? Not in the least." She took Jace's offered hand and rose, straightening her rumpled skirt.

Rachel considered Anna's reaction and then said, "Maybe you aren't so prim and proper after all."

Anna smiled. Perhaps she was off to a good start.

❧

By suppertime, Anna had toured the house and made mental notes about the cleaning jobs ahead. The rugs and drapes needed a good beating, but that would have to wait until the weather cleared. And since she wouldn't be here by then, God willing, she didn't worry about those. Most things throughout the house needed a good wash or dusting, but the potential for a lovely, comfortable home was evident in the well-made furniture and in the musty-scented linens and china and silver stashed away in a large wardrobe.

She and Rachel scrubbed away most of the kitchen grime and slapped together a passable supper. Tomorrow she would do better. She was a good cook, thanks to Baba Lily, and missed the delicious recipes her Ukrainian grandmother had brought all the way from her home near the Black Sea.

"What smells so good?" Jace, accompanied by two other young men, stomped through the back door.

Rachel motioned toward the table, her cheeks glowing from the heat of the kitchen. "Anna made her grandma's apple squares."

The three men groaned in appreciation of the rich, cinnamon-scented pastry and headed for the washbasin. As she dished up the meal, Anna watched the brothers jostle and tease, a hitch beneath her ribs. She'd longed for siblings, and though she'd had friends at the boarding school, all were too busy trying to be proper and win the attentions of wealthy beaus to have fun together. Kansas was a different world. She had missed the freedom of the prairies.

Her gaze drifted to Rachel. The girl had worked as hard as she had all afternoon without complaint. If only Anna could stay longer, she and Rachel might become close.

Melancholy overtook her and she remained unusually quiet, although the Bracketts had no way of knowing her normal propensity for chatter. For years at the ladies' academy, she ached to be close to someone. She missed Papa and Baba, missed being loved.

Now the only family she had left not only didn't love her; they wanted her dead. And because of their treachery, she was forced to seek out a husband for reasons other than love.

Stomach in a knot, she took her place at the table, passed bowls heaped with food, and worried about her future. Yes, worry was a sin that she had not yet conquered.

The brothers, she learned, were Wade and Brett, who ate like hungry dogs. Their compliments for the meal amused and pleased her. She noted Rachel's face aglow with pleasure when Jace quietly noted her part in preparing dinner. The girl needed more of that. God bless Jace for his insight. Perhaps he wasn't as arrogant as she'd assumed.

Anna caught his gaze and smiled. He smiled in return, setting off a pleasant warmth inside her.

Throughout the meal, the younger brothers kept up a running argument until one challenged the other to arm wrestling. Elbows thumped onto the tabletop, rattling the china Anna had rescued from the back room.

She spoke up: "Gentlemen, may I suggest you allow us to clear the dishes before beginning the match?"

Both appeared thunderstruck. They looked from Anna to Jace to the good china as though they'd never considered such a thing. "Oh. Yes, ma'am." Their raised arms slid from the table.

She gave them her most regal ladies' academy smile. "Thank you very much."

The room was eerily quiet while Anna began to collect the dishes. Jace scraped back his chair and surprised her by beginning to help. As if taking their cue from their older brother, all three siblings scrambled up and did likewise. In moments, the table was clear.

"Now," she said with an encouraging smile as she retook her seat and folded her hands in her lap, "I should enjoy watching the outcome of your match. You may begin."

❦

Miss Anna Federov was full of surprises. Jace had expected her to run screaming from the disheveled house at first glance. Instead, she claimed to adore the place, regaling him with ideas for cleaning, restoring, and decorating. He didn't give a fig about such things as long as she continued to cook such wonderful meals.

She'd also surprised him with her calm acceptance of his rowdy brothers and her kindness toward Rachel. Anna was not the snobbish, silly city girl he'd expected.

But the surprise turned to amusement the next day when three young farmers appeared on the porch, newspapers in hand, all looking to meet Miss Anastasia Federov.

As she showed the first of the men into the parlor, Jace lingered in the doorway, hoping for a bit of fun, until Anna gave him a look. "Will you please excuse us, Captain?"

Inclining his head, he stepped just out of sight. She didn't know it, but he had no intention of leaving her alone with her "applicants," as she called them.

By Friday of that same week, he was worn out from standing outside the parlor, his ear pressed to the door. As he'd predicted, every cowhand and farmer within twenty miles was braving the elements to meet Miss Anna. As word of her quick wit and charm rippled throughout the countryside, the traffic increased and Jace's mood soured.

To make matters worse, his own brothers were mooning over her cooking, and Rachel had taken to sitting in the parlor each evening while Anna showed her how to sew a simple stitch. Rachel took to Anna like a puppy, a fact that hurt his heart. His baby sister was hungry for a woman's attention, and he hadn't even realized it. Some provider he was.

As a safety precaution, he'd told his brothers about Anna's situation, to which the youngest had replied, "We need a woman around here. Why don't you marry her, Jace?"

Jace had growled like a bear and tossed a forkful of hay at him.

❧❧

On Sunday afternoon, Anna alighted from the hired carriage in front of the Brackett house. The sun had come out that morning, providing a pleasant December day, though the trip to church with her latest caller had bordered on intolerable.

"Church service was lovely, Mr. Fetterman." At least that much was true. "Thank you for escorting me."

"So does that mean you'll marry me?" the farmer asked, his weathered felt hat in hand. "I could sure use another hundred and sixty acres. Being as how your land adjoins mine, it just makes good sense we should join up."

Anna stifled a scream and as gently as possible said, "I'm sorry, Mr. Fetterman. I'm still interviewing applicants."

"Is that a flat no or a maybe? I got a farm to run. I can't be wasting time with courting, 'less'n you're planning to say yes."

Anna burned with embarrassment. But she'd put herself in this position, so no use blaming the man. Trying her best to keep the anger from her voice, she said, "Then, sir, I must decline your kind offer and wish you well. Have a safe trip back to town."

As the rented buggy rumbled away, Anna hiked her rose-colored skirt and started up the steps. At the top, Jace Brackett waited, one shoulder against the doorpost, a smirk on his face. "Another flop?" He seemed to delight in teasing her about her applicants.

With a sniff, she tried to edge around him. He blocked her way.

She glared at him. Yes, glaring was unladylike, but she wasn't feeling too prim today. "Are you intentionally trying to annoy me?"

Every time a man came to call, Jace loitered about, smirking and making little side comments that set her face aflame.

"George Fetterman is a decent fella. You could do worse."

"He wants my land," she blurted, still incensed at the farmer's crass insensitivity. "And he has no notion of romance."

"What did you expect?" He rolled his hat around and around in his hands, liquid eyes locked on hers. "Love?"

His cynical attitude got under her skin in the worst way, because the truth was she *did* want love. Or at least for a man to behave as though he found her attractive for reasons other than 160 acres.

"As you've so often pointed out, people out here on the prairie wed for many reasons, the least of which is love. But I refuse to hitch my wagon, as you so aptly put it, to a man who would probably trade me for a Jersey milk cow and not miss me in the least." Getting worked up at the insult, she poked a finger in his chest. "And another thing. If Mr. Fetterman is thrilled over owning my farm, how do you think he'll react to my bank account?"

Jace caught her fingers in his before she could poke a hole through him. She could feel the thump-thud of his heart beneath her hand.

"What about Thompson? He seemed rather smitten."

He had been. Too much so. He had slobbered all over her hand and declared undying love at their first meeting. She had laughed. Poor fellow.

Anna tugged to release her fingers and was almost disappointed when he let go without the usual tussle. "Not him."

"What about Clifford, then? He's a good man and he

wouldn't be after your money."

Bob Clifford owned the mercantile. His wife had died last June in childbirth. "True. I like Bob."

Jace's eyebrows lifted. The annoying smirk appeared. "Bob, is it?"

"I said I like him." Though he was twenty years her senior.

"It's only three weeks until Christmas. And he's a good candidate."

Anna bit her bottom lip. "I know." Bob *was* a good candidate, but Anna had yet to find a man who really interested her.

Well, there was one. But he didn't count.

Jace pushed the door open. "Better get inside. Wouldn't want you to chill."

"You're just anxious for your dinner," she said with a grin.

Jace laughed and reached for her cape.

Pleased, Anna let him take it. "You shouldn't go off and leave the kitchen smelling so good. Tortures a man."

"If you'd attend church, you wouldn't be here to suffer. The music is heavenly, and Rev. Jacobs is a fine preacher." Anna slid the pin from her hat and placed the feathery confection on a side table. "I wish you would come."

"Why is that, Anna? Are you worried about my mortal soul?" He followed her into the kitchen, where she checked the roast she'd set to bake.

"I am indeed. You need to be an example to your brothers and sister." Wade and Brett attended church mostly to sit with their ladies, though they brought Rachel in the wagon. Jace stayed at home.

Pot holder in hand, Anna opened the oven. A delicious scent of roasted beef and potatoes wafted forth. Bread baked yesterday was ready to slice and slather with freshly churned butter, and Rachel had baked a tasty, if somewhat lopsided, lemon cake to complete their Sunday dinner.

The rest of the siblings clattered in from outside, bringing a welcome draft of cool air into the heated kitchen. Laughter came along, as well, filling the house with the kind of happy family moment Anna had missed for so long.

"Is dinner ready?" Wade asked, nose sniffing the air like a hound.

"Indeed, it is. Everyone wash up. Rachel and I will have the food on the table momentarily."

"Miss Anna," Brett said, "if you keep this up, I may have to marry you myself."

Anna laughed. "And break Miss Betsy's young heart?"

Brett and Betsy were well on their way to the altar, though Jace clouded up every time the matter was mentioned—more proof of his anti-marriage opinion.

Not that she cared one whit. Regardless of the way her stomach fluttered in his presence, Anna required a biddable Christian man, not a stubborn, unbelieving mule like Jace Brackett.

"Come on, now. Let's eat," she said. "I want to bake some cookies before Jess arrives."

Jace made a rude noise. "Jess Brewer is a milksop."

Which was exactly the reason Anna had agreed to see him again.

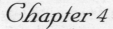

Chapter 4

Lamplight flickered from the sitting room to cast long shadows into the hall. This had become Anna's favorite room in the Brackett house, a place to retreat at night and read or sew. Although she enjoyed the male attention heaped upon her and was truly having the time of her life, the evenings at home with the Bracketts were a needed respite.

Rachel had become an apt sewing pupil, eager to make Christmas gifts for each of her brothers, a thoughtfulness Anna found endearing. The girl took up her sewing from the basket beside her chair, slipped a silver thimble onto her thumb as Anna had instructed, and began weaving the needle in and out.

As Anna reached for her Bible to share the evening devotional, Jace appeared, filling up the room with his size and vitality. And just that quickly, weariness from the day's toils was replaced by a buzz of energy that set her pulse racing and made her heart light.

"Good evening, Captain. Do you care for tea?"

"Got any of those Baba cookies left?" Settling into a chair

near the crackling fireplace, he stretched his long legs out in front of him.

Anna motioned to a plate next to the tea service she'd spent hours polishing. "As you can see. Help yourself."

Baba's cookies, as Jace teasingly called them, were one of her favorite recipes handed down from her grandmother. Snowcapped with meringue, the rich, buttery dough melted in the mouth and had caused more than one moan of appreciation from the Brackett brothers.

"I believe we're ready to read the prophecy from Micah." In preparation for Christmas, she was reading all the scriptures pointing toward Christ's birth. Regardless of her unsettled future and the passage of days in which she still had not chosen a husband, her devotional time with the Lord provided gentle assurance that all things would work to her good.

Sometimes, though, she wished the Lord would hurry up and tell her exactly what to do, but she tried to be thankful. Rupert had not found her. And she had met some very nice gentlemen, all eager to win her hand.

She glanced across at Jace, quiet for once as he thoughtfully nibbled the meringue from a cookie. He caught her gaze and winked.

Flustered, she opened the Bible. "We're reading Micah 5:2. 'But thou, Bethlehem Ephratah, though thou be little among the thousands of Judah, yet out of thee shall he come forth unto me that is to be ruler in Israel; whose goings forth have been from of old, from everlasting.'"

"Don't you think it's interesting," Jace said, tapping a cookie against his lip in thought, "that Jesus descended from Judah?"

"I can't say I've given it much thought. Why?"

"Old Judah was one of the brothers who tossed Joseph into the pit and sold him into slavery, wasn't he? They were both great-grandsons of Abraham, so either one could have carried the line. Joseph was the good son. And yet Jesus descended through the tribe of Judah. I find that interesting."

So did Anna, now that he'd brought the matter to her attention. "For a man who shuns the faith, you're certainly knowledgeable of the scriptures."

Jace hitched a shoulder and popped the rest of the cookie into his mouth.

Eyes on the silver needle weaving in and out of fabric, Rachel said, "Ma read the Bible to us every night."

Jace blinked in surprise at his sister. "You remember that?"

In the lamp's glow, Rachel's doe eyes softened as she nodded. "I know I was little, but I remember a lot about Ma. The way she smelled. Her long flowing skirts that swished when she walked. The way she'd play the piano and sing, especially at Christmas." She laid her sewing in her lap. "Remember the Christmas she hid tiny gifts all over the house and laughed and clapped while we scattered like geese looking for them?"

Jace's face had gone as nostalgic as his sister's.

Anna's heart pinched with empathy. "Those are wonderful memories," she said.

"Every Christmas Eve when I was a boy, we would set up the nativity scene. Each of us took a turn, setting out a piece and telling the story of that character."

"Jace probably chose the donkey," Rachel teased. "And I'm sure I chose the angel."

Anna chuckled. She liked thinking of Jace as a boy, all wide-eyed with wonder. What had happened to make him so cynical, both about marriage and about the Lord?

"Nope, squirt," Jace said, "not the donkey. Wade and I fought over the Baby Jesus every year. Turned into a regular wrestling match."

And so the evening wore on with talk and teasing and laughter until the fire in the grate burned low, and Anna, though reluctant to end the pleasantry, stood and began to collect the teacups.

"It's late," she said needlessly, for Jace had risen, too. She shouldn't be noticing him so much, but Anna couldn't seem to help herself. He was annoying and charming, intelligent and stubborn. And he fascinated her. A man without the Lord, clear in his intentions never to marry, was the only man she'd met who interested her in the least.

A pity. And a fact that could not derail her carefully laid plans.

"I'll say good night, then." He started to the door but stopped in the opening.

Both ladies looked toward him expectantly. He hovered as though something remained on his mind, but then without a word turned and pounded up the stairs.

"He never used to sit around in the parlor at night," Rachel said. "And he sure never used to talk about the Bible. I think he likes you."

And what should have been a compliment only made Anna sad.

The off-key singing was his first clue to her whereabouts. The troublesome belle of Flat Rock, Kansas, couldn't carry a tune in a bucket, but she loved to sing.

Jace shut the back door and trotted up the stairs toward the noise. The door to one of the rooms was open and her back was turned as she scrubbed vigorously at a dirty window glass. The pungent scent of vinegar permeated the air. "Anna."

She jumped and spun around, the hand holding the rag pressed to the lace at her throat. "Jace Bracket! You scared me half silly."

He crossed the room and took the rag from her hand, tossing it aside. "Come with me. I want to show you something."

"What is it?"

"Just come."

"Is this one of your tricks?"

"No." He must have convinced her, for she placed her small hand in his outstretched one and followed. He led her down the stairs, where he looped a cape over her shoulders and then continued outside.

"Oh, it's snowing." Anna lifted a delighted face to the heavens. "I love snow."

He'd figured as much, though this was not his surprise. "There'll be plenty of snow before winter's over. Come on. The surprise is in the barn."

With a curious look, she followed him inside the big wooden structure. Jace wasn't sure why he wanted to share the kittens with Anna, but he knew she'd love them, too.

The hay-scented barn was warm with animal bodies. A young mother cow mooed softly to her calf as Jace pointed to the loft. "Up there."

Anna glanced down at her skirts. "You first."

He scampered quickly up the ladder then reached back to assist her. Bits of hay trickled down, landing in her soft-looking hair. She always kept the honey brown locks swept back in a chignon. Just once Jace wished he could see it down.

Leading the way, he carefully moved a barrel to one side then knelt beside a pile of loose straw. "We'd best keep our voices low. Bright Eyes might not appreciate a lot of noise right now."

He watched Anna's face, knowing the minute she saw the cozy scene in the straw. Voice filled with wonder, she murmured, "Oh, Jace, how many?"

The gray-and-white-striped mama cat had apparently been courting long before Anna had. She blinked up at them with alert green eyes.

"Five. Only a few days old, best as I can tell."

Anna knelt on the rough planks next to him to watch. "They're so tiny. Do you think she'll mind if I hold one?"

Jace reached in among the wiggling, mewing babies and plucked a tiger stripe. He'd been squirting milk into the mama's bowl for so long, she trusted him.

Carefully Anna took the kitten against her shoulder and began to make sweet baby noises to the tiny animal. Something turned over inside Jace. Anna was going to make some man a fine wife, and within a year or two, she'd be making baby noises to her own little one. She'd be a good mama, he was sure of it, from the changes he'd seen in his little sister.

He watched her, his chest tight, for a long time while she stroked and murmured. Then when Bright Eyes shed the suckling kittens to stretch a paw toward her absent baby, he took the kitten from Anna and tucked it into the warm nest of hay and cats.

Shoulder to shoulder, he and Anna watched the kittens, a kind of hush settling over the barn. A wind rattled the loft door. Cool air drifted through the cracks while outside the snow fell in light, fluffy flakes.

"You have straw in your hair," he said and reached for it.

She stilled, a half smile on her lips.

He touched her hair, his fingers lingering there on the softness he'd only imagined. Their eyes met and held. They'd never been this close, and Jace could feel the rise and fall of her breathing, see the flecks of green in her beguiling, long-lashed eyes. He had the sudden, insane, and completely inappropriate urge to kiss her.

"Anna!" They both jumped when Rachel's voice came from somewhere outside. "Mr. Brewer is here."

"Oh my." Anna glanced toward the loft entrance. Voice a little too breathless, she murmured, "I plumb forgot. Mr. Brewer has come for tea."

Jace wanted to kick himself. What was he doing up in the loft, staring into Anna Federov's face like a lovesick pup, when she fully intended to marry someone else by Christmas?

His hand fell away from her hair. Putting on his best smirk, he stepped back. "Better get on out there and see good old milksop Jess. Wouldn't want to scare off one of your best beaus."

In a swirl of skirts and petticoats, Anna hurried down the ladder.

Jace stood at the top of the ladder, a sour taste in his mouth. Flighty thing. Like a honeybee flitting from flower to flower looking for the sweetest nectar. No different than Merilee Simpkins.

Ah, what was wrong with him? One minute he was philosophizing about what a fine wife and mother she would be, and the next he was comparing her to Merilee.

The woman was making him crazy.

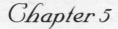

Chapter 5

Days later, Anna was still mortified by the events in the barn loft. Why, she'd wished for Captain Brackett to kiss her. Shameful. All her life, Baba and Papa had warned her against the danger of an unequal yoke. Jace was not a believer. Regardless of his knowledge of the Bible, he'd told her more than once he could handle his life just fine. He didn't need God's help. Of all the awful things to say.

Furthermore, he was not the least interested in marriage and she must have a husband. Her very life depended upon it. And yet she'd almost kissed Captain Brackett.

All during that afternoon tea with Mr. Brewer, she'd been distracted, thinking about the barn and the kittens and Jace. Finally, when poor Jess had left, she'd nearly fainted with relief.

To make matters worse, since that fateful afternoon, the evenings in the parlor had grown ripe with tension. Even Rachel had noticed. So much so that Anna considered taking to her bedroom before dark.

Her only consolation came in the knowledge that time

with Jace—with all of the Bracketts, of whom she'd grown increasingly fond—would soon be at an end. With Christmas only a week away, she had to choose a husband and do it quickly. No doubt Cousin Rupert was scouring all of Kansas in search of his Christmas bride. She simply must beat him to the punch and be wed before he discovered her whereabouts.

The thought depressed her. Whatever was wrong with her that the only man who made her heart sing and filled her with a yearning to be kissed was not among her gentlemen callers?

It was a puzzle, a dilemma, and a worry. She'd asked the Lord more than once to take Jace Brackett out of her mind, but how could He when she was washing the man's shirts and spending every evening in his company? She really must stop the latter. But how?

Tonight, at least, would be a reprieve. Other than the up-coming nativity play at church, the taffy pull at Maude and Karl Hoffman's farmhouse was the most anticipated event of the Christmas season. In addition to the candy making, there would be music and refreshments and a holiday cookie exchange, not to mention a crowd of delightful company. Captain Brackett had sourly refused to attend, a declaration that had caused considerable comment among his siblings. Anna was both relieved and disappointed, more proof of her confused state of mind.

Just then Rachel appeared in the doorway of Anna's room.

"How do I look?" Rachel, appearing nervous and a tad bit awkward, turned in a slow circle.

During a cleaning spree, Anna had found a trunk filled with dresses in the attic. Together, she and Rachel had remade one of them into a Christmas party dress.

"You look spectacular, my dear."

The bright red fabric accented Rachel's dark coloring. With the addition of ringlets and ribbons, Miss Rachel, the tomboy, was transformed. "Do you think Joseph Hoffman will notice me?"

"Why, Rachel," Anna answered mildly, "I had no idea you had eyes for young Mr. Hoffman."

Rachel blushed and hiked one shoulder. "He's very handsome. The other girls at school think so, too."

"A fine Christian boy, too. And if he isn't blind, he'll see that you're the prettiest girl at the party."

"You'll be the prettiest."

Anna laughed. "Not to Joseph, I'm sure."

"I'm glad you're riding with us instead of with stuffy old Mr. Clifford."

"Rachel, Mr. Clifford is a nice man."

"But he's old, Anna." She leaned forward in a sincere plea, taking hold of Anna's upper arm with both hands. "I don't want you to marry him. You can't possibly love him, can you? Wouldn't it be better if you married someone younger? Someone like Jace, so you could live here forever?" Knowing she'd gone too far, the child stopped and bit down on her bottom lip.

Anna's heart flipped and flopped like a banked perch. "Oh, Rachel, some things simply are not possible."

"But why?"

"Your brother has made himself very clear on the subject of marriage—and, unfortunately, on the subject of the Lord."

"But he likes you."

Anna searched for a way to end the conversation without hurting Rachel's feelings. Thinking about Jace in such a manner was too painful to pursue. "Of course he does. And I like him. He's a fine man." She hugged Rachel's shoulders. "Now get your wrap and come along. Brett and Wade will be chomping at the bit to get going."

Jace stood in the darkened corner next to the front door of the Hoffman house. He hadn't planned on coming tonight. He was not in the Christmas spirit. But after the rest of the family, including their Belle of Kansas housekeeper, rattled down the drive, he'd changed his mind, saddled his buckskin, and ridden over to the homestead. The cold wind had slapped him around some, and he'd arrived, if not cheered, at least invigorated.

Like most of the citizens of Flat Rock, the Hoffmans were simple prairie folk, a jolly lot who enjoyed making merry, especially for Christmas. Josiah Tompkins had brought his fiddle, and now and again, a jolly tune caused a round of singing. Anna's off-key voice joined in and brought some small measure of amusement to Jace's dour mood. The sweet smell of boiling molasses and the sounds of laughter and happy talk warmed the crowded space.

The rooms of the Hoffman homestead were smaller than those in his house, and Jace suffered a pinch of guilt for not offering his place for the gathering. He had one of the largest houses in the area, but he'd never considered throwing a party until Anna Federov had come along. She had likened him to Ebenezer Scrooge, Charles Dickens's stingy character in *A Christmas Carol*.

Anna. His mouth twisted ruefully as the sound of her voice once again reached his ears. He seemed especially attuned to that prim little voice, so that he could pick her out in the most crowded room. Tonight she was one of only three unattached females in a room filled with married couples, children, and single males.

His gaze fell upon her, festive in a deep green color that turned her hazel eyes to emeralds. Old milksop Jess stood before her, waving his hands as he told some big tale that had her giggling.

Jace's lip curled. What would she want with that watered-down excuse of a man? Sure, he was a hard worker with a good reputation, but he was as scrawny and bandy-legged as a chicken.

He crossed his arms and watched as yet another gentleman crowded into the conversation. When Miss Anna turned her smile to the newcomer, Jace's belly dipped south. She had a smile bright enough to light the sun.

This wasn't the first time Jace had watched her without her knowledge, though he comforted himself with the fact that he was her bodyguard. Watching her was his responsibility. But if he told the truth, he liked looking at her. He enjoyed watching her cook and sew, too, and enjoyed the elegance of her fingers when she poured his coffee. He even liked the cheerful sound of her constant, off-key singing. When she'd arrived, he'd thought her an empty-headed city girl. He'd been wrong. She'd taken to his ranch and to his little sister as if starved for this kind of life.

She had him thinking, too, a fact that kept a burr in his saddle blanket most of the time. Her faith in the Lord was as strong as Ma's had been. Nothing could shake her, not even the intentional arguments he started every night during devotionals. He reckoned he still believed in God, but after Ma and Pa died and the woman he'd loved jilted him, Jace figured God wasn't paying much attention anyhow. Why bother? He had a ranch to run and enough work to keep a man busy throughout eternity. He could handle whatever came his way just fine without any help from anyone.

But Anna set a lot of store in going to church and talking about the Lord. Even with the threat of danger over her head, she remained cheerful and confident and full of trust that everything would work to her good.

Jace frowned. Sometimes she trusted a mite too much, to his way of thinking. But then, that's why he'd stepped up to be her protector. He'd known she would have her share of callers, but the parade of female-lonely males to his doorstep was now a source of constant annoyance. Like a rock in his boot. He hadn't been in a good mood since. . .well, since that day in the barn with the kittens.

To tell the truth, he wondered sometimes about Anna's story of a ruthless, conniving family and the forced betrothal to Cousin Rupert. He'd kept his ear to the ground and no one had as much as inquired about Miss Anna Federov. Could it all be a ploy to capture a suitable husband?

He disliked thinking such a thing, but it was on his mind. Along with a lot of other thoughts about Miss Anna.

"Is that you, Cap'n?" The sugary sweet, giggly voice of Matilda Weatherby came to him through the dimness. "What are you doing hiding in the corner?"

Jace bit back a groan. For a married woman well into her forties, Matilda sometimes was a bit too friendly for his comfort. He didn't cotton to the idea of going toe to toe with her blacksmith husband. "Not hiding. Just standing."

"Well now, Cap'n, a gentleman such as yourself can't be standing all alone in the dark. Come on into the living room and let me get you some cookies and coffee." She took his elbow and tugged.

Teeth clenched, Jace let her lead him several steps, all the while searching for a means of escape. Finally, he said, "Mrs. Weatherby, you'll have to excuse me. I need to have a word with my sister."

The bewildered Matilda glanced around. "I don't see Rachel."

"I do." Actually, he didn't. Swiftly he strode away, searching for his sister. Dressed in red, she should have been easy to spot. Maybe Anna knew where she was.

And just like that he found himself standing with Anna and milksop Jess. The other fella had wandered off.

Anna looked up at him quizzically. "Captain? Is everything all right?"

"I need to have a word with you." Well, it was true, wasn't it? He wanted to find his sister. There was no other reason why he would interrupt Anna and her beau. "It's important."

"Oh. Well. Of course, Captain." A worried expression brought her delicate golden eyebrows together. She cast Jess an apologetic glance. "Excuse me, please."

Jess, the milksop, stepped back without a complaint. Jace's opinion of the man fell even lower. He was no good for Anna. What was she thinking?

Taking her elbow, Jace guided her rapidly across the room away from the chairs being scraped together for the taffy pull. Josiah struck up a jaunty fiddle rendition of "God Rest Ye Merry, Gentlemen," which Jace found especially appropriate considering his sudden desire to see any number of gentlemen laid to rest—especially milksop Jess and bald Bob.

"Is something wrong, Jace? You look as cranky as a sore-pawed bear."

"A real man worthy of your affections wouldn't have let me steal you away like that."

Anna offered him a look of mild reproof. "I thought you weren't coming tonight."

"Changed my mind."

"So I see." She cocked her head to one side. "So what is so urgent that you had to drag me over here?"

"Your hair is different." Why had he said that? What did he care about hair? Instead of her usual simple chignon, soft, fluffy curls framed her face. Her eyes looked twice as big. A man could drown in them. No wonder old Jess followed her around like a pup.

"I don't think my hairstyle constitutes a sufficient reason to whisk me into a corner."

"I didn't. . ." His voice trailed away, for he had, indeed, guided her into a corner. "It looks pretty." There. He'd paid the compliment.

"Thank you. Now, if I may, I'll return to the party." She pushed at his chest.

He didn't budge. "Where's Rachel?"

"Upstairs with the Hoffmans' daughter, I think, helping dress her hair."

When had Rachel become interested in such things? When had he? "Good. She's safe, then."

"Quite safe."

Another beat passed while Jace tried to decide how he'd gotten into this conversation and how to get out. Finally, he said, "Let's go pull taffy."

He was mildly surprised when Anna smiled. And then she laughed. The sound, tinkling high and sweet like the upper keys of a piano, stunned him completely.

"Yes," she said, "let's."

Chapter 6

Anna unclipped her mother's cameo brooch and gently placed it on the dresser. Papa had given the brooch to Mama for Christmas when they'd first married. He had loved Mama all the days of his life—from the moment he'd first laid eyes on her, he claimed. A love he'd carried with him to the grave.

Tears gathered at the corners of Anna's eyes. She wanted a love like that. The trouble was, she feared she'd found it with the wrong man.

The party tonight had been delightful. Sharing recipes with the other ladies, planning Christmas dinners and the program at church. But most of all she'd enjoyed the moment Jace had appeared. Buttered hands reddened from the heat, they'd pulled taffy, teased, and laughed until the candy was ready to cut into pieces. Though the sweet was being made for the sacks at church on Christmas Eve, everyone who'd participated enjoyed a bite or two. Jace, as she already knew, had a sweet tooth.

Afterward, they'd played parlor games and sung Christmas

carols until everyone was too tired to continue. She'd sat on a bench between Jace and Jess, admiring the rich baritone of each one. Jess Brewer was a good man. But he wasn't Jace, a truth that had hit her hard tonight, as if all the wind had been knocked from her.

What was she going to do with this growing emotion? *Dear Lord, please give me guidance.*

Later, they'd traveled the two miles home with Jace riding alongside the wagon. She'd felt him there beside her in the lantern-lit darkness and had experienced a sense of safety unlike anything she'd ever felt before.

With the stars bright above and her heart light and happy, Cousin Rupert seemed a million miles away.

Her hands clenched the edge of the dresser. Yes, she was safe now, but for how much longer? With Christmas so near, she had no doubt her relatives were searching with determined ferocity.

She crossed the room, lit only by a small oil lamp, and prepared for bed. The hour was late, and morning on a ranch came early.

Her time had run out. A decision had to be made. Now. She clasped her hands beneath her chin and prayed herself to sleep.

⤝⤞

"What is all this?"

Jace strode into the parlor, the scent of the cold outdoors clinging to his sheepskin coat.

Anna, busy weaving red ribbon in and out of a long garland

of evergreen, paused to look up at the tall, handsome rancher. Her throat filled with emotion, but she forced a smile. "Decorations. Wade and Brett cut these branches this afternoon. Aren't they wonderful?"

"The branches or my brothers?" Jace grinned and tossed his hat onto a chair.

She widened her eyes in appreciation of the joke. "Both, of course."

"Where is everyone?"

She handed him one end of the garland and motioned toward the fireplace. "Rachel is in the kitchen checking the *kolach*."

"The what?"

"Braided sweet bread. It's a Christmas tradition from the old country. Baba taught me. The dough is wound into three braids to symbolize the Trinity, and the bread itself represents Jesus, the bread of life. You'll like it. It's sweet."

"Couldn't be as good as your Baba cookies. Did you make more of those?"

She laughed. "I taught Rachel. That way, you can have Baba cookies long after I'm gone." Saying the words pricked her heart like a thorn, but she couldn't hide from the truth. She was leaving. Soon.

Jace hesitated at the comment but didn't ask the obvious question: When? Instead, he held the garland while she climbed onto a chair. "Where are my lazy brothers? In the kitchen, too?"

"No, silly, they're upstairs searching for your mother's box of decorations." Using a small wire hook, she looped the greenery above the mantel and gazed down at him with a smile. "And later, Captain Brackett, we are all going out to find the perfect Christmas tree."

He stood with one hand on the back of the chair, face tilted upward with an expression she couldn't quite read. "What about your beaus? Won't Jess or Bob or some other sop be here to entertain you this evening?"

"No indeed. Tonight is about family." She caught herself and said, "Your family, I mean."

"But it's not Christmas Eve."

"It soon will be, and since I—" Anna stopped, not ready to tell him. She wanted this evening to be perfect and wonderful, an evening they could all remember for a long time, maybe their entire lives. Placing a hand on his shoulder as support, she stepped off the chair. "You and your family have treated me wonderfully. The least I can do is to prepare a Christmas celebration for all of you as my gift of thanks."

Jace's glance drifted to the half-hung garlands, the candles waiting on the table, and the tiny crocheted ornaments she and Rachel had made. When his gaze returned to her, Anna suspected he knew the truth—that she'd made her decision and would be leaving before Christmas. He would be right. But she was not about to spoil the evening with the news. Tomorrow would be soon enough. Tomorrow, after she'd had this night with the Bracketts.

She was saved from further explanation when Wade and Brett thundered down the stairs, their voices raised in friendly argument, as usual.

"They were sugarplums," Brett insisted.

"Gumdrops," came Wade's reply.

Anna and Jace exchanged amused glances.

"Do they ever stop?" she asked.

"Not in all the time I've known them."

"Which would be all their lives." Her smile widened.

"Exactly."

"Here are those decorations you wanted, Miss Anna," Wade said. "They were buried under a bunch of other boxes."

"It's been a long time since they were used," Rachel said, coming in from the kitchen, her cheeks rosy and dark eyes bright with enjoyment. "I can't wait to see them again. Christmas will almost feel the way it did when Ma was here."

A miniature pause came over the brothers, but Anna was determined that no melancholy should take place tonight, not from them or from her.

"Your wonderful mother would be delighted to see her children gathered in this room preparing for Christ's birthday with her ornaments." Anna motioned to a spot she'd cleared near the window. "Put the box there, if you please. And let's all bundle up and go find a tree before it's too dark outside."

"Uh, Miss Anna"—Wade's eyes shifted to Brett—"me and Brett have something to tell you."

"What is it?"

"You won't be mad, will you? I know you had your heart set on going after the tree, but. . .well, you see. . ."

Brett groaned in disgust. "What he's stammering about, Miss Anna, is the tree waiting outside. We found it when we cut these branches."

Anna clapped her hands. "That's wonderful. Oh, what a lovely surprise."

"You're not mad?"

"Of course not. It's bitterly cold out there. You've done us all a favor. Bring it in; bring it in!"

Amid much maneuvering and laughter and discussion about the correct procedure for securing a Christmas tree, the pungent cedar soon stood tall and elegant alongside the half-decorated mantel.

"It's beautiful, boys. Just perfect."

"You think so?" Both of the young men seemed eager for her opinion.

"The loveliest I've ever seen."

"Come on, then," Jace said, the twinkle in his eye belying his gruff tone. "We'll be up all night if we don't get started."

Anna bumped him with her side. "Why, Mr. Scrooge, I do believe you're enjoying yourself."

He tapped her on the nose. "Your fault."

They stood like scheming children, grinning into each other's eyes.

Oh my, Anna thought. *This is both wonderful and awful.*

"Look what I found," Wade said, waving something in the air. "Mistletoe. Want to borrow it, big brother?"

Jace stiffened but recovered quickly and put a bit of space between him and Anna. "I fear one of her gentleman friends would have my hide."

"Coward," Wade taunted. "But if you won't use it. . ."

When Wade started toward her with a gleam in his eye, Anna

was grateful for the diversion. Striking a silly pose, she presented her cheek. Wade gave her a loud, innocent smack then turned toward his sister, cackling with nonsense and good cheer.

"Don't you dare, you loon," Rachel squealed. She won a reprieve when Brett snatched the mistletoe and shoved it into his pocket.

A deflated but cheerful Wade relented, coming back to help with the tree.

"I don't know why we ever stopped doing this." Rachel's expression was filled with a happiness reflected on all three of her brothers' faces.

Jace tied one of the crocheted angels onto a limb and studied it as he said, "After Ma was gone, there didn't seem to be any point."

"Maybe we were wrong about that," Brett said as he situated a candle in the front window.

"You absolutely were," Anna said. "There is nothing like a Christmas celebration to bond a family together."

Jace locked eyes with her.

Anna found it hard to look away.

"Family is important," he said.

"The most important earthly thing we have." What she would give to have Papa and Mama and Baba back for one more Christmas. Rather than allow the sad thought to linger, she said, "Let's sing something."

To cover her emotion, she launched into "The Twelve Days of Christmas." Four voices joined in, and by the chorus, Wade was sashaying around the room, swinging his arms in dramatic fashion like a conductor. On the last line, all five singers threw their arms out to the side and in their best operatic imitation belted, "And a partridge in a pear tree."

By the time they had wrapped their tongues around all twelve verses, they were breathless and laughing, and Anna's momentary loneliness for her family was forgotten.

"I declare, I fear our singing may have curdled the milk," Rachel said.

"The chickens will stop laying, that's for sure," Jace said. And the funny comments brought more chuckles.

In fact, the mood was so festive, Anna wished it would never end. As time passed and the decorations dwindled, she found herself stalling for time, finding more and more tiny additions to the tree, to the mantel, to the windows, until at last, only the star remained.

"You do it, Miss Anna."

"No. It's not my place." She turned to Rachel, holding out the shiny tinsel star. "Jace, will you assist your sister?"

"Me?" Rachel's smile was as bright as the Star of Bethlehem as she took the gilded ornament and accepted Jace's hand up onto the chair. Once the star was situated, Jace handed around the matches and they carefully lit each candle.

Wade then doused the lamp until only flickering candles and the golden glow of the fireplace illuminated the cozy, festive parlor. The ornaments glittered, the star on high shone, and a hush fell upon the happy little group.

"It's beautiful," whispered Rachel. "Thank you, Anna, for making us remember."

Anna's very full heart felt near to bursting. If for no other reason, the Lord had led her here to this place for Rachel. She could leave, knowing the young girl would carry on the old family traditions and maybe a few of Baba's, too.

"I love Christmas," Anna said. "When Jesus came as the Light of the world, the greatest gift of all, there was no room for Him in the inn. Tonight, my fondest prayer is that we all have room for Him in our hearts." Voice wobbly with emotion, Anna went on, "To all of you, I want to say thank you. You've made my Christmas very special."

And if any of them heard the good-bye in her tone, they kept it to themselves.

"Could we sing 'Silent Night'?" Rachel asked, her voice hushed, too. "Ma always did."

Jace's deep, rich baritone began to sing:

Silent night, holy night,
All is calm, all is bright.

As the others joined in, Anna choked back the tears threatening to fall. Tears of joy and happiness, tears of love and worship, and tears of sadness for the only Christmas she would spend with this family she'd come to love.

Chapter 7

"I need to tell you something."

Anna's hands twisted in the folds of her apron. She and Jace were alone in the parlor after the noon meal the next day. Brett and Wade had headed out to repair a fence, and Rachel was at the church preparing for the Christmas Eve play.

"After last night, I figured as much." Coat at his side, ready to get back to work, Jace sat on the edge of a chair, rolling his Stetson round and round in his fingers.

"Last night with all your family was special," Anna began. "I'll always be grateful for the memory."

Jace's expression was thoughtful. "You've made a difference here."

"Have I?" She glanced up, hopeful.

"You know you have. You will be missed."

She wanted to ask if he, specifically, would miss her, but with a sinking heart, Anna knew there was no point in prolonging her own agony. She couldn't wait another day hoping for him to have a sudden revelation of his need for God or to decide that marriage wasn't a dirty word. Her time had run out. "I've decided to accept Jess Brewer's proposal. We'll be married tomorrow if everything can be arranged."

A tiny muscle twitched beneath the captain's left eye. Otherwise, he displayed no emotion. "I see."

Did he? Did he really? Did he see that she was dying for him to give her a reason to stay? "Jess is a good man."

"He is."

"He'll treat me kindly."

"And allow you to run your own business affairs?"

"Yes. We've discussed it. He's agreeable."

"So he knows about your inheritance?"

"Not yet. I plan to tell him this evening when I accept his proposal."

Jace looked away then to stare into the fireplace. Orange flames danced beneath the decorated hearth. A log snapped and fell, sending out sparks and the homey scent of wood smoke. The room was prepared for the coming Christmas, as well as for the leaving housekeeper. For that's all she was. Jace's housekeeper.

As hard as she tried to be chipper, sadness had crept into the parlor and hung in the space between them.

"So you love him, then?" Jace's tone was serious, his profile set in a grim line.

Anna's heart had taken up a heavy pulse beat in her throat and ears. She swallowed hard. "In time, I'm sure I shall grow to care deeply for him."

When she'd first come to Flat Rock, this had been enough.

Now the idea of marrying a man she didn't love with all her heart seemed wrong.

Still, Jace didn't turn, didn't look at her. He stared into the fire as though the flames held the mysteries of life. His jaw worked, and she saw him swallow. What was he feeling? Relief to see her go? Regret at having to find another housekeeper? Would he miss her even a little?

But Anna kept all the questions in her heart. If Jace cared for her at all, he would have said so. "Jace?"

As if she'd poked him with a needle, Jace jerked to a stand. "That's it, then. I'd best get to work." And still without looking at her, he slapped his hat on his head and left the house.

Anna sat staring at the pretty, cheerful Christmas tree for a long time after his departure. Her apron was fairly wadded to pieces beneath her twisting hands. She felt as if she'd swallowed a rock that lay heavy and hot in her midsection.

But the decision was made. Jess Brewer would be a fine husband. As soon as they were wed, she could breathe a sigh of relief, knowing she was safe from Cousin Rupert and his parents. For that, she should be thankful.

With a deep, cleansing huff, she stood and straightened her skirts. She glanced again at the brightly decorated cedar and inhaled the clean Christmas aroma. Last night had been such fun. She would never forget.

But in all the decorations, they had not found Mrs. Brackett's nativity to set beneath the tree. Rachel, in particular, had been disappointed. And so, rather than stand there feeling sorry for herself, Anna determined to find the figurines before Jess's arrival.

She glanced at the mantel clock. She had some other things to do, as well, to keep her mind occupied and her spirits high. She wanted to leave plenty of cookies and a baked ham for the Bracketts' Christmas dinner. She also had small gifts to wrap and hang on the tree for each one. And then she would pack her things.

Because tomorrow was her wedding day. And she *would* be happy and thankful, no matter what.

⁂

"Where is that box?" Anna rubbed her upper arms against the chill. The attic was colder than a mountain spring, but she would not leave until she found the Bracketts' nativity. They needed it, especially Jace, to remind them of the true meaning of Christmas.

It was the least she could do to repay their kindness. And the hunt had put her in a lighter mood.

She lifted dusty lids and pushed aside trunks until at last the treasure was revealed. With a happy cry, she carried the box of figurines down the stairs. Cobwebs clung to her dress, but she hummed a Christmas carol just the same. Time enough to freshen up before Mr. Brewer arrived. Jace and his siblings would be thrilled that she'd found their mother's special crèche. Before she left with Jess Brewer, Anna would remind the captain of their family tradition, and once again on Christmas Eve, the Bracketts would tell the story of Jesus' birth.

The notion lifted her spirits considerably. Life was good. God was good. Even if He hadn't worked things out to suit her,

He had kept her safe. And He had used her to bring Christmas back to the Brackett family. She was thankful. Truly, she was.

As she set the box on the damask-covered table in the parlor, the strains of "Angels We Have Heard on High" trilled from her throat.

The French doors swung open, and Anna spun to share the good news. "Oh, Captain, guess what I found—"

The words died in throat. There before her was her worst nightmare.

"Rupert," she gasped.

A malicious smile lifted the corners of his mouth. "Surprised to see me, cousin?"

A shiver of fear ran through Anna's body. "How did you find me?"

Snow melted on Rupert's beaver hat and the shoulders of his coat. His usually ruddy complexion was windburned, and his beady blue eyes were watery and reddened. "That's not important. Get your things. We're leaving."

"No." Hands fisted to hide their shaking, Anna hitched her chin. "I'm not going to marry you, Rupert. You have to understand that now. I will not leave with you."

Her cousin's eyes narrowed. He grabbed her arm and yanked until they were nose to nose. Spittle gathered at the corners of his lips. Anna caught the whiff of whiskey. Her stomach churned. She yanked back, but the heavy, hulking man didn't budge.

"I've had all the trouble I'm going to tolerate from you, Anna. Either get your belongings or go out into the freezing weather with nothing but that apron to warm you."

"I would freeze to death in this."

"Makes no difference to me. Fact of the business, I'm starting to think you'll be more trouble than you're worth."

The chill of truth was in his words. He didn't care if she lived or died.

She started up the stairs, hoping to find a way to escape. Her mind raced. Cossacks were warriors. Cossack blood flowed in her veins. She would fight. She would not give in to this madman.

His boot steps tromped behind her. She picked up her pace, an idea forming. As she reached her room, she rushed inside and slammed the door.

Too late. A black boot toe poked inside. She pushed harder. But Rupert was far too strong. With a heave, he shoved the door open with a resounding bang. Anna fell back against the dresser, striking her side. She cried out.

Rupert laughed, though the sound was anything but pleasant. "I told you I'm not putting up with your tricks anymore. You've caused enough trouble for my family. All we wanted to do was take care of you, but you had to run off like this."

"You never wanted to take care of me. You wanted my money."

His hand came at her so quickly she had no time to duck. He struck her across the cheek. "You agreed to a Christmas wedding. Mother sent out the invitations. You *will* be there."

Fingers pressed to her stinging skin, Anna knew there was no point in reminding him that she had never agreed to any such thing. "We can't get to St. Louis by tomorrow."

He yanked the wardrobe open and began tossing out her dresses. "Pack them or leave them."

Though trembling like a leaf in the wind, Anna refused to back down. A life with this odious man was out of the question. "I'm not going, Rupert. The Bracketts will be here any minute. They will not let you take me this way."

She could only pray it was true, that Jace or Wade or Brett would come home. And dear Jess. Oh, if he would only arrive early instead of at the appointed time.

To her horror, Rupert removed a long-barreled pistol from beneath his overcoat. "Then I'll have to take care of them, won't I?"

"You would be hanged."

"Not if I claimed you were my fiancée and these people had kidnapped you."

"But that's not true."

"Oh, but it is. The announcement is in the *St. Louis Dispatch* this very week. And Dr. Strothers is convinced you are unbalanced and need care, so no one will listen to your ramblings about a forced wedding."

"Unbalanced?"

"Female nervous disorder, he calls it. He believes, as we do, that you need to be cared for. I'm willing to do that for you, my dear, but if you don't cooperate, I fear we shall be forced to have you committed to an asylum. That is, if you don't take your own life in a fit of insanity on the way home."

She had no doubt at all that Rupert had offered Dr. Strothers a large sum of her money to "believe" that she was mentally unbalanced and capable of such destructive behavior. Horrified by the very real threat, Anna bent to gather up her dresses with trembling hands and thundering pulse. Rupert's wet boots had left a filthy print on one garment.

"So what's it to be, Anna? Are you going quietly? Or do we plan a little surprise party for this nice family that's taken you in?"

Heartsick, Anna knew the answer. She couldn't be the cause of any harm coming to the Brackett family.

She took her carpetbag from under the bed and began to pack.

Jace kicked the barn door closed and stomped across the yard toward the house. The snow had started again, adding to his sour mood. The women and children wished for a white Christmas, but farmers and ranchers knew the snow was nothing but trouble. Lost calves and frozen ponds and grass buried too deep for grazing.

All afternoon he'd worked himself into a sweat preparing his cattle for the worst. The harder he worked, the more it snowed, the worse his mood.

Miss Anna was marrying Jess Brewer. He should be glad about that. She'd be safe with Jess. The scrawny fella was prairie tough and he could shoot the eye out of a rat at fifty paces. No cousin or uncle would harm Anna with old Jess on the job. He'd be good to Anna, too. Take her to church the way she liked. Buy her green ribbons for her hair.

Yes, sir, he should be happy with the news. But he was as

sour as milk left in the sun for a week.

He figured the housekeeper situation was the reason. Sure. That was it. He'd have to ride all the way into town and place another advertisement and then hope someone would apply. Now that Anna had the place spiffed up, another woman could step in easily.

He frowned at the Christmas tree he could see through the parlor window. Rachel wouldn't want another woman stepping into Anna's shoes.

Neither did he.

He kicked the door open, ready to offer Anna a new deal. He'd protect her until she reached the age of majority and could handle her own affairs. In exchange, she'd stay on at the Brackett ranch. Sounded fair to him.

He stopped in the entryway to stomp snow from his boots. Anna would have his head if he tracked on her shiny floor. He grinned at the thought of her scolding, feeling better now that he'd come up with a new idea. "Anna!" he yelled.

Rachel came in from the kitchen. "She's gone."

"What do you mean, she's gone?"

His sister shrugged. "When I came home from practice, she wasn't here."

Jace's sour mood returned. "The eager bridegroom arrived early, I suppose."

Dismay leaped into Rachel's eyes. "What bridegroom?"

As soon as he'd spilled the news, Jace wanted to kick himself. Or better yet, let someone kick him. The last thing he wanted to do was spoil Rachel's Christmas Eve. "I meant to tell you later.

Anna's getting married tomorrow." At Rachel's look of betrayal, he reminded her of what they all knew. "That's why she came, Rachel. No use getting sentimental."

Tears gathered in his sister's eyes. "She wouldn't leave us if you weren't so thickheaded."

"What are you talking about?" Jace hung his coat on a peg and sniffed the air. Something good was on the stove. He started that direction.

"You. You're too stubborn to admit you're in love with her."

Jace stopped dead still in the doorway to the kitchen. He was already in a bad mood. Rachel was pushing it. "My feelings," he said through clenched teeth, "have nothing to do with her decision."

But his cold glare didn't dissuade Rachel. "Yes, they do, you idiotic cowpuncher. Haven't you seen the way she looks at you? The way her eyes follow you all over the room? The way she takes care to be sure your coffee and your shirts and your everything are just the way you like them?"

"She's the housekeeper."

Dark eyes so like Ma's snapped at him. "And you're a fool."

"I'm not going to stand here and take a dressing down from a twelve-year-old. Go to your room."

Rachel glared, hands on her hips as if she wouldn't obey, but after several miserable seconds, she burst into tears and flounced up the stairs.

Frustrated, angry, and depressed, Jace lost his appetite. Swinging around, he stalked into the parlor to get warm and, if he'd admit it, to sulk.

As soon as the fragrance of cedar hit him, he was taken back to last night, to the sound of Anna's laughter and her off-key singing. He was going to miss that.

With a groan, he collapsed onto the couch and propped his boots on a table. Anna wasn't here to chew him out. It was his table. He could put his feet up if he pleased.

He was staring morosely at the Christmas tree when his gaze fell upon an overturned box with contents spilling out. Curious, he crossed the room and knelt beneath the tree, picking up a painted glass statue of the manger and Baby Jesus.

"Ma's nativity," he said softly.

Anna, sweet Anna had found the cherished set for them. But why had she left the pieces scattered on the floor this way? She knew their significance.

As he gathered the figures, wrapping them one by one in paper, the dog barked, and then he heard the rattle of harness and wheel.

Going to the door, Jace frowned out at the visitor. What was Jess Brewer doing here? And why wasn't Anna with him? "Brewer," Jace said. "What brings you here?"

The little man leaped from the buggy and bounded happily up the steps to where Jace stood in the doorway. Thin flakes of snow swirled around his boots. "Come to see Miss Anna. Is she ready?"

"I thought she was with you."

"She's not here?" Jess blinked in bewilderment. "Then where is she?"

Anna's beau peered around Jace as if he didn't believe she wasn't inside.

Just then Rachel came pounding the stairs. "Jace, you'd better come upstairs and look at something."

"What is it?"

"Just come. Hurry. Something's wrong."

With a deep and terrible dread, Jace raced up the steps with Jess Brewer close behind. Rachel led the way into Anna's room. And what he saw there froze the very blood in his veins.

The usually neat-as-a-pin room was in disarray. The wardrobe door hung open, dresses on the floor, toiletry items on the dresser overturned.

"Anna would never have left the room like this," Rachel said, eyes wide and worried.

Grimly, Jace agreed. "Not unless she was forced."

"Do you think her cousin—"

Jace cut her off. "Who else? She's not with Brewer." He whirled on the man. "Are you certain you haven't seen her? You don't know where she is?"

"No. I promise you." At the suppressed fury on Jace's face, Jess started to babble. "We had plans this evening. She said she had something important to tell me."

With a sinking heart, Jace knew what had happened. Upset that Anna was going to settle for marriage to someone she didn't love, he'd let his guard down. Just when Cousin Rupert had found her.

And that's when the truth hit him like a falling tree limb. He was in love with Anna Federov. That's why he'd been so upset about her leaving. Rachel was right, after all. He *was* a fool.

If he didn't find her in a hurry, either Anna would be married to her evil cousin, or she would be dead.

Sick to his stomach at the thought, he practically pushed Jess Brewer out of the room. "Ride into Flat Rock and tell the sheriff Miss Anna has been kidnapped. Rachel will explain."

"What are you going to do?"

"I'm going after her."

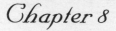

Rupert Johnson was insane. This was the conclusion Anna drew as she jounced and bounced beside him in the buggy. Her cheek stung where he'd struck her. And her wrists chafed against the rope he'd used to tie them together. To his fury, she hadn't gone without a tussle. She had kicked and fought and ripped her fingernails across his face when he'd set out to tie her hands. Even now the red streak across his cheek cheered her. But that was the only thing.

In truth, she was in deep trouble. Rupert had lost his mind. She was certain. And he would stop at nothing now to gain her wealth.

He had the horses lathered already but continued to flay them with the buggy whip. His fury radiated from him in waves, usually accompanied by a diatribe against her and her father.

Somehow he had become the victim and she the perpetrator. It was her fault he was cold. It was her fault he would spend Christmas somewhere on this ugly, barren, uncivilized prairie.

"All I wanted was to love you. Ungrateful wretch. Mother

warned me you wouldn't be docile. Too much Cossack, she said. She was right. Trouble. That's all you are. Do you realize the stories we had to concoct to explain your absence?"

"Then let me go, Rupert, if I'm so terrible."

They had traveled for a while, and darkness had fallen. Light snow continued, but thankfully, the wind had died down at dusk and intermittently the moon broke through the clouds. They'd passed farmhouses and skirted a town, but she had no idea where they were now.

"I have obligations. You must be my wife."

"I'll give you money, Rupert, if that's what you want."

Face set, he glared down at her. "I love you, Anna. I want your money, but I want you, too. And I will have you or no one will. Ours will be the wedding of the year. A celebration society will gossip about for months to come."

Yes, the man was as mad as a hatter.

He slapped the reins, but the tired horses couldn't respond. "You'll learn to be a good wife. I've been congratulated by all my friends for finding an heiress. You *will* marry me. You will love me. Mother, Father, and I have planned everything."

Cold fear, far icier than the snow, pricked her nerve endings. Cousin Rupert's ramblings grew more confused and troubled by the minute.

"Captain Brackett will come after me, Rupert. He will find me. You will not get away with this."

"Captain Brackett?" His head snapped toward her. "Exactly who is Captain Brackett?"

She hitched her chin and told the truth. "He's the man

I love. The man I want to marry."

With a growl, Rupert grabbed her upper arm and squeezed. "You love me. You will marry me. Understand that, Anna. Once we are married, you will legally belong to me. Your captain can do nothing."

With vicious strength, he shoved her away from him. She fell to the side, half lying in the seat. Frightened and helpless, she closed her eyes and prayed for God to help her.

❧

Jace rode hard and fast, his buckskin an excellent mount for distance and speed. Now and then, snow struck his face and melted on contact. More flakes gathered on the saddle and in the horse's mane. He was glad for the occasional snow. The four-wheeled tracks of a light buggy and a pair of horses were easy to follow. As long as he moved fast before snow covered the tracks, he could catch them.

After a while, the snow ended and a full moon peeked between the clouds, reflecting off the snow in a soft, golden glow that shed enough light to travel. Mysterious shadows rose out of the darkness along the trail, but Jace paid them no mind. During his cavalry days, he and his men had ridden many nights with less light than this.

The air was cold but not painfully so. He hoped Anna was warm. Doubtless the buggy she was riding in had a lantern, but had the brute thought to bring a lap robe to keep her warm? Would he care if she was cold?

The thought caught beneath his rib cage like a hitch from

running too hard. His mind chanted her name. *Anna, Anna, Anna.*

Why had he been such a thickheaded cowpuncher, as Rachel had called him? Why had he not seen the gift right in front of his nose? He loved her. And she loved him. He was sure of it now, as he looked back on their days together. Hadn't everything she'd done spoken of love?

He'd been so blind. So blind. He'd let one youthful experience harden his heart.

"Oh God," he groaned into the moonlit sky, "please keep her safe."

It was the first time he'd prayed in years. And it wasn't enough. Not near enough.

Anna had been right about his relationship with the Lord, too. All these years, he'd thought he was in control. He was Captain Brackett, a man in control, a man who could handle anything by himself. But now he saw the truth. Without God's help, he would not find Anna in time. Without God's help, he could not right this wrong he had done to her, to his family, and to himself.

"I need You, Lord. Forgive me," he muttered through lips stiff with cold.

With those simple words, the floodgates of Jace's heart opened. He poured out his anguish, his sorrows, his brokenness to God. And when the wall of sin that had separated him from Jesus came down, he prayed for Anna.

"Help me find her, Jesus. I'll take good care of her from now on. You have my word. If she'll forgive me, too, if she'll have this thickheaded cowpuncher."

The buckskin's ears twitched, but he galloped on down the long, flat road, breath huffing rhythmically to the beat of his hooves. An owl hooted as Jace passed a scrubby stand of trees. Far in the distance, the lights of a town twinkled.

The situation hadn't changed. The night was still dark and cold. Snow still fell. And Anna was still somewhere in the grips of a kidnapper.

But Captain Jace Brackett was a new man. With an assurance that made no sense at all, he knew the Lord would lead him to Anna.

"Get up."

Anna awakened with a start and blinked up at the cruel face of Rupert Johnson. With a shiver, the memory of the last hours raced into her consciousness. At some point, they'd stopped in a town. Disoriented by sleep, Anna didn't know how long ago that had been. Rupert had gone inside a business, a saloon, she suspected, because he'd returned to the buggy smelling of liquor. He'd bound and gagged her, leaving her out in the cold for so long she'd fallen asleep.

And now they had stopped again. Furtively she glanced out at the shadowy night. This was not a town.

She'd dreamed, hoped, prayed that someone would help her. She'd prayed for Jace to come. Only he knew the danger she was in. Only he was strong and brave and stubborn enough to search for her.

But would he realize she'd been taken? And if he did, how

would he know where to look?

"Get up, I said." This time Rupert tugged at her shoulder.

She shrank away from his touch. "Where are we? What are we doing?" she asked as she struggled to sit up in the seat. Pins and needles stung her feet. Her side ached. "Are we stopping to rest?"

He laughed that strange, ugly laugh again and lifted her down. "You might say that."

Anna swayed, her feet too numb to hold her. Gritting her teeth, she leaned against the buggy wheel and waited for feeling to return.

They were in front of a house, though she had no way of knowing where. A light glowed yellow in the front window.

Hope leaped into her throat. She held her wrists out. "Will you remove this, please?"

"Will you behave yourself?"

She swallowed, mind racing. A lie was a bad thing. She hoped the Lord would forgive her. "Yes."

"Good girl. I knew you'd come around. You just needed a little time." He leaned in to untie the knots. As the rope came loose, he pocketed it then leaned closer, trapping her between his bulk and the wheel.

And then to her horror, Rupert pushed his mouth against hers. The whiskey stench was overwhelming. Anna's stomach rolled. She shoved her now-freed fists against the rough wool of his overcoat, but he caught her hands in a cruel grip, his face a mere inch from hers.

Eyes gleaming in the moonlight, he said, "My sweet bride.

Welcome to our wedding."

Icy fear snaked down her spine. "What are you talking about?"

"A fine justice of the peace resides in this humble abode. He has graciously agreed to marry two eloping sweethearts."

"I'll tell him the truth. He'll send for the sheriff."

Rupert didn't seem the least concerned with her threat. He reached into the buggy and removed a large jug of liquor. "Fellas in town say Mr. Jenkins is fond of his whiskey. Will do most anything for a jug and a few dollars. So I don't think I'll worry too much about your ramblings. He's already in his cups, from what I just observed inside. Likely he won't even remember you in the morning."

Panic crept up her windpipe. "I won't marry you, Rupert. I won't say the vows."

The long-barreled gun flashed from beneath his coat. He tapped it beneath her chin. "Then you will die. You and anyone inside this house. You don't want to be responsible for a child's death, do you?"

Oh Lord, please help. "You wouldn't shoot a child."

"Yes, Anna, I would. It's a shame, I know, to be so foolishly in love with you, but I will have you or no one will."

Anna's shoulders sagged along with her hope. Part of her couldn't believe Rupert would resort to murder, but she was afraid to take a chance.

Taking her elbow, he propelled her across the snow and into the house. Pleasant warmth struck her, along with the faint smell of kerosene and burnt grease. The room was small, lit by a single lantern and a fireplace.

A round man with a red, bulbous nose struggled up from a chair next to the fireplace, swaying unsteadily on his feet. Anna's heart sunk lower. As Rupert claimed, the man was drunk.

"Is zis your little bride?"

"Yes, sir. All ready for the wedding."

"Eloping, are you?"

"Yes, sir. Now can we get on with it before her parents catch up?"

The justice of the peace cackled. "You're in a heap of a hurry, son. She must be a real prize."

Rupert shot her a loving look that curdled her blood. "That she is. Her pa didn't want us to marry, but she had her heart set on Christmas Eve. I sure enough didn't want to disappoint her, if you know what I mean. This being her Christmas present and all."

Anna stared at Rupert, thunderstruck at the smooth lies and the country bumpkin accent.

"Well, give me a shot of that jug you got there and we'll get started. I'll have you two hitched and on your way in two shakes of a lamb's tail."

He took a long pull on the jug, shuddered, and then dragged a sleeve across his mouth. "Ahhh. Mighty fine whiskey. Warms a man on a night like this."

"The ceremony, Mr. Jenkins," Rupert insisted, setting the whiskey on the table. "We'll celebrate afterwards, and then this jug is all yours."

"And the hundred dollars?"

Anna gasped, finding her voice for the first time. "A hundred dollars!"

"All yours, Mr. Jenkins, as soon as Anna and I are legally man and wife." Rupert extracted a wad of bills from inside his coat and tossed it on the table.

Mr. Jenkins cackled. "You're worth a lot to this fine man, miss."

"You have no idea how much," she muttered.

Rupert pulled her close, his arm around her waist. He still wore his coat, and she felt the hard tip of the gun barrel against her side.

"Then shall we begin?" Weaving but upright, the justice of the peace stood in front of the fireplace, hands clasped over a protruding belly. "Tell me your names."

"Rupert Johnson and Anastasia Federov."

"Wait," Anna said, desperately stalling for time.

Rupert turned a warning gaze in her direction. Through clenched teeth and a false smile, he said, "We need to proceed, darling."

"I—I have to go to the necessary."

The gun barrel jabbed harder. "After the ceremony, dear one. It will only take a minute." He nodded toward the justice of the peace. "Continue, please."

"Rupert Johnson, do you take this woman to be your wife?"

"I do."

Too fast. It was happening too fast. Anna stared wildly around the room, looking for escape but finding none. In a few more minutes, she would be legally bound to a man who only wanted her fortune. She shuddered to think what would become of her under his control. After the night's events, she was certain she would be mistreated, penniless, and a virtual slave for the rest of her life.

"Miss Anastasia Federov, do you take this man to be your husband?"

Oh dear Lord Jesus, can You hear me?

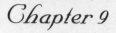

Chapter 9

Mr. Jenkins cleared his throat. "Miss Anna, all brides are nervous. Think nothing of it. A simple 'I do' is all you have to say."

Rupert pulled her tighter against him, his fingers digging deep on one side while the pistol threatened on the other. Mouth nuzzling her ear as if to kiss her, he whispered, "Say it or he dies."

Blood pounded in her temples, her head roaring with fear. "Will you repeat the question, please?"

Her breathless voice sounded for all the world like that of a nervous bride, not a kidnapped one.

Mr. Jenkins's drunken smile was indulgent. "Of course, my dear. Will you take this man to be your husband?"

Anna's breath grew short. Her throat clogged. "I—"

Suddenly the door slammed open, cold air whirled inside, and someone shouted, "Stop!"

Anna would know that beloved voice anywhere. She twisted toward him. "Jace," she cried. "He has a gun!"

Then with all the Cossack blood in her veins urging her on, she slammed an elbow into Rupert's side and a sharp heel down on his instep. He yelped in shocked pain and loosened his hold.

Jace was across the room so quickly Rupert had no time to recover. A man wearing a badge rushed in behind Jace, gun drawn.

In minutes Rupert was bound with his own rope and carted off to jail. The drunk justice of the peace blubbered and stammered, denying any knowledge of the kidnapped bride. When it became clear that he wasn't being blamed, he collapsed on the sofa and promptly passed out. Anna was stunned to learn that the man lived alone. Rupert had lied about the wife and child.

Legs as weak as dishwater, she sank onto a chair. It was over. She was safe. And Jace was here.

"Are you all right?" Jace asked, going to one knee beside her.

She nodded. "I am now. How did you find me?"

"I prayed."

Her heart leaped into her throat. "You prayed?"

"And the Lord heard me." He clasped her hands between his own, his dark eyes boring into hers. "I've been a foolish man, Anna. I thought I could live without God's help, but I was wrong. I asked Him to forgive me, to set me straight."

"Oh, Jace, that's the most wonderful news." Unable to stop herself, she lovingly touched his cheek. He had come for her. Surely that meant something.

"I was wrong about some other things, too. When I realized

you were gone, that Rupert had kidnapped you, I'd never felt so helpless in my life. My heart stopped beating. I died a little in those few minutes."

"You did?"

"The thought of never seeing you again, of never hearing you sing or seeing you smile, is unbearable. I love you, Anastasia Federov. Please don't marry Jess."

"I don't have to marry anyone now."

"No, you don't have to. . .but I was hoping you'd want to."

"Why, Captain Brackett, what are you trying to say?"

"Will you marry me, Anna? Tomorrow on Christmas with all my family there to celebrate? Will you?"

With a joyful laugh, Anna threw her arms around his neck. "Yes."

And then she did what she'd only dreamed of for so long. . . . She kissed him.

❦

Never was a Christmas Day so perfect, at least to Anna's way of thinking. She should have been weary from the previous night's terror, but instead, she awoke invigorated, filled to the brim with the knowledge that Jace loved her. And today she would be his bride.

The Reverend Jacobs had been most agreeable to perform the ceremony following the Christmas service. All those wishing to stay for the wedding were thus invited to do so.

Candles flickered around the altar. To one side, a tin star hung over the manger scene where the children had reenacted the birth of Christ. Outside, the sun glistened on newly fallen snow.

And here in the front of the small schoolhouse church, the Cossack bride and her hero groom would be wed.

She glanced at Jace, standing so straight and tall at her side. Resplendent in black coat and pants, gold vest, and snow-white shirt, his black hair oiled and combed, he took her breath away. He was the handsomest man she'd ever seen.

"Ready?" he whispered, dark, teasing eyes meeting hers.

"Oh yes. Very ready." With only a jitter of nerves, she ran her hands over the velvet dress she'd made especially for Christmas. She hadn't known then that this would be her wedding gown, but she loved it. Jace had said the green turned her eyes to emeralds.

At her throat she wore Mama's brooch, the one Papa had given her. Baba's lace hanky was tucked inside her sleeve. She felt them all there with her, their memories rich and precious. They would approve of Jace, she was certain.

With a slight turn of her head, she smiled at Rachel, sitting ladylike and proud between her handsome brothers. All three beamed as if they were about to burst with joy.

She understood the feeling, for her heart was full to overflowing.

Jace took her hand and gazed lovingly into her eyes. "I love you," he said, as though he couldn't say it often enough now that he'd begun.

"I love you, too," she whispered.

The minister began the ceremony, and Anna listened to the

beautiful words from the Bible that would join her forever to this fine, strong man.

When the time came to exchange vows, Anna answered in a strong, clear voice, "I do. Oh yes, I do."

A titter ran through the church, but Anna didn't mind. She loved her captain, and she didn't care who knew.

Jace laughed softly down at her and then thrilled her through and through by responding, "I do, too. Oh yes, I do."

And suddenly the ceremony was over and she was in Jace's arms, right where she had belonged for so long.

The church bell began to peal, and someone—Rachel, she thought—began to sing "Joy to the World." A dozen voices joined in until the chorus swelled with a beauty that brought tears to her eyes. Joy bubbled up inside her and spilled over into thanksgiving.

Hand in hand, the bride and her handsome groom strolled, laughing, out into the snow-kissed day to begin their life journey. As Jace lifted her into the buggy festooned with red bows and cedar boughs, Anna knew her faith had been confirmed.

For what Rupert had meant for harm, God had turned for her good. He'd brought her to Kansas and to the Bracketts. He'd protected her. He'd even opened Jace's eyes to love and renewed faith.

And to the Cossack bride, that was the best Christmas gift of all.

LINDA GOODNIGHT

Linda is the author of more than twenty-five books that have been translated into a dozen languages. Recent awards include the Booksellers' Best, ACFW Book of the Year, a Reviewers' Choice Award from *Romantic Times Magazine* and a RITA nomination. Linda's life scriptures are Isaiah 58 and Matthew 25: the commands to care for the needy. As such, she and her husband are active in orphan ministry. A former nurse and teacher, Linda feels blessed to write fiction that carries a message of hope and light in a sometimes dark world. She and husband, Gene, live on a farm in Oklahoma where they are proud parents of six children and grandparents of another six. Readers may contact her through her Web site: www.lindagoodnight.com.

A Letter to Our Readers

Dear Readers:

In order that we might better contribute to your reading enjoyment, we would appreciate your taking a few minutes to respond to the following questions. When completed, please return to the following: Fiction Editor, Barbour Publishing, Inc., P.O. Box 719, Uhrichsville, OH 44683.

1. Did you enjoy reading *A Bride by Christmas*?
   ❏ Very much—I would like to see more books like this.
   ❏ Moderately—I would have enjoyed it more if _____

   _____

   _____

2. What influenced your decision to purchase this book?
   (Check those that apply.)
   ❏ Cover   ❏ Back cover copy   ❏ Title   ❏ Price
   ❏ Friends   ❏ Publicity   ❏ Other

3. Which story was your favorite?
   ❏ *An Irish Bride for Christmas*   ❏ *An English Bride Goes West*
   ❏ *Little Dutch Bride*   ❏ *The Cossack Bride*

4. Please check your age range:
   ❏ Under 18   ❏ 18–24   ❏ 25–34
   ❏ 35–45   ❏ 46–55   ❏ Over 55

5. How many hours per week do you read? _____

Name _____

Occupation _____

Address _____

City _____ State _____ Zip _____

E-mail _____

If you enjoyed

A BRIDE BY

Christmas

then read

A CONNECTICUT CHRISTMAS

Four Modern Romances Develop at a Christmas Collectibles Shop

Santa's Prayer, by Diane Ashley
The Cookie Jar, by Janet Lee Barton
Stuck on You, by Rhonda Gibson
Snowbound for Christmas, by Gail Sattler